2 | Cross My Heart

Author's Note

This book took a lot longer than I expected it to and I can't even give a reason as to why that is, but like Sofia Renaud, I believe everything happens for a reason.

I started writing this book in 2016 after Blood Secrets was published, but that was also a year where a lot changed for me in real life. Some not so good, but it brought me to where I am now, and I believe everything we do in life serves a purpose.

I had been chipping away at this story since 2016, but it wasn't until this year, 2020, when the world stopped and every day life ground to a halt that I was able to find my way back to this world again.

COVID-19 has been horrendous and has affected every single one of us in one way or another, but if there is one thing that I will take away from this scary, crazy time – a silver-lining, dare I say – is it has helped put my priorities in perspective. And in having to isolate and therefore not worry or stress about everyday tasks and responsibilities, I have been able to focus on what I love, which is writing, telling stories.

This book was never planned but was essential. Elle and Than's story runs alongside the events of Blood Secrets. It doesn't matter if you haven't read book two in the series or even the prequel, She-Wolf. But I would highly recommend that for your own enjoyment and to understand the events of this book, you have at least read book one, Cranberry Blood.

I'm so happy to finally be sharing this instalment with you and hope you enjoy every second of it and find it worth the wait.

Elizabeth Morgan xx

Blood Series
She-Wolf
Cranberry Blood
Cross My Heart
Blood Secrets

Cross My Heart

10 | Cross My Heart

Prologue

~ Nathan ~

The sky was a mixture of orange and pink making the scattered, wispy clouds look like candy floss. It was hot, with next to no breeze, and somewhere in the distance, birds sang. But as always, our haven was as silent as a grave.

I had never really understood that saying. Of course, a grave was silent—it was a patch of ground marked by a slab of stone ... and we were surrounded by them.

"This isn't fair. Switzerland is practically on the other side of the world," I huffed, aiming the pebble in my hand toward the thin arch window in front of me.

"Your geography is terrible," Elle replied, climbing along the wall of what was once the left side of the friar's house. "It's not that far."

The monastic site had closed hours ago, a tourist attraction by day and our haven in the evenings. Sure, it was a graveyard, but it was historic and had a tower which allowed you to see far off into the distance. It had been the site where we had slain dragons and hid from the monsters lurking in the nearby forest. Where we had braved great peril to rescue the princess locked up in that very tall tower ... which Elle had never offered to play the part of. She'd always preferred to be on the ground, fighting by my side.

We had played here as children and had hung out here as teens. It was our special spot, and right now, I had no idea if I would ever see this place again.

"Still—" I reached down and grabbed another small stone from amongst the grass. "—I don't understand why my da had t'take a job in a different country."

"I don't think it's necessarily his choice where the promotion's based."

I snorted. "It's his choice on whether t'take it or not, and he has, and now we're off t'bloody Switzerland." I lobbed the stone toward the glassless window.

It wasn't fair. How could my father just change our lives without even asking if I was okay about it?

"It's better money, isn't it?" Turning, Elle lowered herself so she was sat on the uneven stones. "That's why he's taken it because he wants you and your Mamai to have a better life. That's not a bad thing, Than."

"It's easy for you to say. Your family has plenty of money."

Elle's family were loaded—big house with acres of land... Not that I had ever gotten to see any of it, but from what I could see through the gaps in the iron gates at their entrance, it looked pretty damn cool. Her parents weren't snobs, well, at least they didn't seem to be, but they never allowed 'strangers' into their home. Not that I was a stranger; Elle and I had been friends since reception. You'd think ten years of friendship would mean that you would at least be allowed to play in their garden occasionally, but apparently not. It didn't matter, though—we had our own land to explore.

"Besides, you're supposed t'be on my side and be equally pissed off about this."

"I *am* on your side, butthead." She sighed. "But it's not like I can do anything about it."

"You could kidnap me?"

A chuckle escaped her. "And take you where?"

"Your house. Seems like the most secure place in the world." I threw a stone over her head. "No one gets in, and hardly anyone gets out."

"My house would be the first place they'd come looking for you."

"They wouldn't find me, though, because your father wouldn't let them past the gates. It's a perfect place to hide."

Her expression flattened. "Yeah, I guess it is."

"So, it's settled, then." My next aimed pebble hit her shin. "You're kidnapping me."

"I kinda think you're missing the silver lining here." She threw her arms in the air, her hands indicating to everything around us. "You're getting out of Wicklow and getting to see a different part of the world, a new ... adventure."

I rolled my eyes and threw another pebble toward her. "You always go on that our hometown's so boring."

She caught the small stone. "It is. Hardly anything happens around here."

"You mean other than the fact there are Vampires creeping around at night?"

"Shush." She lobbed the stone at my upper arm. "I told you that in secret."

I shrugged, resisting the urge to rub the spot she'd hit. "We're alone. No one can hear me."

"You'd be surprised."

A small shiver crawled down my spine. It creeped me out when she said stuff like that.

I glanced over my shoulder, gaze darting around the sparse tombstones. "Remind me again why it's safe t'hang out in a graveyard? Aren't Vampires supposed t'burst through their coffins and claw their way through the dirt?"

As cool as the idea sounded and looked on TV, standing alone on top of graves suddenly didn't seem like such a smart idea.

She cocked her eyebrow. "You've seen way too much *Buffy the Vampire Slayer*."

"Duh, that's because Sarah Michelle Gellar is hot." I casually and quickly made my way around the side of the crumbled building until I reached what remained of the front entrance.

"Theory is Vamps can't come on t'sacred ground. That's why it's safe."

With the help of a large slab of stone, I pulled myself up onto the uneven wall and carefully climbed toward her. "But you don't know for sure?"

"Let's just say it boils down to superstition because I don't think anyone has tested the theory in a long time."

I wanted to laugh but knew better by now. This was a fantasy world that Elle had lived in for six years and simply refused to step out of despite being older. Not to mention she would bite my head off for teasing her about any of it. No, I had learnt by now to just play along.

It was creepy how serious she was about the whole Vampire mythology thing, but at the same time, interesting. Fun when we were children, but now we were teens, it was kinda bordering on obsession. Maybe the loon would eventually become a writer and put all these details to good use, because I highly doubted she was going to find paid work as a Vampire Slayer.

I stopped by her side, standing tall on top of the ancient wall. The rays of the sun were already slithering away as the big ball of heat slowly sank behind the mountains. Since the light was withdrawing, it meant the shadows had sprung to life, crawling from the base of the below gravestones. Yeah, it was easy to believe in the undead when you stood in a graveyard amongst super old ruins.

"God, if anyone could hear us, they would think we were both crazy."

"You believe me, though, don't you?"

I looked down to find her staring up at me.

"Of course I do. That's what friends are for." I thumped down beside her, ignoring the discomfort of the uneven stones beneath my butt. "Sticking by each other, even if one of them is a little mad."

I laughed, grasping onto the jagged stone as she shoved me.

"I'm not mad, you eejit. I just know more about the world than most people."

"I don't think believing in Vampire means you know more about the world than anyone else."

"It's not a belief, it's a fact."

"Sure, sure." Another fact: Danielle Renaud was crazy, but at least she was fun.

The shadows had already crawled to the bottom of the wall—just a little farther, and they would touch our Converse-clad feet dangling above. It was almost time to go. Her father always wanted her home before it got dark. Apparently, Vampire hunting was a family activity. All my family ever did was go bowling or to the cinema.

"There will be Vampires in Switzerland, y'know."

She spoke softly, unusually so, as if she didn't want me to hear her.

I nodded and gave a small sigh. "I wonder if they yodel before or after slaughtering all the mountain goats?"

"You're not funny."

I slanted a look at her. "Then why can I see a smile hiding at the corner of your lips?"

She reached up and wiped her mouth as if trying to rub the evidence of her amusement away. "You might not want t'believe I'm telling the truth, but trust me, if you ever see one, you wouldn't be making jokes. They're ugly and violent creatures."

"Who look like the guy from Salem's Lot?" I placed my hands to my mouth, using my index fingers as fangs.

"The Master from Salem's Lot is similar, but firstly, Vampires aren't blue, and secondly, they only lose their hair when they transform."

"Because they actually look like normal people?"

"Yes. When they transform, their eyes turn black, their jaws dislocate to accommodate their fangs, and their tongues fork and extend."

"Like a snake?"

"Yes." She didn't bat an eyelid, didn't stutter, didn't even look like she was going to laugh at the idiocy of what had just come out of her mouth. She was serious, as always.

"Come on, Elle." I rolled my eyes. "That doesn't sound like a Vampire at all."

"That's because you're use to watching Hollywood's representation." She pushed her palms into the stone and carefully stood up. "Trust me, they're hideous."

"Uh-huh, and how many have you seen to date?"

"Four." She wiped her palms against her denim dungarees.

"And how many have you killed again?"

"Three."

There came that chill down my spine again. "Y'know, you scare me sometimes."

"Just promise me you will carry a pocketknife around with you when you're out at night and get yourself something silver to wear."

"Because they're allergic?"

"Yes, and if you manage t'shove the item into their throats, it would buy you enough time to get away—"

"Jesus, Elle." I pushed myself up until I was eye to eye with her. "I'm not about t'start throwing jewellery down people's throats."

"Not peoples. Vampires." Her left hand landed on my right arm, steadying me. "I can't ... I can't protect you in Switzerland, Than." Her green eyes suddenly looked bigger, wetter.

In all the years we had been friends, I had never seen her cry, but right now, I was pretty sure she was close. It was an uncomfortable sight, and I was pretty sure that if I took the mickey out of her, she would push me off this wall, which wasn't that high but high enough to still bloody hurt.

"It's alright, Elle." I gave her a smile and took hold of her elbow, squeezing gently. "I know that you're going t'miss me. I am your only friend, after all."

That earned me an eye roll. "Besides Heather."

"She's your second cousin, so she doesn't really count as a friend."

I knew she and Elle were close, but Heather hardly ever left the house, which had to suck especially because she was home-schooled. Ten years old and no friends. Her mother had committed suicide only two years prior; it was sad. The few times Elle had brought her out with us, she'd always looked so damn uncomfortable and worried. Poor kid.

"Well?" I gave her a little shake. "You going to admit that you will miss me, or do I have t'force it out of you?"

Her gaze didn't leave mine, her fingers flexing on my arm. "I'm scared I will never see you again."

My stomach flip-flopped at the whispered reply, and my earlier frustration reared its head again. My parents were moving me away from my hometown, my school, grandparents, and friends, from Elle. Did they even care or know what they were doing?

"I'll visit. My grandma is still here so we will be back at least a couple times a year, but more importantly, I will email you. We can be pen friends."

It wasn't fair. My parents were ruining my life all for the sake of a job—a job my father started in a month, which meant we only had three weeks to pack up and do whatever the hell people did when they moved countries.

I had to start all over again: new school, new friends, and I would be all alone. No Elle and her idiotic stories and crazy drama to make it all easier. This was one of the last times we would hang out … maybe the last time we would properly hang out.

I suddenly felt sick. I wanted to shout and cry, break something or run, do anything that would stop the churning in my stomach. My forehead was pressed against hers before I realized I'd even moved. It wasn't fair. How were you supposed to say goodbye to someone you had known for your whole life?

My grip tightened on her arm. "I promise we will see each other again."

The shadows had finally reached us. The cold cradled my left side while the dying warmth of the almost-set sun still touched my right.

Tears had formed in her green eyes, and I was pretty sure I could feel them brimming in my own.

She placed her right hand on my chest. "Cross your heart?"

A smirk curled the corner of my mouth. "And hope to die."

She tilted her head and pressed her mouth to mine. Her lips were soft and gentle—words I would never use to describe Danielle. My brain seemed to go blank, unable to register the fact that my best friend was kissing me, and before I could decide what the heck to do, she had pulled away.

My focus remained on her as she slipped her arm from my grasp.

Her attention went to the gravestones below. "You should be careful what you wish for, Than."

Chapter One

The dream darkened. The images disintegrated to ash as something deep inside me stirred. That unusual, invisible tug I had quickly learnt was my new alarm clock, my body telling me that I now had to be awake, and therefore, without my consent, it pulled me into the realm of semi-consciousness. The innocent dream got lost in darkness.

No, not a dream. I didn't have the luxury of dreaming anymore. It was just a memory, and one that kept replaying in my mind every time I closed my eyes—my subconscious telling me that I owed an old friend one big, fat apology; an apology that would surely get me an 'I told you so' as a reply, and that was presuming I ever got to see her again.

It was the truth. Everything she'd ever told me ... *It's all real.*

The past seemed like a pleasant place to live, but then again, anything was better than my current predicament, which proved nothing short of a nightmare. A cold, dark, twisted nightmare.

"I told you t'be careful what you wish for."

Her voice rang in a soft and sweet whisper that I could feel dance across my skin, the usual taunting tone accompanying her words.

"Go away, Elle."

"Make me."

A lock clicked. Hinges whined as heavy, rusted metal scraped against concrete. Light briefly touched my face, only to be overtaken by an unfamiliar presence that filled my door frame. My eyeballs hurt behind my lids, but I didn't bother opening my eyes and indulging in the mild curiosity that involuntary tickled the back of my mind. Truth be told, I didn't have the bloody energy to even try to look. Then again, if I had learnt one thing during my time in purgatory, it was that nothing ever good happened when you opened your eyes and that the things you did see weren't always real.

A crinkle of plastic accompanied the odd squeak and shuffle of clumsy feet. My visitor moved into the room, allowing the overhead lighting from the outer corridor to slither into my cell. Not as good as daylight, nowhere near, and yet being locked in the dark for such long periods of time had made my skin super-sensitive. That horrid illumination was all I had, all I could use to delude myself into pretending that I was really lay on a rock-hard stretcher in my back garden, and not some dank room in a strange facility in God only knows where the hell I could be. The light was cold and pale, not like the warmth from the sun, but regardless, I could feel it on my skin, feel its energy in a way I couldn't before.

Iron clamped around my jaw, breaking my momentary delusion. Not to mention the impact was so sudden, my lids snapped open, and my eyeballs practically bulged from their sockets. *Jesus, talk about a wakeup call.*

The left side of my friend's face remained in the shadows of the room, but the right ... The light barely touched him as if almost afraid to. His jaw was square, and from the patch of skin that was illuminated, he was as pale as every other Vampire I'd had the pleasure of meeting during my time here. His hair seemed dark, and he looked to be wearing black—the meatier fellows all seemed to wear black and have the role of 'the muscle' in this joint. Clearly, they were prison guards, and one other thing I had learnt during my stay? These guards didn't have patience, not that human bouncers or security guards rarely did, but then again, humans couldn't go around biting or beating the crap out of the people they were responsible for.

He raised his left hand, and the red, opaque silhouette of my feeding tube caught the corner of my eye, a droplet ready to fall from the slit. The scent of blood touched my nostrils ... *Jesus* ... how I hated that I even knew that smell.

"I'm not thirsty."

The words didn't quite make it past my lips. Instead, they remained locked between my throat and teeth, but my new friend seemed to understand—this was made obvious by the tick in the visible side of his neck. Not that he gave a shite, which he proved by digging his ice-cold fingertips into my cheeks, pushing my flesh into my teeth so violently that I was sure they would have shattered, but being a compromising soul, I obliged and opened my mouth. Although I doubted anyone would class my mouth as being opened since my lips were vertical and the top lip was stuck in the opposite direction of the bottom. I no doubt looked like a fish mid-breath.

"*More like a fish with a botched lip job, mid-breath.*"

I said go away, Elle. I slanted my gaze to the right corner of the room, watching as the shadows solidified.

"*And I said, make me.*"

The tube was pushed between my teeth, the tip grazing along my tongue and pushed farther, until it was stuck halfway down my gullet. Blood, cold and thick, coated my throat, slithering into my system. My throat flexed, more from the slight discomfort than the need to drink or even to retch. Retching would be the right thing to do when someone force-fed you blood, but since I'd woken up, it was all I could eat—well, drink. Even though my mind was still plagued with disgust and the madness of the situation, a part of me had accepted the inevitable and ridiculous truth ... I was a Vampire.

Then again, my captors had drilled this life-changing fact into me repeatedly since the moment I had first woken up and had refused to believe, refused to drink, which they had loved. Tormenting was apparently no fun if your victim was accepting of their situation. It had been somewhat hard, not to mention physically painful, to digest, especially since I couldn't recall a flash of fangs or being filled with terror as one of the undead pounced from the shadows in order to feed from me. Nor could I remember being fed blood or the agony of death or waking up reborn—all of which was supposed to take place according to Elle.

"*So maybe I lied. Maybe I was wrong.*"

My focus stayed fixed on that corner of the room, to her form which became more solid with each second. *You would never admit you were wrong.*

"Maybe not when we were kids, but maybe now, I would admit such a thing, especially since a Vampire didn't feed off you and baptize you with its blood. That certainly didn't happen t'you, did it?"

No, all I could remember was rain ... A dark street, Freddie singing the Spice Girls, 'If you wanna be my lover' severely off-key beside me as we stumbled back to the hostel in London. Being knocked to the ground; blood trickling into my eyes ... Freddie on the floor next to me, someone in black pining him down. Darkness followed by flashes of light and faces; being naked and so freaking cold. The glint of needle tips and ... *fuck* ... the pain; slices into my ball sack, and then my heart, hammering so quickly and so damn hard, as if it were about to explode out of my chest or just give up on me altogether ... and then a whole lot of nothing before I woke up in this dark, dank room.

The Hollywood take on being turned into a creature of the night hadn't happened, and sure, I had always though Elle had been crazy, obsessed with Vampires, but in a cute, supernatural fanatic kind of way since she went into fascinating details which were so elaborate, it was always like being told a scary story. I had always believed her overactive imagination to be just that—while we played in the fields and forests near our hometown, she wished we were roaming through a more dangerous and thrilling world. A world she had been invested in since we were eight, a world I humoured her with because she was my best friend and had enough crazy stuff going on at home, but ...

"Vampires exist, Than. It doesn't matter if you don't believe in them. Lack of belief doesn't make them any less real." She snorted. *"I've told you this a million times."*

Vampires existed. I had seen far too many fangs, too much blood, and a bunch of other freaky shite over my stay to not believe that this brand of fiction was cold, hard, un-bleeding-believable fact, but I was one. Evident by the pinch in my gums or the stab of my canines against my tongue every time I smelled blood; evident by the fact that I no longer had a beating heart, no urge to breathe or eat, or even to go to the toilet. And as sexy as Hollywood made Vampires out to be ... the reality was a total turn-off.

The click-clacking of heels echoed in the corridor, announcing that the red-headed she-devil was about to pay me another visit. Her last visit with a spiked blood cocktail had almost killed me, but sadly, fate had decided to spare me and just gift me with the mother of all hangovers. A Vampire with a hangover—who'd have thought such a thing would be possible, but Christ almighty, it was nasty blood. Well, not nasty. Different, energetic, intoxicating, and freaking painful. It sure as hell burnt my insides. It was like being on fire and yet having a sledgehammer hitting your head at the same time. The messed-up part was that I liked it, because it was the closest I had felt to being human in ... days, weeks; I had no idea.

My focus shifted to the open doorway as the click-clacking ceased. Instead of the redhead, an entirely different demon stood in the doorway.

"Smells like trouble."

"So, this is what the alternative solution to our evolution looks like." She wandered into the room with a predatory grace, circling me and my new nursemaid. "I must admit I expected ... well, something a little more impressive."

I cocked my eyebrow at the Spanish she-devil as she came back into my line of view.

"If you really want t'be impressed, then fetch me the harmonica from my backpack, I'm known for having a very talented mouth," I gurgled through the still-flowing course of blood and as best as I could through the death grip of my new friend who didn't look like he was going to release my cheeks until I had finished the drink he had brought me.

"You are Irish."

Her laughter rang throaty, with a delightful edge. She gave off an air of carnal delight, and the way the light curved around her shape as she paused by my right ... curves in all the right places. The longer I stared at her, the sharper my sight became, adjusting to the light and shadows surrounding me. This Vampire was beautiful, every bit the image of the temptress from the Christopher Lee versions of Dracula. She had a fantastic rack, dark, long hair, big, almond-shaped eyes, and full lips ... my dick twitched.

Just the blood, Nathan. Just side effects of this stupid blood.

Elle had never mentioned that drinking blood could make you as horny as a bleedin' schoolboy, but then again, maybe she didn't know everything.

"*Or maybe the sickos lace the stuff with Viagra for cheap thrills? Either way, it might be an idea to stop devouring her with your eyes before your jeans become a tent and you start drooling.*"

My gaze shot to the corner, to the petite, slender, auburn-haired thirteen-year-old leaning against the metal wall. One strap of her denim dungarees hung loose, a three-quarter-length top beneath, moss green to match the Converse she sported. She was too vibrant and solid, like a sticker stuck to a black sheet of paper; she was too obvious, too out of place to be real. *You're too young t'know what Viagra is.*

"How many times do we have t'go through this? I'm not actually this age anymore. I'm just a figment of your sad little imagination, you nut job."

She—the real Elle—had once told me that victims could go a little crazy after being turned, become recluses, or blood-thirsty murderers. I just hadn't realized imaginary friends were one of the benefits of being fucked up in the head.

"Oh, they're not. You're just special, Than."

"How delightful." The female Vampire slid up alongside my nursemaid. Her hand landed on his arm, and with that simple gesture, he released my face and exited the room.

I opened my mouth wide, stretching my aching jaw, only to regurgitate as the tube slid farther down my throat. "Why am I here?"

"Surely, you have figured that out by now?"

"Apart from being told I'm a Vamp, which I kinda guessed since I have no heartbeat but now have fangs, Red and Skinny have done nothing but feed me blood and prod me with needles." I gulped, swallowing more blood from the tube, wishing I could spit it out, but it was too far down my throat to even try. "If I'm one of you, then why aren't I frolicking around this place with you all? Why am I being kept locked up? I'm hardly dangerous."

"That is obvious." She moved closer. "But the reason you are in here is because you are not technically one of us."

"So, I'm not a Vampire?"

"Jesus, Than, you're dead and yet you're talking. Of course, you're a bleedin' Vampire."

I could be a zombie.

"Please don't tell me you're crazy enough to believe zombies actually exist?"

What's crazy about it? Vampires are a myth just like zombies, but guess what, there's a freaking Vampire standing right in front of me. So, who knows what else might be out there? And wasn't that a terrifying thought? Vampires might not be the only piece of folklore that walked the Earth.

A throaty laugh escaped the female. "You are proof that our kind can be created ... differently."

"Well, I already gathered I was an experiment."

"And a fairly cute one, at that." She plucked the tube from my lips and slid it from my throat. "And sadly, the only one left living in this place."

I gulped, forcing the remaining blood in my mouth to vanish. "That depends on your definition of 'living'."

"Well, mobile then." She brought the tube to her own lips. A disgusted grunt sounded at the back of her throat. "No wonder you are reluctant to drink. Stored blood is dreadful."

"Yeah, I'm not against drinking it because it's stored blood. The whole drinking any blood in general is freakin' disgusting."

"You only feel that way because you are a new-born who has yet to conquer your conscious, or at least that is what the good doctor's notes say." She slipped the tube between my lips, and despite my so-called conscious, my teeth closed lightly over the plastic, holding the tube in place. "But you will lose that once you get to drink from the source."

"I'm not sure I want to lose it."

"Not when you've already lost your sanity."

I glared in Elle's direction. *Have you got nothing better to do?*

"You want me t'go? I will go. I'm only here because you want me here and you know that."

The female stepped closer, her slender hand resting on my bare chest.

"But you do want to feed from a human, *si*?" Her fingers wandered up, dancing across my collarbone. "Sink your fangs into the soft flesh of a woman's neck, pierce her delicate vein and feel that first, hot gush of blood fill your mouth?" She dragged her nails down my torso, slicing through my skin, which healed as quickly as it split. "To taste the essence of human life, the spark—" she slid her hand over my jean-clad crotch, cupping my semi, "—nothing can compare."

"Oh, gross." Elle retched.

"So I've heard," I bit out around the tube. "Sadly, no human women come t'visit me here. So—"

"It can be arranged, if you are a very good boy and tell me what I need to know."

"Question. Why are you even talking to her?"

Because despite being undead, she's here in this room with me, and talking to someone who is physically here occasionally, despite them being Vampires, is the only reason I haven't completely lost my bloody mind. Does that answer your question, ghost of friendships past?

"Just ask her what it is she needs to know before this turns into an X-rated movie and I spew ectoplasm everywhere."

"And what is it you need t'know?" I sucked a little harder on the tube, trying hard to concentrate on the rush of blood entering my body and not the fact that every drop was heading down south.

"What happened here?"

I felt my brow furrow. "What d'ya mean?"

"Do not play coy." Her hand slipped under the waistline of my jeans, her fingers wrapped greedily around my junk, which leapt eagerly into her curious palm.

Fucking blood.

"You still seriously blaming this on the blood?"

Yes, blood causes reactions.

"Having your dick touched by a female after months of neglect would also be a reason why you're almost as hard as rock." Elle gagged. *"But she's a dead female, Than. She's one step away from being a corpse. I mean, that's just nasty. That's practically necrophilia."*

I know. Jesus Christ, Elle. I've been fucking kidnapped, turned into a Vampire against my will. I'm strapped up, being force-fed blood and getting sexually assaulted here, and you're making out like I'm bloody well enjoying this!

She held her hands up. *"Hey, don't yell at me. Try telling your dick all that. He's the one who's letting you down."*

"What did they want? What did you overhear?"

"Lady, I have no freakin' idea what you're on about."

"The Wolves." The words left her mouth on a hiss.

"Wolves? What—"

She squeezed harder. "They were here only days ago. They killed almost all of the Vampires who Nested here."

"Fuck." I grit my teeth. "What?"

"You expect me to believe you heard nothing? No grunting." Her strokes became quicker, firmer. "No growling, or screaming?"

"I heard nothing. Last thing I remember was the redhead hooking up blood to my drip and then rolling me into a white room—"

"And then you went bat shit crazy for hours, as if someone had given you a mixture of chocolate and cocaine."

"And then what?"

"I woke up in here like ... fuck." I bit the inside of my cheek as her nails dug into the underside of my junk. "I don't know how long I've been in here. I blacked out. The blood she gave me tasted weird—"

"So, you heard nothing?" Her hand disappeared. "That is a shame for you. I only reward good boys." She moved closer, so her breasts were squashed against my chest. Her hair felt like silk as it brushed against my shoulders. "Then again, I suppose it was not your fault. Your notes do indicate that the Were's blood was not kind to your system." She popped the button on my jeans. "You have apparently been in and out of consciousness for days."

"What blood? I don't ..." My words died as she sank down to her knees.

"Okay, I'm going into the hall. I can't watch this shite. She could bite your dick off or anything."

Bite my dick off? My gaze snapped to Elle's back as she left the room, before dropping down to the wicked, black gaze of the temptress.

"You really did not hear anything?" She pulled my zipper down. "Even in your futile state, nothing sank through?"

What the fuck? Elle? The Vampire's fingers curled around the seam of my jeans. *Will it grow back if she does bite it off? Elle!*

Every muscle in my body was already tense, but I was rigid. Unable to do anything but helplessly look down toward my prize jewels. Would this be it? Would I die from having my dick torn off? Or would I be a dickless Vampire for all eternity?

"You're already one, if you ask me. What kind of Vampire puts up with being strapped up for so long?"

Fuck you, Elle! You have no idea what I'm going through right now!

"Woman, I haven't a damn clue what you're fucking on about, but if I did—"

"Constance?" a male called.

A sigh escaped her.

"To be continued." She straightened, zipped up my jeans, and gave my crotch a pat. "Drink up, N. That is the last batch you will get before we leave."

"Leave?" I gritted. forcing myself to focus on what I was saying and not the raging boner I was now sporting—or the relief that was building up so rapidly, I was scared I was going to black out again. "You can't leave me like this. What's going t'happen t'me if everyone here is dead-dead?"

"Oh, do not worry, we still have use for you yet." Twisting on her heel, she exited my cell, closing the door and leaving me in the dark once more. Not to mention leaving me even more fucked up than when she had walked in here.

"What the fuck?"

A slurping noise met my ears, and that's when I realized I had sucked the blood bag dry. I spat the tube out and settled for whacking my head against my platform. A pulse of pain swam round my skull, but the pain was short-lived compared to the throbbing agony currently taking place in my jeans.

"What the fuck's wrong with you?" Elle passed through the metal of the door, pausing in front of me, arms folded and her right eyebrow cocked. *"Bad enough you're a Vampire, but you don't have t'be attracted to them either."*

"Who says I'm attracted? I'm still a guy, and surprisingly, my parts still work. More to the point, it's been a while since I had sex, so—"

She held her hands up. *"TMI."*

What was wrong with these creatures? They were insane, violent, greedy or horny. Most of the time, they were all fucking four.

Christ. "I gotta get out of here, Elle."

"That's what I keep telling you."

"Well, tell me how? How do I get out of here, Little Miss Smarty Pants? What do I do?"

"She said, "Drink up. That is the last batch you will get before

we leave."

"And?"

She rolled her eyes. *"They are taking you out of here."*

"Shit, you're right. Where the hell do you think they are planning on taking me?"

She walked over to the sleep platform fixed to the wall on my left and took a seat. *"No idea, but if I were you, I would make my move when we're all out in the open. That's if, you know, they don't sedate you again."*

"Fuck."

***

Time meant nothing here. A second could have easily been an hour when you were alone in the dark, staring at nothing, listening to every sound outside. Except it was quieter now; quieter than it had been before. I couldn't make out distant chatter, or footsteps. Nothing but silence, which made it worse, made the isolation even more suffocating.

No, time meant nothing when you were locked away, the only benefit being that it gave a man a chance to think and put his life in perspective. Do some soul searching. *Did I even have a soul anymore?* When time was all you had, what else was there to do but reminisce, regret, and wish?

"You're reminiscing too damn much lately. It's making me nauseous."

"Well, what else would you have me think about?"

"Duh, a way t'get out of here."

"Erm, duh, I'm strapped down, and in case you haven't noticed, the metal of these straps burns my skin."

"Jesus, did you ever pay any attention to anything that I told you about Vampires?"

"I did, actually, especially the part where you said that they had to bite people to turn them. So, what in the name of merciful

Jesus has happened to me?"

"I don't know."

I glanced at her, lying on the platform. "Yet again, you'd never admit that you didn't know something."

"Yet again, that's because I'm not the real Elle. I'm a memory of her, and I'm only relaying information that teen Elle told you. If you had bothered talking to adult Elle—"

"We kept in touch."

"But you haven't spoken for the last four years. An email essay on her birthday and at Christmas hardly counts as keeping in touch."

"Look, that's beside the point. You said Vamps bite people t'turn them. You were wrong."

"You're clearly special. The female just said you were an experiment t'prove they could create Vampires differently."

"Okay, so I'm different, but why?"

"I don't know, but don't y'think you need t'find out? You've been kidnapped, turned—"

"Molested."

"I don't think that counts."

"Does too. Do you really think I'd have let her do that if I was free from these restraints?"

She turned her attention to me, eyebrows arched. *"Is that a serious question?"*

My focus strayed back to the door. "I don't want t'die here, Elle. I don't want t'die in some cell or wherever the hell they're planning on taking me."

"I'm afraid it's too late for that, Than. You're already dead."

A bitter taste rose on my tongue. Horrid reality snuck up on me once more. "I'm dead."

How long had Freddie and I been missing? Had anyone even noticed? Had our parents? I had been sending postcards to my mother every week since our little backpacking trek across Europe had begun. Surely, she would know something was up by now. How would she find me?

"She can't, Than. Hard enough for police t'find people in the country they live in. Backpacking ... you two could be anywhere. More to the point, you're undead. You can't see her or anyone else y'knew ever again. They wouldn't accept you, and shit would really hit the fan if people found out Vampires existed."

"So, what's the point in escaping then? There's nothing for me."

"You can still have a life, Than. You can have a very long life if you get away from this place. Being dead sucks, being a Vampire has a lot of complications, but being free and immortal is still something you can achieve and work with."

"I am not wheeling him through the forest. That is a ridiculous idea." Voices echoed in the hallway.

"What do you suggest? He needs to be detained. We have no idea what he is capable of." Constance's voice was easy to recognise.

"And neither does he by the sounds of his paperwork or from the look of him," a male replied. "I say we kill him."

"No, Michael will want him alive."

"For all Michael knows, he could be dead already like the other one."

The back of my head hit the platform. "Freddie."

They had brought us here together as far as I was aware; he had been 'turned' like I had. We had passed each other on many occasions as we were wheeled in and out of laboratories. He had been incoherent most of the time, but like me, he had still been mobile, which was better than nothing.

"The Pack could have killed him. Michael is not going to know either way, and I hardly think he is going to care."

"We take him with us. Michael is already pissed that the Infected Cunt got away, at Lance for not being more careful or swift, and that Marko has refused to give our Colony a second chance."

"And do you not think that Marko would be pissed if he were to hear that Lance was straying from his orders? This facility was for harvesting, testing, and preservation, and yet, Lance was not only conducting his own experiments, but—"

"Lance got what he deserved." Constance cut the male off with a grunt. "He is dead, and our discovery of his outside projects are shocking, but will at least give some form of explanation to what went on here and how the Pack were able to find this place. All of which will no doubt piss both our Master and Marko off, but regardless of this evidence, it will not change Marko's mind. Our Colony is to have no further involvement in his plans. Lance blew it for all of us."

"I cannot understand how he figured out how to isolate and keep the virus alive."

"Did you not see the stamp on the envelope? They were findings from the facility in Italy. That stupid bastard had eyes over there as I suspect someone was planted here, which would be the only reason Marko found out so quickly that the Infected had been rescued."

"It is wrong when you cannot even trust your own kind."

Their voices grew louder, as did the echo of their footsteps.

"Do not be so naive, Jonathan. Our kind have never trusted each other, but since Marko revealed his plan ... these last ten years have been different."

I glanced at Elle. "What are they on about?"

She hopped off the platform and stopped by my side. *"Beats me, but since they're talking about you, I would say you're involved in something pretty big."*

The distinct sound of chains filled the hallway right before the door to my cell was pushed open. Constance was the first to walk into my room, followed closely by two males, one of which held a long silver chain in his gloved hands, two thick shackles hanging from each end.

"Time to go already?" I looked at Constance.

"No time like the present, as the saying goes."

The other male moved closer, pulling gloves onto his large hands. In quick succession, he gripped each of the padlocks attached to each strip of metal holding me place, and with a whine and sharp tug, broke each one, throwing them to the floor as he went. He pulled open each strap, and as soon as my ankles were released, my body slumped like a sack of potatoes to the floor.

"You really want to bring him?" asked the male who had just released me from my bindings.

"He has been locked up for days. You know the silver particles in the restraints can weaken our kind even if they have been fed, which he has," Constance replied. "He will be fine in a few minutes."

"Well, we are not waiting for him to recuperate." The male, who I had to presume was Jonathan, caught my arms in his gloved grip and pulled me up as if I weighed nothing. With me sagged against his chest, he gripped my arms and held them out before me so the other male was able to cuff me.

The thick metal sat on my skin, and within an instant, the hot prick of a thousand needles bit into my wrists as the silver laced inside got to work. I gritted my teeth, fighting past the burning pain, ignoring as the rank scent of singed flesh fluttered in the air.

"Be strong, Than." Elle moved beside the chain master. *"The pain will subside in a minute. Y'need t'focus on walking so that you can get out of here, so man up."*

I scowled at her as the male Vampire finished locking my ankle cuffs. With a tug on the chain to check I was secure, he led me out of my prison cell. I tripped over my feet, my shoulder landing right into the rusty, metal-panelled wall of the hall. The lighting strip hummed above us, and even though it wasn't the brightest light, it still smarted my eyes.

"Move." Jonathan yanked me off the wall and shoved me forward.

I kept my eyes downcast, focused on the dirty concrete floor, waiting for my eyes to adjust to the light.

"This place is so quiet."

I shifted my gaze to the pair of green Converse walking in step beside me, her footfalls making no sound, not like the three

Vampires I was currently with, but she was right. Apart from their footfalls, the place was deadly silent. In all the time I had been here, there had always been signs of habitation, subtle background noises.

Blinking, I lifted my head as the male led me through a set of double doors. The underlying hint of musty damp still lingered in the atmosphere, but even the air didn't smell the same. We turned left, and Constance's earlier questions suddenly made sense.

"What the hell?"

Large black patches stained the walls and floor of the corridor we moved down. Strange silver weapons lay abandoned on the ground.

"You sure you do not remember hearing our kind being butchered?" Constance asked from behind me.

"So that's what the black stuff is, Vampire blood?"

Shouldn't you know that? I angled a look at Elle.

"I only know what you know, remember?"

Well, whatever it is, it smells vile.

"Last thing I remember is being in that white room," I replied to the she-devil.

"What could have done this?"

Beats me.

My guard stopped as we reached a large door at the end of the corridor with a single window. He hit a red button, and the door rolled open to reveal a rickety cage, which he stepped into, pulling me right along with him, before shoving me into the left corner so Constance and Jonathan could step inside also. Picking up a yellow remote that was on the end of a long black wire, he flipped the switch. The door slid shut. The cage rattled then started to ascend.

"Well, this is a huge health and safety risk," Elle commented, eyeing the top of the cage.

After a moment, the makeshift elevator came to a grinding halt. Jonathan rolled the door open and stepped out into the small scruffy room, followed by Constance. My guard stepped out before me, giving the chain a firm tug. My gaze clocked bricks and ivy before I was pulled out of the single door and into the great outdoors.

It was magnificent. My eyes couldn't absorb enough. Everything was so alive and lush. The air felt cool and soft against my skin, but the caress remained only skin deep. I didn't feel a tremble as the chill surely should have gone straight through to my bones, nor did I feel the urge to drink in the fresh air. I'd been locked up for ... weeks surely. I should want to breathe, to refill myself, and yet, despite how wonderful it was to be back outside, my body felt empty. *Dead.*

"Move." My guard tugged on the chain, pulling me away from the odd little building nestled away in the vast forest that surrounded us.

"Did you get everything?" Constance asked two Vampires leaning against a nearby pine.

"Everything we could," replied the female who held a box filled with papers.

"Well, that will have to do."

"Let us get out of here," Jonathan interjected, taking the lead on our 'escape route.'

The two Vampires fell in step behind me as we followed.

The undergrowth of the forest was dry and brittle against my bare feet, but it felt like Heaven to have grass sliding between my toes, and the dry scratch of earth. I mindlessly continued to follow the Vampire in front of me who had a strong grip on the chain wrapped in his gloved hand.

"Now's your chance." Elle appeared beside me, walking backward.

For what?

"To escape."

I snorted. "How do you suppose I do that?"

"Silence." The Vampire leading me snapped his head round and glared, bringing to my attention that I had just spoken out loud.

"You're a Vampire; you're strong and fast. You need t'kill the guard with his chain. Wrap it around his neck and yank hard. You will decapitate him."

What?

"You don't have much choice. If you continue t'be a little bitch, they will just take you somewhere else, lock you up, and eventually kill you for real since that's what the big guy at the front wanted to do to begin with. It sounds like you should already be dead and buried."

Did you just call me a bitch? You can't use language like that at your age.

"Realistically, I'm now twenty-five, and for all y'know, I could cuss like a sailor."

Still. I glanced down the line at the three Vampires before me. One against five—Vampire or not, I didn't like my chances. *Say I do it. Say I manage to decapitate this guy, then what?*

"Run, obviously. Run, and if they chase you, it will be easy t'take them one on one, but you need t'run and to not stop until you're far away from here."

What if I can't decapitate him? What if I'm not that strong?

"Then they will either kill you now or knock you out for the rest of the trip."

I'm not liking my odds.

"That's only because you still think you're human. You're not."

I'm not.

"No, they took your humanity away from you. You can't age. You can't go out in the sun or eat food. You can't see your family ever again. You can't have kids of your own. You will be forever twenty-six. You're stuck like this, because they kidnapped you and turned you against your will. You must drink blood t'survive, hurt people t'survive. Why aren't you angry about that?"

"I am."

"Shut up."

"You don't seem angry. You've been locked up for weeks.

You've clearly gone mad because you're talking t'yourself—"

"I'm talking t'you." Irritation wound round my spine.

"And I said shut up," my guard grumbled.

"What, and that's not insane? I'm a figment of your goddamn imagination, Nathan. I'm not actually here, talking t'you. You're alone with a bunch of Vampires. You're dead. You're cursed. These bastards have taken your life from you, your human rights from you, and you're fucking scared of hurting them, of decapitating one of them t'get away. Jesus, you are *a little bitch."*

My eyes narrowed to slits as I glared at her. "Shut up, Elle."

A punch hit my back. "Are you deaf?"

I threw a dirty look to the dickhead behind me.

"Deaf and stupid, like a little bitch. Scared t'fight the creatures that have taken everything from you. They wouldn't have taken me without a fight, but then, I'm not useless. No wonder we're not friends anymore. You're a fucking pussy, Nathan."

"I said shut up!"

Something popped inside me, the irritation bursting through my arms, and before I knew it, I was in front of the guard with the chain. Only, it wasn't a glistening length between us, but a thick necklace around his neck. His eyes had already started to bulge, and tendrils of smoke were rising from beneath the links of metal.

"Pull!" Elle screamed.

So I did.

Time seemed to slow down, or was it already slow? It wasn't like I could count a second since I had no pulse.

The male's face went slack as the chain slid through skin, cartridge, and bone, like cheese wire on a block of cheddar. Blood splattered across my face, black, rancid, and thick. His head toppled off his shoulders.

The female behind us lost her grip on the box she was carrying. Files slid, spilling to the ground, her expression stunned as she watched the male's body sinking to the forest undergrowth.

"That file has your name on it." Elle's voice was all I could hear. *"Grab it and run."*

The blood-stained chains dropped before me, the weight pulling my arms down hard, the heft causing the shackles to rub further into my wrist. Sizzling pain bit me. Gravity felt as though it was standing on my shoulder. All I wanted to do was fall, but Elle wouldn't let me.

"Nathan! Grab it!"

One look at Elle's startled eyes was all the motivation I need. Even though my legs were about to buckle, I lunged forward. My right knee smacked the ground as I reached for the folder Elle was pointing at. The shackles pressed against my skin, sending blazing pain up the back of my calves.

"Run!"

At that command, I seemed to have lost control over my entire body. Before I could even think, my feet were hitting the forest floor in short, awkward strides. My arms stretched out in front of me while I pressed my folder tight between my palms.

"After him," Constance shouted in the near-distance.

Hands still bound, the silver chain followed, slashing against my upper arms and back. Each hit felt like fire licking across my skin, the agony short-lived for as quick as a cut was delivered, I could feel tightness as my flesh knitted back together and wounds were gone.

Footfalls sounded swiftly behind me.

"Run faster." Elle ran beside me.

"I can't," I growled through clenched teeth.

A howl split the night sky, the sound so unexpected, I lost my footing and ended face first on the ground.

"Get up, you eejit," Elle screamed.

I propped myself on my elbows and twisted to see the other male mere feet away, his eyes lost on the treetops, searching.

"Leave him," I heard Jonathan call. "Let the Pack have him. As far as anyone is concerned, they killed him when they came for the girl."

The guard sneered at me and quickly ran back to the group.

I watched as the four remaining Vampires disappeared into the wilderness.

"They're letting me go. Why?" I looked toward Elle. Her focus moved across the trees that surrounded us, staring into the darkness.

"So something else can finish you off."

I rolled back onto my stomach and crawled toward the nearest tree. "Would it hurt you t'say something like dumb luck?"

Another howl split the sky, followed by dead silence. Nothing in the forest moved, not even the trees.

"Wolves."

Twisting, my back hit the rough bark. "Wolves in London. Don't be crazy."

That was presuming we were still anywhere near London, near where Freddie and I had been jumped. *Poor Freddie ... What had they done with his body?*

"The female Vamp didn't seem t'think it was a crazy idea."

Constance had gone out of her way and said that Wolves were to blame for what had happened at the facility. But how would Wolves even get in? Surely, they would be helpless against Vampires?

"You need t'get out of here, Than."

"And go where exactly? My mum's probably worried sick about me since I haven't called for weeks. I don't know how long I've bloody been like this. What t'hell am I supposed t'say? How can I—"

"You can't go home."

Her words were a dead weight that hit me right in the chest. If I couldn't go home—and deep down, I knew that. Of course I knew it—where else could I go?

I sagged against the tree, defeated. Part of me wanted to feel it, that sinking feeling that was despair and grief. I had the notion deep inside the cavern that was my stomach that I should feel devastated by the fact, that such feelings were right, but I just felt empty, numb.

My focus wandered to the brown folder that had slipped from my grasp while I had face-planted into the undergrowth. I could see my name scribbled fancily across the front. I reached for it, and opening the flap, pulled the wad of pages out. A photograph of me was clipped to the top of the first page—a naked, unconscious me, lying on a stretcher. It reminded me of a post-mortem report, the type you saw on CSI and other such shows. I read my details, the first page just information I imagined they had pulled from my wallet and passport. It was the second page I was stuck on.

"They removed my—" The sides of the pages crumbled in my grip. I couldn't finish the sentence. My throat seemed to be closing over, but I remembered the pain, in between my legs, knowing when I came to that something wasn't right down there. The bastards had taunted me about losing my balls, but I'd just presumed it was part and parcel of the ridicule. It looks like they'd meant it. "They fucking ... They fucking castrated me."

"Why, that doesn't make sense?"

"What t'hell are you asking me for?" I glared up at her, tension cradling my jaw. "How t'hell should I know? You're the fucking Vampire Expert. Why don't you tell me?"

I wanted to scream, cry, but I couldn't feel the build-up even though I knew it was there somewhere, lost in the abyss that was now my dead body. I should feel something, be able to react. I'd been kidnapped, murdered, neutered, cursed to be undead, unable to eat or sleep, or see my family ever again ...

"Come and find me."

I looked up at her. "What?"

"Like you said, I'm the Vamp expert. So come find me."

I laughed, short and shallow. "Get real."

"Where else are you going t'go? Who else will believe you?"

Another howl ripped through the night sky, that wild, haunting sound making the darkness more isolating.

I was alone, and I had nowhere to go. I couldn't go home. My friend was dead, for real this time, and I was currently shackled and half-naked. I had no money. I had no balls. No heartbeat. I had nothing.

"Firstly, you need t'stop feeling sorry for yourself."

"Are you freaking kidding me?" I held up the folder. "I'm absorbing my situation here."

"You've been absorbing your situation for weeks. If you haven't got it in your head by now that you're undead and your life will never be the same ... then you will never get it." She walked over to me and knelt, her moss-green eyes on level with mine. *"I know this is bad, but it could be worse."*

I snorted. "How?"

"You could be dead and buried in a field."

Okay, you have a point.

"But you're not. You're still here for a reason, and sure it's complicated, but at least you get t'find out why t'hell this happened t'you. You can get answers for yourself and Freddie." She straightened. *"So, you need t'get your arse up and get out of this forest. Secondly, you need t'find somewhere indoors t'hold up before sunrise, and then, you need t'come find me. I'll know what t'do."*

"You really think you're going t'help me after all these years?"

"Maybe, maybe not, but I'm the only Vampire Hunter you know. Who else can you go to like this?"

I looked back down at the folder, at the photograph of my naked, lifeless body.

"You want t'know why, don't you? Why this happened? What all of it means?"

Part of me did. Part of me just wanted to wake up and find that it was just a long nightmare. "I'm not sure what I want."

Something rustled in the distance.

"Well, for now, I suggest you figure it out somewhere else, because in this forest, there seems t'be more than one type of monster that you need t'be worried about."

I placed the folder on the ground. "It's going t'be tricky t'move while I'm still cuffed."

"As long as you're able t'move t'some degree, that's all that matters."

Ignoring the bite of metal against my wrists and ankles, I pushed myself up, using the tree as support.

Twigs snapped to my left.

"I'd be quick about it, if I were you." Elle pointed at the folder while backing away from me, her focus in the direction of the rustling undergrowth. *"It doesn't look like we have time t' take in the scenery."*

I had no idea what happened next, what my future held, if I could even have a future. I was a changed man—no, I wasn't even a man anymore, and according to the she-devil, I was a different class of Vampire, whatever the hell that meant. Elle was right; only she would know the answers. Question was, would the real her give them to me?

Bending down, I collected the folder, grasping it to my chest. "Lead on, spirit. Lead on."

Chapter Two

~ Danielle ~

Sunday 11th October, 2015
Wicklow, Ireland

I awoke to the sound of rain hammering against my window, one of my all-time favourite sounds, especially when snuggled beneath my duvet. The world beyond my partly closed wooden blinds looked grey and wet—why would anyone want to leave the comfort of their bed for such a day? Why did anyone want to leave their bed most days? My bed had to be my all-time favourite place in the world, and I would gladly hibernate in it all year round if I thought I could, but my parents wouldn't forget about me so easily.

A glance at my digital alarm clock informed me it was past noon, so regardless of the lethargy hugging my limbs and the want to just stay put for the rest of the day, I really needed to get up.

Before I could change my mind, I threw my thick, blue duvet to one side, letting the cool air of my bedroom hit me, chasing away the want to hibernate. Hands firmly planted on my mattress, I pushed myself up. A groan escaped me upon catching sight of my face in my freestanding, black mirror across the way from my bed. Mascara was smeared all over my eyes, my hair resembled a bird's nest, and I was still wearing last night's white T-shirt.

When had getting ready for bed become such a chore?

Swinging my legs over the side of the bed, I forced myself to stand up. Last night's jeans and boots were pooled on the cream carpet along with my black bra. Shedding my knickers and top, I wandered into my bathroom, disposing the items in the bamboo wash basket. Grabbing my hairbrush, I set to work on the bird's nest, pausing to untangle the stray bobby pins caught in the auburn strands.

"You need to sort yourself out, Elle," I told my dishevelled reflection. I had been telling my reflection that a lot lately.

Hair untangled and tied in a high ponytail, I flicked the power on to the shower and walked inside, washing away the crust that was my make-up and the scent of cigarette smoke and lager, wondering yet again why these ordinary every day smells seemed a million times worse than Vampire blood.

Because you're not used to the smell yet. Give it time.

Not used to the smell of everyday vices, and yet Vampire blood ... I could have been coated in the rancid black gunge and it didn't bother me, and, well, when I stopped to think about it, that just seemed wrong. So very wrong ... Then again, not like my family were normal.

Washed and dressed in black leggings, a vest top, trainers, and smelling of sweet cherry blossom instead of a brewery, I headed down the hall toward the kitchen where I could hear my mother humming away, the scent of chicken broth wafting in the air.

"I didn't hear you come in last night," she commented as I stepped through the doorway.

The skylights beamed from the tall, arched ceilings, the white light more effective next to the roof window that revealed storm clouds and the ongoing slaughter of rain that heavily hit the double-glazed panes.

I made a b-line straight to the coffee pot, retrieving a clean mug from the silver stand which stood beside the green machine situated at the corner of the counter. "Well, I wouldn't be a very good hunter if I couldn't sneak around undetected."

"I've never known a hunter to waste their time standing behind a bar serving men pints," my father said from the kitchen table.

"That's because normal hunters never run out of prey," I retorted, pouring the fresh brewed caffeine into my mug.

Not even an ''Afternoon, dear daughter. I trust you slept well?'

It was straight in with the snide remarks. *He couldn't just drop this, for one day.*

My father hadn't been too happy when I went and got myself a part-time job at the local pub. Vampire Slayers weren't supposed to do anything else with their time but train, hunt, and talk about training and hunting for Vampires. I was one of many in a long-standing family business—an isolating, crazy-dangerous business which he much preferred me to be doing over the safety and monotony of standing in a building, serving customers, and earning money.

"You haven't run out of prey—"

"For the last time—" I put the pot back on its stand and turned to face him. "—I'm not going t'continue driving t'every corner of Ireland just t'look for Vampires. *That* was a big waste of time, not t'mention your money."

Fuel costs alone had been crazy. Throw in the fact that I needed to eat and occasionally sleep, it was costing a damn fortune to make sure the whole of Ireland was safe.

He lowered the newspaper, his dark eyes fixed on me beneath the two caterpillars that were his crazy, thick eyebrows. Lines marked the corners of his thin mouth, which was set in its usual line of disapproval. His fading brown hair was damp and combed back, and at least two days' worth of stubble claimed his tense jaw. "It is your duty—"

"Do you have t'discuss this again?" My mother stopped peeling the apple in her hand and glanced over her shoulder. She didn't move from her spot besides the cooker, but her gaze wandered between us. "Danielle is fully aware of her responsibilities."

"She could have fooled me." His tired gaze moved back to the paper in his hands.

"What do you want me t'do, Da?" I leant against the counter. "Go over to the UK and pay some Vampires t'come over here so I can hunt and slay them? It's not my fault that the undead find our lovely emerald island too boring to stay in. We all know the only reason activity was so high for all those years was because Alexis and Heather were with us."

He dropped the newspaper to the table. "This has nothing to do —"

"It has *everything* to do with Heather." I moved over to the table and took a seat opposite him. "She was the special one. The one they all wanted. When she moved, they moved." I took a swig of my coffee, before resting my arms on the table. "You should be happy there's no more activity over here. Isn't that what we all want, a Vampire-free zone?"

"What we want is to see Marko dead." He stabbed his finger against the wooden tabletop with each word spoken.

"He *is* dead," I remarked before taking another big swig of my coffee.

"Don't get smart with me, missy." His index finger now pointed at me, his French accent rearing its head as his irritation doubled. "You were trained to kill Vampires, like I was. Like—"

"Like every damn member of this family has been, and yet where are the rest of our family?" I put my mug on the table. "Is it left up to just us t'look for Marko? Are none of us allowed an ordinary life?"

"So, that's it?" He slumped back in his chair, hands gesturing to the 'outside' world. "You plan to work in the local pub for the rest of your life, ignoring what happens outside your door?"

My father thought I'd abandoned him and everything he had taught me, or at least that's what it sounded like recently, since I had come home from my hunting trip a few months back and declared that the undead had well and truly gone from Ireland. He was under the impression that I wanted to spend the rest of my life as a bar maid, and I had no clue what had given him that idea. All I wanted was to fill my time before I ended up going crazy, because what was I supposed to do with my time if all the Vampires had vanished? Was I just supposed to sit and wait for them to come back? Was I supposed to spend the rest of my life just existing?

Taking hold of my mug, I stood. "No, just until I find a job where my skill set will actually be some use."

Without another glance at my father, I moved round the table and headed toward the basement door.

"Danielle, dinner's almost ready."

"I will eat later, Ma," I called, halfway down the stairs.

***

"You've been down here a long time."

My mother's apron was gone. Left in jeans and a cream sweater, she looked like she belonged down here in the family training room. Arms folded, she leant against the door frame, watching me.

"Just training," I replied, and threw a punch at the red leather bag hanging before me. "Don't want my dull day job to cause my joints and abilities t'rust up."

To an outsider, this space would look like a gym—whitewashed walls, white spotlights beaming from the ceiling, grey carpet, and all the usual exercise equipment knocking around the place, plus a sparring area and fridge full of water. At the other end of the room, through the thick wooden door, you'd find the sauna and showers. Yeah, it was all just a harmless home gym with some added luxuries.

However, if they had chosen the door across the way from the one my mother leant against, the more serious-looking aluminium door, which was stood next to the second security panel—the first one being situated at the basement door at the bottom of the stairs leading from our kitchen—they would be surprised to find an armoury, slash family museum, slash archive that basically took up the remaining space of the basement.

As a child, our freakishly large basement had reminded me of those rooms you saw in James Bond films, the ones that were hidden and full of gadgets and men experimenting with them. Our basement was very much a secret agent's headquarters, or rather, a Vampire Hunter's training ground.

"You should just ignore your Da." My mother moved farther into the room. "He's still adjusting to the fact y'have a job."

A sharp laugh escaped me.

"Do you have any idea how ridiculous that sounds? You don't adjust to the idea of your twenty-five-year-old daughter getting a job." I belted the bag once more. "Having a job is normal. It's a normal part of a person's life."

"Not for his family."

"So, are we all just doomed t'walk in the same steps as everyone before us? Times have changed. Being a Vampire Hunter might have worked well in the medieval ages where you were going t'die young anyway." I walked over to the fridge, pulling the door open and retrieving a bottle of water. "Plus, you were poor and career options were practically non-existent for women, but this is the twenty-first century, which means I really only have two options: I either move somewhere with more activity and continue t'fight the good fight and fulfil my apparent, ongoing purpose in this age old family legacy, or …"

"Or?" she promoted after a moment.

I unscrewed the lid and turned to face her.

"I lay down my sword and try and have a normal, Vampire-free, life." I shrugged. "Is it so wrong that I might want that?"

"No."

"Well, you should let Da know." I took a mouthful of water and swallowed. "He acts as if I've stabbed him in the back."

"I love your father, Lord knows I do, but it would be a lie for me t'say that this was how I envisaged my life. So, I'd be a damn hypocrite if I said I didn't want something better for you, sweet pea." She perched on the edge of the bench press. "Naturally, I want you t'be alive and happy, not fighting your way to an early grave, but just know that if you're really meant t'do a certain something with your life, go somewhere, be with someone, fate is going to take you there regardless of how hard you fight against her."

"What are you getting at, Ma?"

"It's not wrong for you t'want t'have a 'normal' life, but honestly, I don't think this family will ever truly be free t'have any form of life until Marko is dead."

"And once he is?"

"None of us know for sure, but we all believe, have done, that there should at least be less Vampires walking the Earth after his demise, weaker ones, which after the last four centuries, I think it is safe t'say we have made our peace with that."

So many members of our family had died for this insane cause—my uncle Jean and cousin Alexis being the more recent two. Sofia at least had died from normal causes, not that cancer was a good way for anyone to die, but it was more natural than being shredded to pieces by one of the undead.

I slumped on the chair of the weight machine, elbows on my knees.

"I'm so fed-up, Ma, and I'm sick of sitting around, twiddling my god damn thumbs waiting day after day for a Vamp t'show up just so I can kill it and kid myself into thinking that the world is a little safer." I rolled the plastic bottle between my palms, watching the water move on the inside. "There are traces of evil everywhere. It's not just the undead we should be concerned about."

"Then become a supernatural private investigator."

I laughed. "Da wasn't too thrilled when I decided t'go and get m'self a part-time job just to fill the void. What makes you think he would be pleased if I decided to teeter off the path and put my unusual skill set t'some actual use?"

It shouldn't have mattered what my father thought, but it annoyed me that he couldn't see past this life, that he couldn't want more than what he had been thrust into. He'd already lost the use of his legs due to a fatal blow to his spine during a Vampire attack which occurred when I was fourteen. You'd have thought that—amongst a million other reasons and family deaths—would have hit home for him, made him realize that life is fragile and this crazy family legacy of ours was really freaking dangerous, life-threatening.

But no, the loss of his legs naturally pissed him off and therefore made him more determined for revenge, for vengeance.

52 | Cross My Heart

Unfortunately, he couldn't comprehend the reality of our current situation. The Vampires had vanished once Heather and Sofia had left. It had been two years, and activity hadn't picked up. Staying here in Wicklow was pointless if any of us wanted to be any use. None of us could fulfil our purpose where we were. I couldn't do shit here.

"Has this current evaluation of your life got anything t'do with Nathan?"

My chest tightened ever so slightly at the question.

Five days ago, I'd found out that my childhood best friend—well, the only friend I'd ever had—was missing. According to his mother, he had been missing for six weeks, or at least that was what she presumed since it had been over a month since his last postcard. I had been surprised to hear Lorna's voice through the receiver; it had been years. Twelve to be exact.

She'd forgotten all about me, which was why she was only just calling to see if I'd heard off her son. I'd wanted to be hurt at her words, at the idea that I was so forgettable ... *which at least explains why Than never contacts you anymore. He's forgotten all about you ...* but I could hear the panic and exhaustion in her voice, and I'd hated having to kill that hint of hope that had rung in between her words, but it was the truth: I hadn't seen Than for at least ten years.

We had made a promise that we would keep in touch, that we would see each other as much as we could, and he had visited for the first two years after he and his family had left, until his grandmother died, last family member and actual blood tie they had to Ireland. He and his parents never came back after that, and there was no way that my father was ever going to let me visit Switzerland, at least not until I was eighteen, but by that point, I was lucky if I even received an email from Than twice a year.

"Nathan could be dead," I uttered, not sure if I was saying that to myself or to my mother.

I was torn between not wanting to care and wanting to just jump in my Range Rover and go find him even though I was pissed that he had all but forgotten about me. He had been the only person—who wasn't family—I had actually, genuinely cared about, and even though he might not have ever thought about me after leaving, the idea that he could be dead somewhere out in the world, away from his family, from people who actually cared about him ... scared me. It scared me more than it should have.

"And Lord knows what Heather could be involved in," I added. "And what am I doing? Sitting around waiting for my next shift to start." I looked up, staring at the blank wall across the way from me. "I should be out there looking for him, helping Heather? Isn't that what Da is getting at? Isn't that one of the points for our training, so we can help those who need it?"

"Say you did go t'look for Nathan. Where would you even start? His mother has no idea where he was travelling to next. He could be anywhere in the whole world."

A needle in one massive haystack.

"I know." I sagged against the back rest. "But not looking for him just feels so wrong."

"But without a starting point ..." she trailed off.

Without a hint of where he could be ... I couldn't do anything for Nathan but pray. *And what good will that do?* He had last been in London, and I wasn't sure if that was the only place you visited in the UK before moving off to another country, or if you explored a little. Had he gone up north? Was he planning to visit Ireland? Visit me?

Get real. As if he cares about you. Don't be such a fool.

I shouldn't care what had happened to him. His mother not hearing from him didn't have to mean something had happened to him—his postcards could have been delayed or lost in the post. It happened. And yet, telling myself all that didn't stop the little niggle at the back of my head, the unease that sat in the pit of my stomach.

I pushed myself up, feeling agitated once more. "If Da wants me t'be of some use, then the least I can do is go help Heather. We weren't there for her when Sofia passed—"

"It was Sofia's wish that only Heather be present for the

funeral."

"Regardless, we should have gone over and stayed for a while. Just been there for Heather. She's lost enough loved ones in her short life, and now to be alone ..."

She'd lost her mother when she was eight, never knew her father, and now Sofia, who had practically raised her due to Alexis slowly losing her mind because she had been infected by the Vampyricc Virus. Heather was all alone. Sofia's wishes or not, we shouldn't have left her on her own, not when the Vampires had a personal interest in her.

"Sofia never did anything without a reason. Even if her actions and choices sometimes came across as selfish or uncaring, there was always a reason, and I believe there was a reason why she didn't want us at her funeral. We just have t'respect that. Besides, Heather is stronger than she looks and can easily take care of herself."

I paced, tapping the base of the water bottle against my left palm. "It's not like she has a choice."

She brushed a chunk of hair behind her ear, her hair a lighter shade than mine, almost bordering on dark ginger. "I spoke t'her the other week. She knows you will go if she needs you."

"Ack, she would never ask for help. The girl has a hero complex thanks to Sofia, which is probably the main reason she was pissed that Sofia had sent a Werewolf t'help her."

How did Sofia even know a Werewolf?

"She's not happy about that, but I don't think any of us would be happy t'wake up and find a stranger in our home, let alone a Werewolf who claims Sofia asked him to be there. She's confused, and I hate the fact that I'm not able t'shed any light on the situation for her. Sofia was extremely private."

That's an understatement.

"Well, Sofia should have spoken t'me. I should be the one who is there helping, not some stranger. This family legacy is as much mine to undertake as it is Heather's, yours, Da, and any other family members who are still living."

Not that our distant relatives seemed to give as much of a shit as my family did. Even though he said he was in touch with those who were left, I doubted they were doing anything to help this age-old cause of ours. No, they had probably given up long ago, realizing how crazy it all was and choosing to fight for a life instead.

"So why am I stuck here while she's off trying t'take down an entire species?"

"I dare say she wants t'be out there on her own." She pushed herself off the bench. "None of this is t'be taken lightly, Elle."

"Christ, Ma, give me some credit." I stopped, my hands coming to rest on my hips. "I've never been foolish enough t'believe I'm indestructible or t'want more than anything to run into the United Colony with my metaphorical guns blazing, but that's not t'say Heather won't do that. I can't imagine her head's in a good place at the moment."

"She sounded fine." Uncertainty flashed in her eyes, her expression less convincing than her words.

"Saying you're okay doesn't mean you actually are, Ma. Regardless of what she thinks, what she has been made to think, she needs all the help she can get, and I can't sit back and expect her t'do what we have both been trained t'do."

My mother pointed at herself and then me. "What we have all been trained t'do."

"She could have a life too. I know she has always believed that t'be impossible considering her ... mutation, but I think she could. I think we both could, and as easy as it would be for me t'hide here in Ireland... It's not fair of me t'let her sacrifice that possibility just so I can get on with my own life."

For all the speeches my father gave about getting out there and fighting the good fight, he had chosen a strange location to set up house. Don't get me wrong—my home was lovely, and our land was beautiful, breath-taking, so much so it could be quite easy to hide here in between the forest, loch, and mountains. We were snuggled away in nature, a purposeful choice as we were safe and cut off from our neighbours so when trouble did come knocking and it had ... our land was private, but still, you could easily forget about the rest of the world in this safe haven. Forget that there were bad things lurking out there in the dark.

"Something's brewing, Ma. It has t'be for Sofia t'ask a Werewolf t'help out."

She walked over to me, placing her hands on my upper arms. "I know, sweet. That's what I'm worried about, especially as Heather mentioned that Sofia had seen Luca in London."

And she *was* worried—I could see it swirling in her eyes, that beautiful mix of olive and hazel. My mother had kind eyes, caring eyes. Not the eyes of someone who had killed monsters, but I had seen for myself how handy she was, how her fire had died a little once my father had lost his legs.

My father wanted me to continue the good fight whereas the appeal had vanished a long time ago for my mother, and she was quite content in this sanctuary, hidden away behind walls and shrubbery. I hated to admit it, but perhaps I was more like my father than I wanted to be, because I couldn't live like this, not any longer.

Especially not now. Not when my cousin was out there looking for a second-generation Vampire who had a direct link to Marko. It was foolish of me to leave it to Heather and this stranger. I should have gone sooner.

"I can't just continue t'sit here. I'm restless. I need t'go to her. Regardless of if she says no, I think it's the right thing t'do."

"I'll give her a call now and see if she's home." She leant forward and pressed a kiss against my hairline, released me, and started to make her way toward the door. "You may have t'go to work and quit, seeing as you don't know how long you will be with Heather."

"Well—" I walked back to the punch bag. "—at least Da will be happy."

Chapter Three

~ Nathan ~

Tuesday 13th October, 2015
8:49pm

It was crazy how going back to a place after years brought a dream-like haze with it, how it seemed and felt as though you had stepped back in time, or into a memory. The odd sensation that stirred in your stomach because the scents in the air were the same and you remembered every step down the road and every house or tree as if you had only seen them yesterday. A large dose of nostalgia had swamped me the moment I'd passed the 'Welcome to Wicklow' sign, and even though it was night, I could recall every walk I had taken with Elle along the streets of our hometown.

Nothing seemed to have changed except me—a fact that I had spent the last two nights trying to wrap my head around. On reading through the rest of my file, I had learnt that something named VV had been injected into my heart, which was what had both killed me and kept me in this undead state. The rest was records of my appetite and the types of blood I'd been fed. There were more details about my balls—the Vampires had put my sperm on ice for some crazy reason.

The rest of it, well, I didn't really understand. Why did Vampires have a facility for experimenting? I thought they just liked to stalk graveyards and nightclubs, drink blood, and depending on which era and stereotype you wanted to roll with, have a lot of sex.

A lot of the facts that I already knew about Vampires had become more evident now I was out in the open. My sight was insane; it was almost as if I had a built-in telescope because if I looked long enough, I could see the details of a leaf, I could see the bug that was currently walking along the side of the wall even though he was as black as the night sky and I was five feet and eight inches taller than him. My hearing was what I imagined dogs' to be—I could hear people snoring in the houses I passed ... and I could run incredibly fast, even when shackled with silver, which was actually a blessing when you were running through a strange forest in the middle of the night trying to get away from Vampires and Wolves. Not to mention a little voice telling you that you had to get somewhere safe before sunrise otherwise you would be dust—a worrying thought especially because I had no idea at the time if there was anywhere safe for me to go.

"There had been no need for you to panic." Elle walked alongside me, her hands shoved in the pockets of her dungarees.

"Not panicking isn't an option when I had you going on all night, stressing that if I got caught by the Vampires, they would kill me, so would wolves, and getting killed by either would be Heaven compared to what it would feel like t'be burnt t'death by the sun."

"Just laying out some home truths," she replied with a shrug. *"Besides, we found you somewhere nice and safe."*

"I don't really class breaking and entering into the first unoccupied house we came across as safe."

"You're still alive, aren't you?"

"Alive?"

"Excuse me, Mr Sensitive, mobile." She shook her head. *"Jesus, you're so tetchy."*

"You would be, too, if you were the living dead."

She angled a look at me. *"I'm not even real."*

Which was another key point added to my list of new superpowers ... I appeared to have gone mad because I was talking to an imaginary teenage Elle. Had been talking to her for weeks, and even though part of me was fully aware she wasn't real, I was still able to see and hear her. Although, could you still be classed as insane if you were aware you were seeing things, if you knew you were talking to yourself?

"Yes."

"Oh, hush you." Being undead had another perk: the ability to not feel the cold, which was a blessing considering I was still topless and barefoot.

"Even if we found you a top, how would you have put it on? Your shackles are in the way."

"Yeah, I realize that." Apparently, I had the strength to bend metal, but that didn't include silver, which was what my cuffs were laced with. I vaguely remember Elle mentioning such allergies to me ...

"Plus, it was mentioned at the facility."

"Knowing I have a new allergy doesn't help me. What I need is a spare set of hands and a chainsaw t'get me out of these damn things." And my only hope was the real Elle who I was praying would have some form of tools to free me.

"Guess we will find out shortly."

My feet knew the way to Elle's family home, and without having to concentrate on a single step, I found myself there in no time, but I wouldn't step any further than the large, black, iron gate that marked the entryway to their estate. Guarded by six-foot walls, the place was completely cut off from public view, not that I imagined many people would travel down this back road. The next house was at least five miles away, the Renauds' nearest neighbours separated by fields and woodland.

It was crazy. As children, I wasn't allowed past this point. I wasn't allowed down that drive or in the house at the end of the long garden. Elle's parents knew me, knew we were friends, knew my parents, but it was a no-entry zone for anyone who wasn't family. Her father was a very private man, though Elle had once admitted the reason they never allowed guests in their home was because none of them wanted to have people associated with them, that it was for everyone's safety. If Vampires caught scent of me, they could come after me to get to them ...

I didn't understand. Apparently, it was mainly to do with her cousin Heather. Something was wrong with the younger girl, not that there seemed to be anything physically wrong with her, but Elle never went into details about it. I knew Heather's father had died before she was born and that her mother was ill which lead to her taking her own life when Heather was eight. Heather hadn't had an easy life, and if she was mixed up in all this Vampire hunting bollocks also, well, no wonder she always seemed so ... aloof.

It was annoying. I could never quite see the entire house from the gate, not through the structure of hedges and trees, but it always looked big and exciting. I guess it was because my house was small and ordinary compared to the manor house that hid behind these walls. Mainly it was because Elle had told me her family were Vampire Hunters and that she had to train in the basement. I used to have all these wild ideas that they had cool equipment down there, swords and arrows, maybe even a stray Vampire locked up in a cage ...

"Like you?"

"No, not like me. Like a bad Vampire, one that actually deserves t'be locked up."

"And you didn't deserve t'be?"

"Why would you even say that?" I scowled at her. "I was on holiday, minding my own business. I didn't deserve what happened t'me."

"Just wanted to make sure you knew that before you started comparing yourself to those original, cool ideas of yours."

Elle had confessed her family secret to me when we were twelve. At the time, I had thought she was joking about being a Vampire Slayer. I'd thought she'd made it all up because things at home had become so bad—her cousin Alexis had committed suicide—and she couldn't escape, couldn't cope, so she made up stories and creatures to amuse herself. Pretending to have another life always seemed like a good idea when you hated the one you had, when you felt there was no way out or to deal. I accepted all the little facts and details, the descriptions of the creatures, the fact she had started her training at eight, but she never let it go. She was adamant that her world was real, and I continued to amuse her, even after I had moved to Switzerland.

"And now, you know better."

Now I knew the truth—that she wasn't mad, or over-imaginative. It was real. All the facts were true. One being that now I was a Vampire, I couldn't enter her house without an invite. I could push the gates open and walk down the drive, something I had wanted to do for years, but I couldn't move. Fear kept my boots planted before the iron gate.

"Well, you can't stand out here forever. Best t'get in there and get this done with."

"Say I go in there and I get to the door and ring the bell. Then what? What am I supposed t'say t'her? *'I'm sorry I haven't seen you in years, that I stopped writing. I know you're probably pissed about it and that I am no doubt the last person you want t'see, but you're right, everything you ever told me about Vampires ... it's all real, which means you probably are a Vampire Hunter and funny story, I'm now a Vampire. Please don't kill me, I need your help."*

"Sounds fine to me."

"Get serious."

"Honesty is the best policy. Besides, it has taken us two nights t'get here. You can't just give up now we're at the end of the line." She passed through the iron gates, turned, and looked up at me. *"Get in here, and when you see her, just apologize for being a shite friend and tell her you're in a fuck load of trouble and she is the only one you know who will be able to help you. Get on your knees and beg if you have to."*

"So, leave out that I'm a Vampire?"

"Just until she invites you in the house. Then again, she has been doing this for years so might also know straight off that you're a Vamp or she might not recognise you ... Either way, the fact that you're topless and in chains might clue her in. So maybe stand a couple feet back from the door so you have room t'move encase she has a weapon at hand."

Elle would have more than one reason to not be happy to see me,

62 | Cross My Heart

the fact that it had been years since we'd last seen each other being the main one, but me being a Vampire and showing up at her door begging for help after years of not seeing her ...

"Maybe it was a mistake t'come here." I stepped away from the gates. "Maybe I should figure this out myself."

"Figure what out? You don't know any other Vampire so you have no one t'guide you and help you get t'grips with 'life as one of the undead,' the Vampires who are aware of you want you dead because they sure as hell didn't see you as an equal ... you were their prisoner, remember? I'm the only person who firstly, knows Vampires exist so I at least won't think you're crazy, secondly, show me the folder and I might actually know how t'find out answers about why Vampires have a facility and are doing experiments."

"*If* the real you chooses t'help me."

"There is only one way of finding out, and that means being a big brave Vampire and walking down this drive."

For weeks, all I had thought about was whether I would get out of that facility ... and how insane everything was, but I had never thought past that. Never thought about what I would do if I was back in the real world. I couldn't go back home to my family, because even though I would love to see them, and they would be happy to know I was okay ... I was dead. What kind of a life could I have? Would I be a danger to anyone? I didn't have the urge to go killing anyone or anything, but would that change? I hadn't drunk any blood for the last two days, and I felt fine. I had no idea what else I was capable of and no idea what I was supposed to do now with my newfound freedom.

"I thought you wanted t'find out why this has happened to you?"

"No, you want to find out why this has happened to me. I don't know if I want to know."

"You were kidnapped, technically murdered, turned into a—"

"I know what has happened t'me, Elle." I lifted my arms, rattling the chain to my cuffs, the folder still in my clutches. "You don't have t'keep reminding me."

"Don't you want answers? Don't you want t'know why?"

I didn't know what I wanted. My focus for the last few nights had been getting far away from that place ... had been on finding Elle, the real Elle, because she was the only one in the world I knew I could trust with what had happened to me. I had questions; I had a shitload of questions. Things that didn't add up to what she had told me when we were young; things I couldn't wrap my head around. Surely, Elle was the perfect person to ask? I knew she was, but now, standing outside sanctuary, I felt unsure.

"I can't do this tonight. I need time. I need to think."

"You've been thinking the last few nights."

"No, I've had you chattering at me for the last few nights, keeping me locked in that cell." I tapped my head. "I need peace and quiet. I need you t'go away."

Arms folded, she gave me a shrug. *"Fine, but just remember without me, you're now all alone in the world."* She started to fade, like the sand in an etcher sketch, only I wasn't shaking her to erase her. She was just blinking out of view. *"So, make sure you use your quiet time wisely and figure out what the fuck you're going t'do."*

My gaze remained on the space which she had currently occupied. Silence engulfed me as I stood in the darkness. "What the heck *am* I going t'do?"

*****

~ Danielle ~

Wednesday 14th October, 2015
6:33am

Glendalough Monastic City hadn't been an active place of worship in almost a century, and despite it being a tourist attraction, not to mention the perfect backdrop for a scene right out of a hammer house film ... there was an echo of something sacred here amongst the crumbled walls and headstones. A security and peace I had never felt anywhere else. Some might have found it strange to sit amongst graves and be at peace, but I suppose it was ironic that I felt safe here in the ancient Celtic cemetery, at home amongst the resting dead.

I had visited this site often in my childhood, ever since I had been dubbed old enough to go exploring on my own. The Round Tower and the accompanying buildings had been mine and Nathan's favourite place to explore as children, and after he left, I'd kept the ritual up, visiting the site at least once a week, once the gates had shut, sneaking in and climbing the wall to watch the sunset.

However, working evening into night had its drawbacks which meant some days, I had to watch the sunrise instead, which was why I sat on the high crumbled wall of what remained of the Friar's House, my back to the Round Tower, huddled in layers with a flask of hot coffee cradled between my gloved hands.

It was an odd ritual, perhaps morbid, but I had never made my mind up whether I believed in God, and for years, I had come here to unburden my soul, first to Nathan, sharing secrets and stories, and once he was gone, to anyone who would listen. I figured, at the very least, if Vampires existed, then a person's spirit could linger and be around their family at times. In my teen years, it had been Alexis I would talk to, about my fears over Heather and the pressure and restrictions Sofia placed on her.

However, I recently found myself talking to Sofia. Mainly because it had been a long time since I had seen her, and I was angry that I hadn't been able to say my goodbyes, that I had been robbed of that part of the grief process. She wasn't my grandparent or my guardian, but she had been an active role model and present every day of my life for nineteen years. It had been strange enough when she and Heather had left, but now, she was gone.

"The thing is, Auntie S, you seem to have forgotten that this family's burden is as much mine t'bear as it is Heather's." I sighed, rolling my flask between my palms. "Clearly, y'knew deep down it was too much for her t'cope with, despite what you drilled into her. Otherwise, why else would you get a Werewolf involved?"

It didn't make any sense why my aunt would go to an outsider over family or why anyone would agree to help a stranger with something so big and, well, dangerous. How did Sofia even know a Werewolf? Clearly, my aunt was a bit of a dark horse.

"You clearly had a lot more secrets than the family's shared lot. I just wish you would have sent for me instead." One way or another, I was determined to find out what the hell was going on with my cousin.

I had gone into work and told the manager I would be working my last week. Not that I could see it happening, but it all depended on the conversation that my mother would be having today with Heather. I'd finished five hours ago, had gone home for a nap, and got back up at six to come here as I knew it would be the last time I would be visiting my haven for a good while. Something was brewing. I wasn't sure what. Maybe it was just my imagination, but I felt restless, helpless. I couldn't help Nathan, and Heather didn't want my help. So I guess it was more to do with the fact I felt useless.

"No more." I wasn't sitting around on my arse any longer while everyone got on with their lives and duties. I was serving no good by staying in Wicklow. It was doing me no good standing here hoping things would change so I could be of some use. I had to go out there and embrace my destiny ... *Jesus, you sound like Sofia.*

"No offence, Auntie S." I tilted my flask to the sky.

"Sorry t'hear the ole girl has passed," a tenor voice commented behind me.

My heart leapt into my throat, and I pushed off the wall to land on my feet on the grass below, dull pain licking my calves on the impact. Dropping my flask by the wall, I grabbed my sword from where it rested in the arched, glassless window, my focus fixed to the remaining half a house as I backed away, searching for my unwelcomed guest. "What kind of a creep stands in the shadows spying on a woman?"

What kind of hunter doesn't hear a creep sneaking up on her? God, I must have been tired or turning lazy with all this sitting around. I hadn't even heard him approach.

"What kind of a woman hangs out in graveyards?" Amusement lit the male's tone.

"One who doesn't want t'be bothered by creeps."

"Lucky for you, I'm not a creep."

"The fact that you're slinking around a graveyard in the early hours of the morning would state otherwise."

"Well, that's hardly fair." The male stopped at the front, right corner of the house, his form pressed against the wall. "You're out here, too, and I'm not calling you names."

Great, creepy and weird. Just my luck.

There was no light out here, the site in complete darkness. The gravestones and buildings around me were blocks of black that only became solid as I moved closer to them. The male was a shadow, almost as lost in the dark as everything else was, and even thought I couldn't see him, see his face, I could feel his eyes on me.

"Why don't you just slither away and leave me be?"

"You're not scared out here on your own?" Something metal rattled.

My muscles tensed. "I've no reason t'be."

"All sorts of ... monsters … lurk in the dark."

"Aye." I raised my sword, unsure if he could see it, but the weight in my hand always felt reassuring. "And I know how t'handle myself."

"You always did."

The words were soft, thoughtful even, and not what you would expect some weird, creepy stranger to come out with. The hairs on the back of my neck stood on end, a chill sweeping down my spine. *What the...?*

My brow furrowed as I stared at the male's form. "Who are you?"

I waited, poised, on edge. Silence seemed to stretch out forever, deafening in the darkness, uncomfortable. He hadn't moved, not an inch, but I could still feel his gaze on me.

"Cat suddenly got your tongue," I found myself saying, needing the strange silence to end. "Or have you suddenly gone deaf? Either tell me who you are and what you want or get lost."

That unsettling scrape of metal was my reply, right before he stepped away from the building. His form moved toward me. "I want your help."

Not the reply I was expecting. "What? Why?"

He paused. "For old times' sake."

Unease washed over me. Confusion beat in my temples. "Stay where you are."

I reached into my left coat pocket and retrieved my mobile. A few taps and bright, white light streamed out in front of me from the phone's torch. I stumbled back at the sight— the light poured over the man in front of me. The pasty-looking, half-naked man.

"Hello, Elle." A small smile lit his pale, exhausted face.

Vague familiarity tickled the back of my mind at the sight of that almost cheeky stretch of his parched lips.

His smile died as he glanced down at himself.

"I realize I'm not looking like my fine self. I didn't expect t'see you so soon, especially not at six-thirty in the morning." He glanced up, his black eyes meeting mine, dark circles beneath them. "Nice t'know this place still means something t'you. It hasn't changed."

My stomach bellowed out. It couldn't be, could it?

"Th-Than?" My heart had stopped, my mind spinning with a million different questions, and yet, the most stupid one managed to escape my mouth first. "Is-is it really you?"

His shoulders relaxed. "Yup, last time I checked."

I lowered my sword, leaving it to hang at my side.

"What-what are y'doing here?" I moved the light over his form. "Why t'hell are you half undressed?"

68 | Cross My Heart

His frame was athletic, arms made up of slender muscles, a subtle six-pack. All in all, an indication of a healthy guy who looked after himself to an extent. But right now, he looked like shite. He looked drained, as if he hadn't slept in a year, his gaze too dark and sad, not how I remembered him. His steel-blue eyes had always shone with such mischief, so very fitting for him as he had been a typical lad, always up to no good. Always joking and laughing.

I'd seen photos of him over the years on social media, but right now, he looked like a ghost of himself. His brown, cropped hair was tatty and flat, smudges of dirt marking his temples, his neck —heck, everywhere that skin was visible, which was pretty much everywhere since all he wore was filthy, ripped jeans. No shoes, no top; he had to be freezing.

"What t'hell happened t'you?"

Nathan moved his arms. That metal scrape sounded, and that's when I noticed the thick cuffs around his wrists, the chain dangling from them. This had to be a lucid dream or the start of some weird nightmare. I was tired and a little amped up on caffeine, clearly worried about Than more than I was letting myself believe because somehow, he was standing right in front of me looking like death in irons.

So surreal that it just *couldn't* be real.

Lifting my gaze from the chains, I looked back at his sickly face. "Why are you in— I don't understand. Are those actual shackles?"

"Oh, you mean my new accessories. Well, more like extremely old." He lifted them. "Yeah, the salesman wouldn't take no for an answer." A dry laugh escaped him. "I-I was actually hoping you might be able t'help me with these?"

I shook my head, my eyebrows surely colliding at the top of my nose from the frown. Even my temples had started to throb. "Wait, I don't understand. How are you here right now? Your mother said you were missing."

He took a step forward, his eyes widening. "You've spoken t'my mamai?"

"Aye."

"Is she okay?"

I blinked. "She's worried sick about you, naturally. She said she hasn't heard from you in six weeks, that you and a friend were backpacking and—"

"Six weeks?" He slumped forward, his face a picture of shock. I moved the light to follow him as he wandered over to the outer wall of the friar's house. His shoulder hit the stone, his wide-eyed focus lost on the ground below. "Six. Weeks."

Unease set in my stomach along with fear and relief, a jumble of emotions that even made my heart feel woozy. "Than, what happened t'you?"

"I, erm—" He lifted his head and looked toward me ... no, not toward me, past me, and he shook his head.

The hairs stood up on the back of my neck. My grip on the hilt of my sword tightened as I cautiously turned, half-worried I was going to find another half-naked person standing behind me, but as I moved my phone torch around the space, I could see nothing, just gravestones.

When I moved the light back to him, he was sat on the grass, his head pressed against the wall, staring off into space.

"Than?" I took a step toward him.

"Truth is I-I do actually need your help, Elle."

"You need *my* help?"

"I had no one else I could turn to." He looked past me again, giving empty space a pointed look. His brow furrowed, and he shook his head once more. "No, scratch that, you're the *only* person I could come to like—" he flicked his hands up and down his chest. "—like this."

"And how exactly did you get like this? A casual hook-up gone wrong? Or perhaps you joined a travelling renaissance fair?"

"What? No." His gaze was firmly fixed on me. "I-I was attacked, Elle. Me and my friend Freddie, we were attacked in London. I-I woke up in this place, in this dark room and, well, we were—" His jaw was trembling; he couldn't get the words out fast enough or without tripping over his own tongue. "—we were fucking kidnapped, fucking experimented on, and now, Freddie's dead—"

"What?"

His eyes grew wide. His words held too much weight, too much clarity, as if he was not only trying to convince me but himself.

"Freddie's dead. He's really dead, like dead-dead." His face fell into his hands, his words muffled. "Shit. Shit, fuck, shit. I've spent the last six weeks locked in a cell in some fucking facility in the middle of a goddamn forest—"

His words became a jumble of curses and broken information beyond comprehensible. My head hurt, my eyes riveted on this mess of a man crumbled on the ground in front of me. This wreck of a man was Nathan. He was safe—well, at least he was now, but he had been locked up for six weeks? What? Why? His friend was dead due to experiments?

I suddenly felt like the scrap of caffeine-fuelled energy that had been circulating in my body the last half an hour had been absorbed. My legs felt like dead weight as exhaustion hit me right in the face. My temples were hurting, and I felt sick as all the built-up worry and frustration I'd had for the last couple weeks dropped to the pit of my stomach.

None of this made any sense. Nathan was no longer missing, but who would have kidnapped him? Why would they lock him up? Did he have enemies? Was he mixed up in something bad, drugs, or maybe he owed someone money? Why hadn't he gone straight to the police? Why had he come here? Why to me? Why—

My thoughts ground to a halted as his hands dropped to his lap.

"That's why Ma hasn't heard from me, why no one has." Black blood streaked his pale skin, seeping from the corners of his dark eyes.

The blood in my own veins froze. I couldn't move. I could hardly breathe. "You're ... you're crying—"

"Grown men can cry under times of stress, Elle. It's not that unusual."

I wasn't sure if I was about to throw-up or pass out. I felt like I had a typhoon in my stomach, and my head had grown light. Maybe it was due to the early hour. Maybe it was the five-hour nap I'd had—short bouts of sleep often made people feel funny, didn't they? And I really was freaking exhausted right now. Maybe it was the unexpected shock of seeing an old friend for the first time in a decade, or more how he had approached me after apparently being missing—naked, ill, and rambling like a mad man.

God, if only it could have been any of those reasons, but it wasn't, and without having to think about it, I'd already tightened the grip on the hilt in my grasp. Despite the tension seizing my muscles, I had already dropped down to one knee, my left arm held high so that the white light of my camera coated his upper body and face.

"Blood." The words were acid on my tongue, the tip of my sword a mere two inches from the Vampire's jugular. "You. Are. Crying. Blood."

***

~ Nathan ~

I don't know why I ended up at the Monastery. I knew the sun would be rising soon and that I needed to find somewhere safe to hold up for the day, but the place seemed to call to me. Or perhaps it was the memories, the ones I had been playing repeatedly in my mind; memories of when I was younger and innocent, and Vampires were just scary, sexy creatures in films. Whatever the reason was for my feet to lead me there, I certainly hadn't been expecting to find a very grown-up Elle lurking in the dark.

Vampire sight was a funny ole thing because I could see her quite clearly. She was made of shadows, but I could make out the angles of her face, the line of her lips, her eyes even though I couldn't see the colour. Not that I needed to. I knew they were moss-green. Her hair was tied up at the back, and she wore a thick scarf round her neck. She smelled of cigarette smoke and lager—not scents I would associate with her, but I didn't know her anymore. A point she was making very clear with her distance.

I couldn't say I knew exactly how she would react to seeing me. I had hoped she'd have been happy in a surprised way, even if it was hidden by anger. A bit of anger was expected, but instead, she was cautious.

"You appeared out of nowhere, it's dark, and you're both in a graveyard. Anyone in her shoes would be cautious," young Elle said in the distance where she leant against a nearby gravestone, arms crossed.

I don't know why I expected her to be bothered about seeing me, why I'd expected a bigger reaction than the one I was currently getting.

Maybe because we were friends ... because she's all I've thought about for weeks? My thoughts and words had run away with me the moment she'd mentioned my mother, told me I had been missing for six weeks.

Despite feeling like I could run for miles or that I could easily lift a truck, I found myself needing physical support. My feet had stumbled over to the nearby wall, shoulder hitting the rough, cold stone as another dose of harsh reality made it through my skull.

I've been like this for six fucking weeks?

My mother knew something was wrong. She was probably worried sick ...

"And there's nothing y'can do about it."

I slid to the floor, my butt hitting the damp grass. My sight blurred slightly, a trail of moisture staining my cheeks. *Six fucking weeks.*

"Get over it, you big cry baby." Young Elle snorted.

I dropped my hands to my lap and scowled at her. "Grown men

can cry under times of stress, Elle. It's not that unusual."

My eyes smarted as the harsh white light of real Elle's mobile torch moved closer to me. My gaze darted to her face as she crouched down in front of me. With the light held at an angle, her face was illuminated, and despite the bags that sat under those large eyes ... she looked amazing. Her creamy pale skin was flushed due to the cool air, a scattering of freckles across her nose and cheeks. Her jaw was tense, her cute button nose flared.

"You're crying blood," she bit out.

"Oh, shit, you really are." Young Elle appeared beside her, wide-eyed.

My brow furrowed as I glanced between them. I reached up to my cheeks which already felt moist, my tears no doubt already dry due to the cool morning air. True enough as I looked down at my fingertips and palms, they were smeared with blood, though it wasn't a watery red as anyone would expect blood to be. No, the liquid was thick and black, tar-like.

Something glinted in my eye. "What the fuck?"

I feebly pushed back, into the wall, trying to get away from the knife which was currently pointed at my throat. No, not a knife.

"Is that a sword?" I glanced down the long strip of sharp metal, stopping when my eyes met hers. "Where the hell did you get a sword from?"

"It's what I use to kill your kind." The words had been ground out, her expression stone-cold as she stared at me.

"My kind?" A nervous laugh fluttered from my throat. "Elle, it's me. It's still me."

"I don't know you. I have no idea what kind of person you are anymore." She shook her head. "Scrap that. You're *not* a person anymore."

Something inside me sank at the truth or her words. It had been one thing to have a Vampire tell you that you weren't human; it had been another for my own fucked up mind to keep reminding me, but to hear someone else clarify it ... Having Elle look at me as if I were a stranger, not even a stranger, just as if I was nothing ... It actually hurt.

"No, you're right. I'm not a person anymore; they've taken that from me." I dropped my hands to my lap. "I know I had no right to come t'you. I've been a lousy friend—"

"A shite friend," she interjected.

"I've been the worst, and believe me, I understand your reluctance t'help me for that reason alone, but I *need* your help."

"I don't help Vampires. I kill them."

"Even ones that didn't ask to be Vampires in the first place?"

Her jaw flexed, a crinkle forming at the bridge of her nose. "Yes."

"You're jokin' right?"

Her grip tightened on the hilt of her sword. "I never joke about Vampires."

I pressed a little further into the wall, ignoring the sharp pricks of the rough, uneven stones on my back. "See, I always thought y'did and then I became one ... Could we just talk without you holding that sword in my face?"

"No."

"Look, up until six weeks ago, Vampires were just folklore t'me, and then I was attacked, Elle. They kept me tied up." I lifted my bound hands up to the side of my face, being careful to not knock her sword. Her gaze moved to the shackles and then back to my face. "They force-fed me, experimented on me. They had a file on me. I've left it by the wall round the corner. I don't understand most of it, but if you read it, you can see what they've done."

"Do you really think I'm that stupid?"

"No, you're smart, and you're the only person who will understand what all the jargon in that file means."

"I turn my back on you and you attack me or run off."

"I'd never attack you, Elle. As for running off, I've spent days trying t'get here, t'you. I've got nowhere t'go, Elle. You're the only one I can trust." My shoulders sagged. "They injected me with something, Elle, and they-they fucking castrated me. Please

—"

"Vampires don't do shite like that."

"They do. I swear t'God they do. Just look at the file. Please, you're the only one I know who knows about this stuff, and the only reason I haven't thrown myself off a cliff is because I spent every second thinking about you."

She blinked. Uncertainty swirled in her eyes. A strange look crossed her features.

"TMI, Than." Teen Elle coughed.

"I mean, knowing that you would believe what had happened to me—"

"You thought wrong." Her fingers flexed on the hilt of the sword. "The only thing I believe is what I see with my own eyes. You're a Vampire, and I kill Vampires."

"Jesus Christ, Elle, it's me. I didn't ask for this, and I have no fucking idea why they chose me." My eyes felt clogged once more, the hint of something slithering down my cheeks. "I don't know what t'do, Elle. Please, for old times' sake, if not for our childhood for my Mamai. I can never see her again, Elle. Not like this. Please just read the file and tell me what it means, and I will go and leave you in peace. I just want t'know what is going on. Why all of this has happened." My voice cracked. "What I'm supposed t'do. Please?"

Silence stretched out before me. Our eyes locked, hers not giving anything away. Suddenly, she straightened, standing with the sword still in my face. "Crawl and get the folder."

She took a couple steps back, the light of her torch following my every movement as I twisted on to my knees and crawled through the grass alongside the crumbled building until I got to the corner where I had stopped earlier. Reaching round, I felt for the manila folder, taking hold of it. I fell back on my knees and held it out to her.

"Open it."

I did as she asked.

Squatting back down, sword now pointed at my midsection, she scanned the first page of my file, her eyes widening slightly when they landed on the autopsy photo. "This has t'be a-a hoax."

"It *isn't* a hoax."

"None of this makes sense. This isn't how Vampires are created." She looked between me and the folder, her brow furrowed. "*Is this* a joke, Than? Are you playing a game?"

"What?"

Her eyes seemed to hold a million questions. "People have been worried about you and—"

I shot up, quicker than intended. She fell back, butt hitting the grass, sword slipping from her grasp. I grabbed her wrist.

"This isn't a fucking joke." I pulled at her arm, flattening her hand against my chest. "I have no fucking heartbeat."

The tension faded from her arm. She relaxed her fingers and pressed her palm firmly against my chest. Her eyes met mine, a hint of moisture hiding in their corners.

"This is *not* a fucking hoax, Elle," I said slowly. "They *killed* me." I could feel the tears seeping from my eyes, and the mixture of horror and pity that claimed her features only made it worse. "And turned me in to this."

A moment passed. Her big, beautiful green eyes searched my face over and over as if she were searching for some vital clue.

"Let me go." The words were practically whispered when she finally replied.

I let go of her wrist. She pushed herself to her feet before leaning down and collecting her sword from the ground. The tip appeared in my face once more. "Y'try and bite me and I *will* kill you, old friends or not. Are we clear on that?"

Relief crashed down on me as I stared at her. "Crystal."

She glanced at her mobile. "The sun is due up in half an hour. I need t'get you somewhere safe."

I just wanted to sink at her feet and cry some more.

"Jesus, you need t'man up."

I slid a scowl to teen Elle who was draped over a nearby

headstone. "Thank you, Elle. Thank you—"

Real Elle held up her hand and cut me off. She nodded at the file on the ground. "Bring that and explain as we go. Start from the night you were attacked, and don't spare any details."

Chapter Four

~ Danielle ~

9.08am

I dropped the file on the bed beside me. My head also wanted to drop that way into my hands … I had brought a Vampire home with me, and not to torture. I'd clearly lost the fucking plot.

No not a Vampire. Nathan.

He's still a Vampire. You still brought a Vampire home with you.

Fuck.

I'd brought Nathan home. Well, he was still resting in the storage space under the backseats of my Range Rover parked on the drive, and he would be staying there until sundown. There was enough physical proof that he was a Leech—crying blood, ice-cold to touch, and the no-longer-having-a-heartbeat was a no-brainer. But the file he had given me, his file, backed up what I could see with my own two eyes, backed up everything he had told me.

He hadn't been turned into a Vampire in the traditional manner, which made no sense. Surely, it was easy to bite a human, let them drink your blood? Why had they done it differently with him? Why go to all the extra trouble?

When a Vampire bit a human, the venom got into the blood stream. If the Vampires were feeding, they easily sucked it back out, but if it was for the purposes of turning—or they were new-born and had no idea what they were doing—then the venom triggered the first stage of the mutation. If a Vampire didn't baptize an Infected with their blood, then the Infected would run wild, but if they did, then the victim's body would go into lockdown as the venom worked its magic. A few days in a cold room, and then the new Vampire would wake up.

The Vampires at the facility had kept Nathan in a cold, dark room, from what he described of his cell. The reference the file kept making to the VV injection I could only presume referred to Vampire Venom. And I couldn't be a hundred percent sure if he had been baptized with a Vampire's blood, or if they had added some into the cocktail, but whatever they had done, they had definitely killed him and somehow made him a Vampire.

I couldn't wrap my head around it, and the only person who might have the slightest clue as to what all this would mean was Heather—she was the only living Infected in the history of Vampires, so I was damn certain that the file that currently lay beside me would make far more sense to her. Besides, she was the only family member I could trust with this information, and could my mother get a hold of her? No. She had gone AWOL, which was worrying enough considering the last thing we knew was a Werewolf had shown up and given her some beyond-the-grave message from my aunt Sofia.

Now Nathan shows up as one of the undead, escaped from a facility that had had a run in with Wolves? Not to mention the word Were-gene had popped up in his file a couple of times. I wasn't a scientist or a Werewolf expert, but I had an inkling that the Vampires were playing with Werewolf DNA. You had to love an obvious name for a substance.

Was all this a coincidence? I really would have loved to believe that, but when you grew up knowing monsters existed and you had your very own family psychic who drummed it into you that everything in life happened for a reason and fate was very real even if she was a bitch at times ... "What t'hell is going on?"

I couldn't go to my mother and father with this information, and telling them about Nathan was a huge no. I couldn't even process how my parents would react, but it wouldn't be in a good way.

If I hadn't already planned to go across to see Heather, well, Nathan had left me no other choice. I had to find my cousin in the hope that she might be able to shed some light on what the Vampires could have done to him. Problem was, would she be willing to help a boy she once knew now that he was a Vampire?

Were you willing? Are you?

80 | Cross My Heart

He wanted answers, and I couldn't give them to him.

I wanted answers, and he sure as hell couldn't give them to me. What option did I have?

Kill him. Put him out of his misery.

Boy, he had looked miserable. He was clueless and helpless ... so not Vampire material. If I'd have just swung without a thought, I could have done it, but it was his eyes ... though they weren't his own anymore. Not the light, mischievous steel-blue I remembered from childhood. They were dark, confused, and lost. Dare I say, sad; the most human, Vampire eyes I had ever seen, if that was even possible.

You could have killed him, should have. You can't trust a Leech.

Every fibre in my body had screamed for me to kill the Vampire in front of me, but I could still see Nathan, and although I was mad at him—still mad at him for how easily he had cast me aside—I couldn't kill the only friend I'd ever had, not when he was begging for my help.

It would have been a mercy killing.

No, I couldn't. Not when he looked so afraid. I was the only one who *could* help him.

"God help me." I fell back on the bed, staring at my ceiling.

I had no choice. I wanted answers. He wanted answers, and if I was being honest, I was damn curious to know why Leeches were suddenly so interested in biology and genetics.

*****

7:57pm

"You can come out now." I exhaled while driving past the county line to state we were leaving Wicklow.

I usual got a rush upon sighting that big sign, since knowing I was getting away from home was always bliss, but tonight, I was filled with uncertainty. It wasn't a feeling I was used to or one that I liked. I was always so certain of everything. Certain that there were no Vampires in Ireland and that their numbers would never grow. Certain that my father was impossible and that our family was truly nuts. Certain that I had made the right choice to go to Heather and be of some use.

My gaze darted to the overhead mirror and partially watched the black seats lifting, Nathan's pale hand sliding along the plastic underside, his fingers curling round the edges as he pulled himself into a sitting position.

It felt almost ironic. Here was my childhood friend who'd questioned me over every detail of Vampires' existence and comparing everything to Hollywood's view on the creatures, and he looked like he was enacting a scene out of Hammer House. Although Christopher Lee was never half-naked or climbing out of car seat storage.

Harbouring a Vampire had not been part of yesterday's plan, let alone helping one. Christ, could I even help him? Was taking him to Heather the right thing to do?

I glanced back as the seats clicked into place, watched as he stretched his arms, the silver cuffs and chains that had been wrapped around his wrists and ankles now gone due to the help of some bolt cutters, a screw driver, and mallet.

"Well, I hope there's more room in my coffin because that's not how the dead should rest." His eyes met mine in the mirror, and a sheepish grin appeared. "Too early for dead jokes?"

Lord, give me strength.

"You have an hour, and then I'm afraid it's back in there." I reached over and grabbed the T-shirt I had pinched from my father's wardrobe. "It will be big on you, but at least it will cover you up for now."

His fingertips were cool as they skimmed my wrist, collecting the T-shirt from my grasp. "Don't like what y'see?"

I snatched my hand back, resting it once more on the wheel. "You look like death."

"Well then, he needs t'take his robes off more often if he's this hot."

He pulled the black T-shirt over his head, but I didn't miss the smirk at his own joke.

Typical Nathan: he had always found himself funny. He was an idiot.

"Where are we going?" He settled in the middle seat.

I exhaled and moved my focus back to the road. "I read your file."

"And you believe me, right?"

"I don't fully understand some of it, but aye—" I met his gaze in the mirror. "—I believe you."

He relaxed, practically sank into the seat, his head hitting the backrest.

"I want t'show it t'Heather. She's the only one who might be able to explain what it all means. However, she moved t'London two years ago. So, we're going t'her. The ferry is at nine-thirty p.m. We should reach Holyhead at eleven-forty-five, and then it's a five-hour trip to London. But at this time of night, we might be able to make it in four."

Seven hours give or take. I could only hope it would go swiftly as small talk had never been a strength of mine.

"Either way, we should be at hers before five a.m."

"Do I have t'go back in the box?"

"Only while we're on the ferry."

Only while we were around other people. Being locked in a car wasn't ideal, but it would at least contain him and mean everyone travelling would be safe. I had no idea if he knew his own strength, if he would be able to break the door off my car or claw his way out of the floor. I had no idea if his thirst was sedated, or when he had last fed. I had offered to find him a hare as there were always plenty running around in the forest bordering my family's land, but he had gagged at the idea.

I had never seen a Vampire retch before, well, without the tendrils of smoke escaping their mouths due to the silver I had just shoved down their throat. It was odd.

"I will see if I can find you some clean clothes on the journey."

"I could really do with a shower. Don't want to scare the poor girl."

"Believe me, Heather doesn't scare easily."

She had seen more freaky shit in her twenty-one years than most people could dream of, but then, hadn't we all.

"Will she try t'kill me, once she figures out what I am?"

No concern or fear accompanied his words. His gaze was on the side window, and he suddenly seemed lost in thought.

"Maybe, but she is more like you than y'think."

Heather had been the closest person my family had known to almost be a Vampire. She was one fatal ingredient away, as had been her mother. In so many ways, Alexis had been more dangerous than any Vampire; she had been an Infected, and they were unpredictable. Yet, my father had let her live in our home, her and Heather. I have no idea if Alexis and Sofia had had to put up a fight for the protection. I could recall the odd whispered discussion between my parents about my cousins, remember one huge argument that had occurred—my father had offered to put Alexis out of her misery.

"My life has never been my own, but you can bet your arse my death will be on my own damn terms. Not theirs, and not yours. This family's having nothing more from me."

She had ended her own life when she'd known she couldn't carry on. I often wondered if Heather would ever reach that point? How did she cope, being so close to the creatures she killed? The creatures that were the cause of both her parents' deaths, the cause of her issues?

"She might sympathize."

"So, you're telling me she's actually a man?"

A sigh escaped me. And just like that, he was back.

"That was another joke."

"It wasn't funny."

He snorted. "Sheesh, I remember you having a better sense of humour."

"And I remember you always thinking you were funny

84 | Cross My Heart

regardless of whether I agreed."

My chest tightened at the sight of him rolling his eyes and huffing. So normal. So Nathan. He seemed so ordinary, so relaxed. Not like any Vampire I had encountered before.

How many times have you carpooled a Vampire? How many times have you had the chance to have a normal conversation with a Vampire? How many Vampires were once your friend?

Reality was starting to catch up. My grip on the wheel tightened.

What was I doing? Driving around with an unrestrained Vampire in my backseat? Taking him to England with me?

"Wait, are y'telling me your cousin's a Vampire?"

His question broke through the whirl of thoughts. My brow furrowed as my focus moved back to the overhead mirror.

"And you wanted t'kill me." He crossed his arms across his chest. "A tad hypocritical, don't y'think?"

Was it?

"She's not a Vampire." But she's not far off being one, and never had I thought of killing her. She had never given me any reason to consider doing such a thing. "She's a born Infected."

And more dangerous than the Vampire who is looking at you like you have just given him a maths equation to answer.

"Yeah, that's right over my head."

Heather was a trained killer. Plus, a born Infected. Without Sofia's special mocktails, then Heather would be worse than a Vampire, wouldn't she? What if she had gone loco? What if she had given in to her thirst? She would be grieving and … God, could I kill her, if it came down to it?

"You a-you remember I told you how Vampires are created?" I turned my attention to the road ahead. "A person is bit by a Vampire and then they have to drink their blood?"

"I remember very clearly, which was why I was baffled when that didn't happen to me. Thought you had been telling fibs."

"They seem t'have found another way of creating Vampires."

"Why would they want that?"

Great question. Why create Vampires differently? Why had Heather survived? Why were the rules suddenly changing?

I shook my head and took a deep breath, needing to concentrate on the conversation we were having instead of the one going on in my head.

"I don't know, but hopefully, we can find out. When a Vampire bites a human, they give them their virus. Now, if the Vampire doesn't baptize the human with their blood, then only one stage of the creation is complete. We refer to humans with the virus as Infected. Basically, the virus is breaking down their body, and if left, they can go insane and—"

"So, it's normal for people t'go insane if they have this virus?"

"Well, it's not their fault. The virus wants t'be fed so it's the need for blood which actually causes the human t'go insane. I mean, think about it. You're human, and you want t'drink blood, it's gross and wrong, but you can smell it and hear it gushing in people's veins ... in your family's veins. You want t'hurt people. So, one way or another, you're more than likely t'crack up. Infecteds are a liability, so if there are any running around, Vampires find them, offer them the change, or kill them because they can't have the human world knowing of their existence. Infecteds are usually created by mistake, often by new Vampires who have no idea what they are doing."

"So, you think I'm an Infected?"

I had no idea what to think; this was out of my box of what was normal.

"I want t'say yes." I glanced back in the mirror. "You seem calm, you're not overly hungry, but your fangs are under half the size and showing without you transforming, which isn't normal."

His eyes widened as if he had just figured something out. "Oh, yeah, the Master out of Salem's lot. That's what I'm supposed t'look like, right?"

I rolled my eyes. "Your fangs are puny. You don't appear t'have any of the Vampires' strength, and apart from your sickly complexion, you look like a regular guy."

And although saying all that out loud helped, it didn't calm me.

It wasn't right. This was not what was supposed to happen. Why did he look like the Hollywood version of a Vampire?

"Are y'done devampulating me?"

"Excuse me?" A laugh escaped me. "What t'hell does that even mean?"

He shrugged. "The same as emasculating, only we aren't talking about my manhood, just my vamphood."

"It's so worrying that you're creating your own terminology."

"I've been locked up for six weeks with nothing t'do but think about this condition that I now have that doesn't fall under the natural law. It seems fitting t'create terms t'simplify the insanity that is my descent into the realms of impossibility. Sue me."

I couldn't help the smirk that curled the corner of my mouth. He was still an idiot, and despite his current predicament, that was a good sign. He was still the Nathan I remembered. Still had his character. There was something strangely reassuring in that. Something comforting.

Yeah, but you being comfortable with a Vampire is not a good sign.

"Anyway, you're not an Infected. However, Heather is, which is why I think she will be able to explain all of this better than I can."

"So, your cousin has this Vamps Virus? How come you never mentioned it?" He almost sounded offended.

"Erm, because you thought I was crazy for believing in Vampires t'begin with, and the idea that I was training t'hunt them sent you into a fit of giggles."

"Well, yeah—" His voice softened. "—That's because Vampires weren't real back then."

"They have always been real."

"Not t'me." His voice dropped to a whisper.

My heart lurched. This was all too surreal, all too crazy.

"Well—" I cleared my throat. "I thought you wouldn't be able t'wrap your childish head around anything else I told you."

That earned me a very defiant look through the mirror. "Try me."

"Heather was born with the virus. My cousin Alexis was bitten when she was pregnant. That's why she, Heather, and my aunt Sofia originally came to live with us. Ireland isn't a hotbed of Vampire activity. It seemed safer over here for them."

I heard him shift in his seat. "So, Alexis was an Infected?"

"For a while, until she put a gun to her head."

"Sorry, I knew she had taken her life. I just didn't know she—"

"It's okay. I mean, it wasn't, but she had been battling with violent thirst for eight years. On top of that, she had mistakenly got her daughter infected, and the night she was bit, well, the reason she got bit was because she went after her husband. He had gone to the United Colony ... they ate him alive."

There was a long pause before he spoke again. "You mean that in the literal sense, don't you?"

I glanced back in the mirror and nodded.

I don't know how it was possible, but he suddenly looked even paler.

"Fuckin' hell. How the shit do you deal with all of this?"

"I've been brought up with it. This is my life."

He scrubbed his hands across his face and through his hair. "Christ, Elle."

"Alexis killed herself, so Sofia raised Heather, fed her blood a few times a day, and I dunno, it seemed t'do the trick. You'd have never known that Heather was an Infected, but then Sofia was very protective over her. The only real reminder was the fact that more and more Vampires seemed t'be coming over. It was great practice for our training, but when Sofia took her back over to London two years ago, all the Leeches went with them."

He rested his elbows on his knees as he leant forward. "So, they were only here for Heather?"

"Like I said, an Infected has two choices: be turned or be killed. The fact that she is a member of this family and the first born Infected, Christ, she was famous amongst the undead."

88 | Cross My Heart

"Do they still want t'kill her?"

"Aye, which is another reason we're going t'London t'find her. Sofia died two months ago, and Heather is all alone, well, apart from the Werewolf my aunt sent to her—"

"I'm sorry, did you say Werewolf? Werewolves exist?"

I glanced over my shoulder at him. "You said there were some at the facility?"

"No, I said there were apparently wolves at the facility."

"Well, there definitely were as there is mention of the Were-gene in your file."

"Were-gene?"

"The—"

"I don't think my head can take any more tonight." He fell against the backrest, eyes wide. "So, you're telling me there are people in this world that can turn into wolves?"

"Not exactly. Think more wolfman."

"So, they just become hairy men."

"Have you seen the film Van Helsing?"

"The one with Hugh Jackman?"

"*That* type of wolfman."

"Oh my god."

"And they don't like Vampires."

"Kinda guessed that from the mess of the facility. So, I'm going t'have a Vampire Slayer and a Werewolf trying t'kill me as soon as we show up to her door."

"I won't let them kill you."

A satisfying 'oh' sounded in his throat. "So, you do care."

"No." I looked at him through the mirror. "I want answers, and having you alive, I mean mobile, will make it easier."

"Are you seriously not happy t'see me?" He held his thumb and index finger up. "Not even a wee bit?"

"I haven't seen you in ten years, Than, and you show up out of the blue as a—" My throat constricted. I looked back at the road.

"I kill Vampires. It's what I do. The fact that I invited you on t'our land, that I'm sat here having a normal conversation with you, it goes against everything I believe, everything I have been trained t'do."

"Elle, it's still me. I haven't changed." His hand landed on my left shoulder, causing tension to seize my spine. "Well, apart from being a little older, a lot hotter, and undead ... but it's still me."

"Talking to you, it's easy t'believe that, but you're a new Vampire, and you've only been 'out' for the last three days. Neither of us knows what exactly has been done t'you or why. Neither of us know what makes you different or if there even is a difference between you and every other Vampire."

"I feel—"

"Vampires don't feel." I rolled my shoulder forward, shifting away from his touch. "They don't care."

His hand fell away, but he remained leaning forward, close enough that I could feel his gaze burning into my cheek.

"I came back for help from my friend, who is the only living person I know would believe me. The only person who knows this craziness t'be true. If I didn't feel or care, why would I do that? Wouldn't I be off plundering villages and murdering people?"

"You didn't come t'me because you care. You came because you had nowhere else to go." It was the truth whether he wanted to admit it or not. "Besides, I'm not a hundred percent sure what a Vampire would do as I've never stopped long enough to have a heart to heart, let alone make friends, with one."

His voice softened, a glimmer of hurt lacing his words. "I was your friend before I was made a Vampire."

Then where have you been when I needed you? I bit my tongue, forcing the pathetic question back down my throat.

"The bottom line is we don't know how dangerous you could be, or what might trigger you. You came t'me for help, and although there is a huge part of me that feels you don't deserve it since I was so easy to forget about—"

"Elle—"

"I agreed t'help you," I cut him off, not wanting this conversation to go on any further, not when we had hours stuck in my car ahead of us. "I'm now responsible for you, and believe me, Than, if you become a danger t'me or my family, I will put you out of your misery."

"Understood." The reply was almost a whisper as he slid to the opposite side of the car.

I watched as his focus turned to the outside world.

"So how come Heather has a Werewolf with her anyway? She's a Vampire Slayer. If she's had the same training as you, surely, she can handle herself."

"The 'why' is what I'm hoping t'find out."

"Your family is insane."

"Aye, I know."

Chapter Five

Thursday 15th October, 2015
4:44am
Wandsworth, London

I'd never been to Alexis and Dorian's house. It was no big deal, and yet, now I was parked up on the curb looking at the terrace beyond the black gates, it suddenly seemed crazy. Families visited one another; they spent time in each other's homes, right? Parties, general visits, mini breaks … Why had I never been here before?

Just looking at the pile of bricks that could very well have been a stranger's house, it was just another reminder of how messed up my family truly was.

"You okay?"

A home was supposed to be a haven. A home was supposed to be the heart of a family, for a family to live and laugh and love together. Not just a rest stop between hunts.

This house had been Alexis and Dorian's attempt at normality, and yet, look where it had got them both. Dead.

"Aye." I cleared my throat and popped the seatbelt. "It's just weird being here, that's all."

This house was a reminder that my family couldn't lead normal lives, at least not for long. No matter how hard we tried to fit in and keep to ourselves, we were dead either way.

"When were you last here?"

"I've never been here before."

"Never?"

His question only clarified how odd I already felt at being here.

"Never." I climbed out my car, shutting the door behind me. My focus shifted to Nathan as he closed the passenger door and stopped by the car bonnet. "What are y'doing?"

"I'm coming with you, obviously."

I shook my head. "No. Vampires—"

"I will behave. I promise. I just need t'stretch my legs after being cooped up for so long."

"I don't know if you'll be able t'come in."

Realization sparked in his expression.

"Ah. Vampire." He pointed to himself. "Right. Got it." He glanced at the house. "Well, I can try, and if I can't, then I will wait right outside for you."

I looked around the street. It was dark and quiet, apart from the gentle glow of the odd streetlights. All the other houses were dark as their owners slept soundly inside, savouring a few more hours of sleep before getting up for work or school. The wall around the house was tall enough that Nathan could stay in the garden without drawing attention to himself, in case there were any early birds around.

"Okay," I agreed as I stepped onto the road and we made our way over.

"There's a car in the drive."

A black Range Rover sat on the other side of the gate. It was a newer model to mine, but still amusing to see. I'd always told her they were the best transport for a hunter. I guess she'd listened.

I swallowed the lump that had formed in my throat. "Just means that she didn't need to take it with her."

I would have liked to believe the presence of a car would indeed indicate someone was home—that was what we all presumed when a vehicle sat on a drive, wasn't it? And considering the time of day, it would be easy to presume that Heather could be safe and sound in her bed.

"Your family really loves a barricade." Nathan folded his arms, eyeing the wrought iron gate fixed between the brick wall that had to be at least six-foot high.

"It's t'stop people getting in."

"Or out, by the looks of it."

I shrugged off his words and opened the gate, stepping through onto the drive, ignoring the inward flinch at his comment. As always, the urge to argue the reasoning behind why my family lived the way they did niggled at me, but it would only make me a hypocrite. Hadn't I recently thought the same about my own home?

Vampires couldn't physically enter a home without an invite, but the land itself ... they could walk right up to the door. So, what was the point in such high walls?

"It's for privacy." The answer slipped from my tongue as we stopped by the front door. "The walls," I continued as Nathan stared at me blankly. "Stops humans from seeing things they shouldn't."

He shrugged. "Yeah, that makes sense."

"It's not just Vampire Hunters who like their privacy. Celebrities and people who are naturally reclusive do the same."

He held up his hands. "Hey, no judgement intended."

"Y'sure?" I punched the code into the key lock safe fixed to the wall beside the porch. Heather had thankfully told my mother the code during one of their phone calls. "You seem t'have a lot t'say about my family."

"Woah. Relax. I'm just trying to understand." He shoved his hands into his jeans pockets. "I spent pretty much all of my teen years thinking this was all made up, and now—"

"You're a Vampire."

"Yeah. That."

I slid the key into the first lock, pushing the porch door open. My grip tightened on the set of keys in my grasp as I stepped inside, pausing in front of the main door. I wasn't even sure what I was looking for. If there would be anything to indicate where Heather was or why she hadn't checked in for days, but this was the best, no, the only place I could start.

I unlocked the front door, pushing it wide open. The house was dark and silent. Not unusual considering it was the early hours of the morning, but it felt a lot eerier than a sleeping house should.

I put the key in my right pocket then slid my hand beneath my coat and retrieved the small blade holstered to my hip before stepping into the landing.

"Am I supposed to feel anything?"

I glanced over my shoulder. Nathan stood in the doorway, his toes right on the threshold. "How d'you mean?"

"I dunno, like an invisible barrier pushing me away, or something?"

Truth be told, I had no idea what an uninvited Vampire was supposed to sense standing at the door of a home. Was there indeed some invisible wall that stopped them from stepping farther? I'd never asked a Vampire to explain it to me, and I highly doubted anyone else in the family had either.

Not that Nathan needed to know that I had no idea what to expect.

"Do you feel that something is pushing you away?"

He shook his head, his eyes scanning the doorframe as if he were going to find instructions or an explanation carved into the wood. "I don't feel a thing."

"Then I guess that means you will have to just take a step and see what happens?"

"I'm not going t'burst in t'flames or anything, am I?"

"Only one way t'find out."

His eyes widened, his expression almost cartoon-like. "Elle, that isn't funny."

The look of horror on his face was indeed funny. I had to bite my inner check to stop from grinning. "I've never heard of a Leech exploding crossing a threshold. They either can't get in due t'being uninvited or they've been invited. There's no in-between."

Despite my amusement at the sheer worry claiming his pale face, every muscle in my body seemed to freeze just waiting to see what would happen. If he couldn't cross the threshold, then that was surely a good sign. I could only presume that the deed for the house had passed from Alexis and Dorian to Sofia, and I had no doubt that Sofia would have passed it to Heather. So, if Nathan couldn't enter, Heather was still alive?

He placed his right bare foot on the dark, wooden floor. His frame went rigid, gaze darting about the hallway as if he expected flames to shoot from the walls.

I suddenly felt sick at the thought. Naturally watching someone burn to death would be a horrible sight, but the thought of Nathan being barbecued before my eyes … The air caught in my throat.

His left foot followed. His hands balled to fists at his side as he yet again waited for something to happen.

Nothing.

All was still.

Complete silence.

He gave himself a once-over. His shoulders slowly relaxed as the tension slipped from his features as he took a few more steps inside.

I exhaled. He was fine. That was good, right?

My heart dropped to the pit of my stomach. Not good. Not good at all. Did that mean Heather was dead? Or was there a chance that Sofia hadn't passed the deed to the house on?

God, I wanted to believe it was the latter, because if the deed was in her name and with her now being deceased … explanation acquired.

"You look confused."

That had to be it. Sofia hadn't passed the deed on.

"I'm just—"

But Sofia knew the future. She knew what was going to happen, which meant she had planned everything. Of course she would have turned the deed over to Heather.

I turned my focus back to the kitchen. "Shut the door, will you?"

The room suddenly felt like it was spinning.

Oh, god, what did it mean that he could step into this house? Had everything we had been taught just been bullshit? Was my cousin dead? Or did it have something to do with the way Nathan had been created? He hadn't been baptized with a Vampire's blood, or at least his file hadn't stated he had gone through the traditional stages of being turned. It just talked about procedures and injections. Successful attempts and a lot of failed ones.

The front door clicked shut. "What are we looking for?"

I took a deep, steadying breath, squeezing my eyes shut in the hopes that the darkness around me would stop vibrating. I exhaled. "A clue."

It was pulling at straws, but maybe, just maybe, Nathan was able to cross the threshold because he wasn't a bog-standard lower level Vampire. He was different. God, I hoped it was that. It wasn't such a stretch of the imagination. He hadn't shown the normal behaviour of a normal Leech. He seemed in control of his thirst. He seemed capable of emotions and normal conversation —well, as normal as conversations had always been with him. He didn't know his strength. He didn't seem crazy.

He was unique, but then, that brought a whole lot of other problems up. If Vampires were experimenting, trying to find ways to create other Vampires differently … Vampires that could enter residential buildings without invites, that didn't go crazy, and could control their thirst … What did that mean?

"What type of clue?"

Nathan's words cut through the avalanche of questions crashing in my mind.

"I need to know where Heather is."

One thing at a time. I had to find Heather first and make sure she was okay. I would give her Nathan's file, and then together, we could answer those dangerous questions.

Stepping inside the kitchen, I reached out, patting the wall, fumbling to find a light switch. The idea of lighting this place up seemed foolish, but a girl couldn't find what she was looking for in the dark. Especially when she had no idea what she was looking for to begin with.

My fingers skimmed the switch. With a flick, the kitchen lights blinked on revealing … a normal kitchen. Not that I would know what an abnormal kitchen would look like … No sleep had clearly turned me a little coocoo.

I stopped at the edge of the breakfast bar, my gaze wandering around the room. It was immaculate. Almost as if it had never been used. There were no plates or cups out to indicate a meal had been eaten in here recently. No heap of mail sitting on the side. Nothing.

I tried to imagine Sofia and Heather sitting at this bar having breakfast. Sitting opposite each other. Sofia with a coffee and Heather with a glass of her mixture.

My focus moved to the right, to the large archway that led into a small dining room. The medium table with four chairs placed around it sat in the dark. Had Alexis and Dorian ever sat there and shared a meal together? The third seat occupied by Sofia and that fourth was to eventually become Heather's?

I rubbed at my eyes as they became irritated by stray tears. Christ, what was wrong with me?

"Hello, my bonny lass."

My heart stopped. Everything inside me seized up at the sound of the familiar female voice.

"This was my idea, the recorded message, and yet, I find myself speechless. I suppose I should start with the obvious."

"Erm, Elle?" Nathan called.

I turned toward the dining room, which was now a little less dark, highlighted by a pale light coming in through another archway that sat to the right.

"The only way you are watching this is if I am dead and you have decided to stay in London, instead of going back to Ireland."

"Elle?" Nathan called again.

I forced my feet to move toward that melodic voice, toward that soft, cold light, not stopping until I stood before the TV in the living room.

"Isn't that—?"

"My aunt," I murmured, my gaze fixated to the screen. This was it. The beyond the grave message.

"The choice is yours, but all I can say is, I am sorry you're on your own. Knowing this day was coming so long before it arrived wasn't easy, and I am sorry I have left you, my darling."

Sofia had sorted the deed to the house, which meant either Nathan was a super special boy or Heather had seen this and gone off and got herself killed.

"What is this?" Nathan asked, the confusion in his voice loud and clear.

"Now, the charming man who is hanging around is Brendan. You won't kill him. At least, I hope you won't."

"Whose Brendan?"

"Must be the Werewolf."

"I'm sorry you have to meet each other like this. Waking up one morning and finding him in the house, but he saved your life, didn't he? He's a good laddie, so please, I know how difficult it is for you to trust. I am to blame for that, but Brendan is there to help, so try to be easy on him. He is mainly there because of me and Carter, his Alpha."

"Alpha?"

I shushed him, needing to hear what Sofia was saying.

"You will be looking at the screen wondering why I have sent him and the answer to the question is the one he has probably already given you. Brendan is there to guard you. Well, to help you. I know you are more than capable of looking after yourself, my dear, but— Things are about to change for the worst, pet. And they will strike while the iron is hot, while you are distracted."

I squeezed the hilt of my blade. My focus transfixed on this younger version of the woman who had had a hand in raising me. A mixture of confusion and anxiety battled in the pit of my stomach. *Why send a stranger, Auntie S? If things are getting worse, why didn't you tell me, send for me?*

"I know you are grieving, my darling, but you must focus. You are more important to them than you realize, Heather. For years, they have watched you carefully; you became a threat only once we completed your training. Maybe it is my fault entirely. Maybe I shouldn't have trained you. Maybe I ..."

I had never seen my aunt like this. Sofia never questioned her choices. Especially when it came to Heather and what was best for her, when it came to our family's duty.

"Elle, what t'hell is this?"

"*Please* shut up," I snapped, not daring to pull my focus from the screen.

"I had to do what I knew was best for you, my dear. And, because of my choice, you became a subject of great interest to them. Your survival has been a great interest to them. You are rare, Heather. Strong. Unique. And, because of that, some will want to change you. Some will simply want you dead. And others ... the others will want to use you."

Use her. How would Vampires use Heather? Change her and wanting her dead, I understood. She was an Infected, after all. She was a Vampire Slayer, and all Vampires wanted our family dead. Simple. But Heather was unique as she was a born Infected, which was why the Vampires followed her to Ireland, why they left when she did.

"Elle, seriously, this is freaking me out. What t'hell is she going on about?"

"Heather is different, special. I told you that."

"Yeah, but this ... this is crazy."

"Heather is the only one of her kind. She's unique." I turned to him. The cold light of the television screen seemed to reach out to him in the darkness; his skin looked translucent. His eyes were dark and wide, his brow furrowed in confusion. The tips of his small fangs pressed against his pale lips. "As are you."

His eyes locked with mine.

He was different, unique. The Vampires had kidnapped him and his friend and used them to experiment on. Was that what Sofia meant? Were the Vampires planning on using Heather in similar ways? If they were experimenting on random humans … What would it mean to experiment on her, the only born Infected they knew of?

Did Sofia know about Nathan? Did she know he would be back and that he would be a Vampire?

A tiny pop of hope tickled my insides as my focus turned back to the screen.

If she knew … well, maybe she had figured out a way to let Nathan in? Maybe Heather was okay?

"I can't tell you any more than that. I want to. God, how I want to tell you, but if you know, you might change everything, Heather, and you can't. No. I mean you must not. It is vital that you do not change the path before you. I have told you, many times, that certain events must happen in a person's life for a reason, always for a reason. The events that will unfold before you ... they must happen, Heather. They have to. Oh, I have seen your future, my dear."

Tears gathered in my aunt's eyes, her expression so pained. There was so much she wanted to say. I could see it in the slight tremble of her jaw, in the tight way her lips pressed together.

A shiver spiralled up my spine. Sofia, what the hell have you seen? What haven't you told us?

"I have seen ... everything. You will see things, sense things—like you always have—but they will be hard to understand. You may not even realize what you are seeing until you are actually within that moment, that situation. But no matter what you do—and I know what you will do because I know you, I know how strong you are—" She smiled slightly. *"You must walk this path. It will be difficult, but trust me. Trust yourself. You must stay on this path and face everything head on. I'm just so sorry that I'm not with you and that I can't help you.*

"That is why I have asked Carter to send Brendan, because I know he is the only one who can help you. Brendan, come here, laddie, so she can see you. Otherwise, she won't believe you are who you say you are."

Shoving my blade back in its holder, I then rummaged in my jacket pocket, retrieving my phone, quickly opening the camera.

"She seems like a pain in the arse," a male replied.

The camera moved, stopping on a man. *"Heather, this is Brendan Daniels."*

He was tall, with broad shoulders, sandy blond hair, striking green eyes. Handsome, if you liked the surfer type.

I knelt down and took a photo of the man on the screen.

Why was he the only one that could help her? She had family. Why did Sofia call upon a stranger?

"Try to be nice, for your own sake. I love you, Heather. So does your mother. She loves you so, so much. Goodbye, my wee pet."

The DVD stopped. Grey static filled the screen.

"Well, that was possibly one of the most messed up things I've ever seen," Nathan stated. "Why t'hell is there a Mission Impossible type message in your cousin's DVD player?"

I fell back onto my calves, my blurred eyes lost in the sea of black, white, and grey dots before me. "How did you—?"

"I wanted to check the news," He cut in quickly. "T'see if me or Freddie … I'm sorry, it just came on, and—"

"It's fine." I pulled my focus from the screen and looked down at the photo on my mobile. "I kind of knew there was a DVD. Heather mentioned it in the last conversation she had with my mum. I just didn't expect it t'be …"

"Completely cryptic and unnerving."

A dry laugh escaped me. "Aye. Exactly that."

Not to mention strange that the DVD would still be in the player. Wouldn't she have put it away somewhere safe, secret?

It wasn't exactly full of helpful information, but still, it wasn't exactly something you would want someone to come across.

"So, Heather's in danger?"

I slid my phone into my pocket and pushed myself up until I was standing. "Heather has always been in danger."

"Which is why she has a Werewolf bodyguard?"

"Aye." How did Sofia know a Werewolf?

"And neither Heather nor this Brendan have been heard from since …?"

I dropped on to the nearby armchair, resting my head against the plump, red material. "September 24th. Exactly three weeks."

"So, we're the back-up team?"

It was only meant to have been me. I was coming over to help Heather who I now needed because I suddenly had a Vampire that required my help, our help. I had no Heather and no clue where she was. I had no clue what had happened to Nathan. No clue what the hell Sofia had seen, or knew, or even planned for. Just no damn clue of what I was supposed to do.

I was still torn over the fact that Nathan was with me. Had I done the right thing keeping him alive, well, mobile? Two heads had always been better than one. And once upon a time, Nathan and I had been a good team. Sure, our foes had been imaginary, but we had been inseparable for years … *Had been. Past tense, girl.*

"I guess we are." Whether I liked it or not.

"Okay."

I glanced at him with an arched eyebrow. "Okay?"

"Just making sure I was up t'speed."

I was glad one of us felt as if we were because my head was about ready to explode. My limbs suddenly felt as if they were made of lead. Sitting down had clearly been a bad idea.

"Do y'mind?" He pointed the remote at the television.

"No." I leaned forward and braced my elbows on my knees, not paying any attention to the images on the screen or what the reporter was saying. All I could think about was the DVD, the fact that my aunt Sofia had basically told my cousin that she knew shit was about to hit the fan, but she purposely wasn't giving her an umbrella.

My gaze drifted to the bookshelf in the left corner, to three photos sitting on the bottom shelf. Forcing myself to stand, I moved closer, picking one up. A young Sofia stood smiling with my uncle Jean and a very young Alexis. I couldn't make out the location, but it was a sunny day.

The next picture was of Alexis and Dorian on what looked like their wedding day. Alexis had a knee-length white Bardot dress on; it was simple. Her hair was down, for a change, dark and wavy. Dorian wore a black suit without a tie, his blond hair slicked back with a stray chunk falling over his brow. I had seen him only once when I was a child. He was handsome. Heather was the spitting image of her mother, but looking at Dorian, I could see the similarities. Heather had his nose and his smile.

My cousin and her husband stood on the steps of what I could only presume was the local town hall. Dorian's arm was round Alexis' waist, her right round his while her left hand rested on his chest. No one else was around them, but they didn't seem to mind, their focus on each other. Genuine smiles rested on their faces. They looked happy.

I couldn't remember seeing Alexis smile while she lived with us. She was always so quiet, serious. Restrained. Unless she was arguing with my father. I thought he had a fiery temper, but Jesus, Alexis gave him a run for his money.

I put down the first frame and picked up the third, a black and white baby scan: Heather.

Once again, I felt my eyes grow sore as I starred at the scan. My cousin had tried so hard for a normal life. She had done everything she was told she had to, everything she was trained to do. She still hunted. She still protected her family and all the innocent, clueless people of this world, but it wasn't enough. The small piece of normality she had put so much effort into moulding toward some resemblance of a happy life had been snatched away from her. Her husband had never even got to meet his baby—a baby that was infected on the night he died. Because he died. Because Alexis was still fighting, still doing her duty even while she was pregnant. Even though Sofia had told her she would lose Dorian. Even while she watched him devoured before her eyes.

She had deserved so much more than what had happened to her. As had Dorian.

104 | Cross My Heart

I put the frame down and wiped my eyes.

"You okay?"

"Fine." I coughed away the lump forming in my throat. "Just a little tired, I guess."

"I'm not surprised. You've been up all night. You should go and get some sleep."

"I'm okay."

"You're not going t'be any good to anyone if you can't keep your eyes open."

As I turned to protest, my gaze fell on a bag wedged between the side table and the end of the sofa. I crossed the few meters and dropped down to my knees, pulling it out. The black sports bag was already open, a man's limited selection of T-shirts, jeans, toiletries, and other necessities all shoved inside.

I held a green T-shirt out to Nathan. "Can you smell anything?"

"You want me t'sniff another dude's top?" He arched an eyebrow at me, his nose wrinkling. "That's nasty."

"Than, if you can get a scent of some kind, then it might help us."

"How?"

"The same way me taking a photo of this Brendan will. You might pick up on it when we're out looking for them."

He pinched the green material between his right thumb and index finger, pulling it slowly from my grasp. He held it up, the material dangling in front of his face. "This isn't right."

I rolled my eyes. "Quit being a wimp."

"If I'm a wimp, what are you?"

"I'm a human whereas you're a Vampire with a heightened sense of smell."

"You always have an answer for everything, don't you?"

"Just smell the damn T-shirt, you big girl."

He leant forward and took a sniff. Disgust crinkled his features.

"Can't smell much. A little BO, a hint of cologne, and a sort of …" He reluctantly sniffed again, "I don't know. A kinda wet dog smell."

"Okay. Good. Try and remember it."

"I don't think I'm going t'be able to forget it." He flung the T-shirt back at me, which I caught before it hit me in the face.

Further searching proved useless. There was no wallet or passport, anything that might tell me where this so-called Werewolf lived. The only helpful thing was a pair of black trainers, which I handed to Nathan.

"Now you want me t'wear his shoes?"

"You want to continue walking around barefoot?"

He took the trainers and glanced inside. "They're two sizes too big."

"Well, either them or I can see if Sofia or Heather have any."

"Because ladies' trainers are so much better?"

"As long as they're not bright pink with hearts and butterflies, who will know?" I stood. "Besides, it's not like you're going t'be seeing anyone y'know."

"Doesn't mean I want t'look like an eejit for the people I may accidentally bump into."

"You look like an eejit regardless of the trainers."

"Takes one to know one," he grumbled before pulling his tongue out at me.

"God, you're such a child." I folded my arms over my chest. "Look, trust me, girls' trainers might draw attention away from the fact you look half dead."

"I *am* dead."

"That's my point." My heart lurched as his expression flattened slightly. "Rummage through the Werewolf's clothes and then go get a shower. I will go and see if I can find some alternative footwear for you, which may be possible as Heather has never been a girly girl."

"I don't think the Werewolf will like me borrowing his clothes."

I couldn't imagine any Werewolf being happy about a Vampire wearing his clothes, but there had been no clothes shops open on the ferry or in the services on the way here. So really, what choice did he have?

"Well, it's between his, Heather's, or Sofia's. Choice is yours."

He pulled the sports bag across the floor and dipped inside. A smile stretched his lips as he pulled out deodorant and cologne. "At least I won't smell like a girl."

"Thank God for small graces." I wandered to the living room door. "Oh, there should be some of Heather's mixture in the fridge. You know, if you're thirsty. It's been a few hours—"

"I will take a look."

Cutting across the hallway, I climbed the stairs, each upward step beating home the fact that I was actually pretty exhausted, but resting wasn't an option.

I paused at the top of the narrow landing. My gaze tripped over the darkened space. Four doors lined the walls, all closed, which seemed odd. Was it normal for people to close all the doors in their house when they weren't home?

If anyone would have been up here that shouldn't have, I'm sure they would have been frightened off by now, or alternatively, they would have come charging down the stairs. Nevertheless, my hand still took its usual position on my right hip mere inches away from the blade I had holstered earlier.

I turned to my left and reached for the handle to the nearest door, pushing the panel wide and glancing into the dark room. My left hand skimmed the wall yet again searching for a light switch. In an instant, the light popped on.

I automatically noted that this room was as void of any character as the kitchen and dining room. Sure, the furniture matched, and the colour scheme was the same for the bedding and curtains—a deep red, which seemed somewhat ironic. For all I knew, I could have been standing in a hotel room right now. There was no personality.

The only tell-tale sign that I had just stepped inside my cousin's bedroom was the odd hair accessory resting on the vanity table situated against the wall facing the end of the bed. That, and a single frame of what I could only presume held a photograph of

Alexis and Dorian, which sat on the bedside table.

I moved around the bed, stopping before the wardrobe, opening the double doors wide. I knew I had been right when I stated that Heather wasn't a girly girl, but luckily, the sight of black footwear confirmed my statement. Mainly boots, which I highly doubted Nathan would want to wear, but luckily, amongst the small selection lay a pair of worn in black trainers. They would no doubt be too small for Nathan, but at least he now had an alternative option if the Werewolf's spare pair turned out too loose for him.

Grabbing hold of the trainers, I straightened, closing the doors and turning back to the room.

The place was spotless. No indication of a struggle. No real indication that anyone actually slept in here. The bed was neat and tidy. The small amount of accessories on the vanity table seemed to all have a place and position. For all I knew, it could have been days since Heather last slept in this room.

It wasn't like I expected some item or note to be conveniently placed somewhere obvious that would scream *"oh hey, just in case I'm missing, and you need to find me, I'm ..."* No, a clue would have been way too kind and made everything way too easy.

I wandered back across the room and out into the hallway, leaving the light on and the door wide open. I wasn't sure why, but closing it felt weird.

I moved to the next door situated on the left. I pushed it open. A hint of musk stirred in the air, indicating that I had just stepped into Sofia's bedroom. I paused, unsure of whether I should even bother looking in the room, but just standing there seemed as close as I was going to get to being near my aunt one last time. The right place to say a proper goodbye.

Turning on the light, I remained in the doorframe. Taking even half a step into the room seemed like a huge invasion of privacy despite how idiotic the thought was. Her room seemed more personal than Heather's, but then again, she had lived a decently long life and had a collection of trinkets and artwork that she had collected over the years.

As my eyes tripped over her belongings, memories began to surface. Just flashes of the few times I would be allowed into her bedroom when she lived with my parents and me. I had always found her jewellery box and perfume bottles interesting—they seemed very elegant and from a classier time.

Now, they almost looked like relics. A fine layer of dust clung to all her belongings. I was sure that if I picked any of the items up, the space beneath would be perfectly clean and framed by the dirt that surrounded it.

It was obvious that Heather hadn't been in this room, most likely since Sofia had passed away. Everything had been left as is, last touched by my aunt and no one else. A shiver raced down my spine. It was almost like looking at a shrine.

I felt as though I was standing in a tomb. Everything was preserved.

"I'm so sorry, Sofia," I whispered, flicking the light off and closing the door behind me. I pressed my head against the wood and sighed. "I'm sorry we weren't there to say goodbye."

My mother was right—Sofia hadn't wanted anyone at her funeral other than Heather. We couldn't understand her reasoning for it, but we had respected her dying wishes. However, we should have been there for Heather. It wasn't fair of Sofia to want her to go through all of this on her own. Grief had a way of affecting people in strange ways. My mother said Heather had sounded fine every time they spoke, but my second cousin had been trained to hide her urges and feelings. I could only hope that Heather hadn't gone and done something stupid.

Turning, I glanced at the final two doors; I reached across and opened the one directly across the way, pulling the cord that swayed in the dark. A pop as the light came on, followed by the gentle hum of the fan.

The bathroom was small and pleasant, your standard bathroom, but it was by far the room that was the most cluttered. A variety of colourful bottled products sat in a shower caddy and in the narrow shelving unit, along with towels and even a first aid kit.

I left the light on so that Nathan would automatically move toward it when he finally came upstairs. I didn't like the idea of him walking straight into my aunt's room, even if it would be by mistake.

The last room was at the opposite end of the hallway facing Heather's room. I pushed the silver handle down with some effort, for the mechanism felt stiff. Using my shoulder, I put my weight on the panel and shoved against the awkward barrier. It took a few tries, but finally, the door fell open. I caught hold of the frame before I fell headfirst through the gap.

My nose wrinkled. The air was a lot staler in here, and although the room was dark due to lack of daylight and electricity, it seemed blacker; crowded, and full. I sought out the light switch only for my hand to hit something solid.

I flicked the hallway light on and opened the door as wide as it would allow me to, which had to be about a foot before the wood hit something behind it. I pressed my back against the door, managing to gain a couple more inches. Staying flat against the wood, I allowed the hallway light into the room—boxes upon boxes, stacks upon stacks, from floor to ceiling, filled the room.

Taking my mobile from my jacket pocket, I tapped the torch option and slid inside. I moved my phone around, the pale white light confirming that the door wouldn't budge any further due to more stacks of boxes piled behind it. I had about a couple of feet to move around in, and that was it. The room was jam-packed.

I stared at the ominous fort of cardboard. I couldn't recall Sofia and Alexis coming to us with many belongings nor did I remember Heather and Sofia having much that they needed to bring back with them. Yet, this room seemed to have enough in here to indicate an entire house move.

I paused as the light from my phone illuminated a word scribbled in black felt-tip on the side of one of the boxes.

A chill crawled down my spine at the sight of the name that accompanied it. *'Dorian's Stuff.'*

Was all this Dorian's and Alexis' belongings?

This had been their house. Had they never gotten round to

unpacking, or had Sofia packed all their belongings up once Dorian had died? Maybe once Alexis had?

I could only recall the odd occasion that Sofia and Alexis had travelled, leaving baby Heather in my parents' care. The first time had been shortly after their arrival for what I could only presume had been Dorian's funeral. I learnt later on that it had been a straightforward mess to sort as his close family had been slaughtered by Infecteds when he was just a child. His father's sister had never wanted custody, so he had bounced around in the system until he was eighteen. Sofia and Alexis had been the only ones at his funeral.

The other time had been once Alexis had passed. Sofia had taken her ashes to where Dorian had been scattered and had stayed away for a short while. Perhaps she had come here? Perhaps she had packed up her daughter and son-in-law and locked them away in this room.

I already knew that the basement in this house would replicate the one at my own house. A glance at the hallway ceiling, and I could see a hatch. Did the attic have more stuff up there? Maybe my Uncle Jean's stuff was up there and there was no more space? An empty room was easy to keep stuff in, I supposed—easier to access, although by the slight warp in the door and how stale the air smelled in here, I would bet money no one had been in here for a long time.

As I looked further, I could make out the odd word here and there. With every scribble I found, the realization that Alexis' and Dorian's entire life was in these boxes burrowed further in my heart. Although they had been together for two years before marriage and just over a year as husband and wife before Dorian was murdered … This is how it had ended for them. Their personal belongings packed up and hidden behind a closed door.

This entire house felt like a mausoleum.

My arm fell like a deadweight to my side. Was this what waited for me? Was this how it would be when my mother and father eventually passed? Would I pack them away and lock up certain rooms in their house? Willing to let them go and yet morbidly trying to hold on to them?

It was almost as if Dorian and Alexis weren't allowed to rest properly if this sad reminder of tragedy had to be always present.

A warning.

"Hey, what have you found?"

I jumped. My phone slipped from my hand and hit the patch of carpet below.

"Shit. You scared me." My heart felt like it was about to burst through my ribcage. "Don't sneak up on me like that."

"Sorry." He peered around the door. "What's all this?"

"Just stuff." I reached down and felt about for my phone, taking hold as my fingers skimmed the cool plastic. "It's not important anymore."

I lifted the light to find him looking at me suspiciously. "If you say so?"

"I do."

"Right, well, I'm going t'head to the shower so, you know, resist the urge to peek."

I rolled my eyes at him. "I'm sure I will be able t'contain myself."

"Any luck with the trainers? This guy's got pretty big feet."

"There's a pair on the chair in Heather's room." I pointed to the open door at the opposite end of the hall.

"Maybe go catch some sleep. You look about ready to drop."

I switched the torch off on my phone. "If I lie down, I might not get back up again."

"Couple of hours will do you no harm."

Did I trust going to sleep while there was a Vampire in the house? It was Nathan, after all, and he hadn't tried anything funny yet, but still …

"I will wake you up if you do." He shrugged, before disappearing back into the hall.

I was tired, and the more I analysed this house, this so-called family home … I knew our lives had been sheltered. So very far from what other young women knew to be as normal. What made it worse was I knew that Heather's life was far worse, if you could call it a life at all. It's as if she was this hollow creature living with the memories of ghosts.

I heard a door click, and a second later, the sound of running water met my ears.

Shimmying back through the gap between the door and frame, I took one more glance at the tower of boxes, my gaze lifting and stopping on the lampshade situated just above where I had been standing. Flicking the torch back on, I angled it, and my heart clenched. Though covered in a thick, dark layer of dust, I could just make out the adorable farm animals lining the bottom of the old plastic shade.

This was meant to be Heather's nursery.

Realizing this, seeing in the flesh what my cousins had truly lost, it was too much.

We had been repeatedly told during our training that we could die. We had been told the story that had been the start of this stupid legacy. We had been told every gruesome detail of our ancestors' deaths in fulfilling this noble vow. Heather had been told all the details of her parents and how, as a hunter in this family with the Vampyricc Virus, it would be a lot harder for her … we knew all of it. And yet, the stories and warnings weren't as bad as seeing this. Even being covered in Vampires' blood, receiving injuries, fighting for survival … It didn't compare to seeing how a person's life was reduced to being shoved into boxes and into storage.

I backed out of the room and pulled the door forcefully to make sure it shut, glanced at my mobile through blurred eyes. Knocking the torch off, I made my way into Heather's bedroom. Closing the door to block out Nathan's terrible singing, I sat on the edge of her bed and dialled my parents' number.

Chapter Six

~ Nathan ~

"You do know that this is creepy, right?"

My gaze momentarily slipped to Teen Elle who lay at the end of the bed, her head and shoulders hanging over the edge, the tips of her pigtails brushing the beige carpet below.

"Like, really creepy. You're standing over a sleeping woman, watching her. It's worrying behaviour."

"I had Vampires watching me do everything for the last six weeks. How is this any different?"

"Erm, well, you were an experiment that they were monitoring. Whereas she's a free, living human woman, and you're a weird dead creepy dude lurking over her while she's vulnerable."

I snorted. Vulnerable was not a word I would use to describe Elle.

"Y'know what I mean."

"I just came t'check up on her. Told her she was tired."

"Well, congrats, you were right. What d'ya want, a medal?"

"No, hearing you say I'm right is reward enough."

Without any effort, she slid off the bed and jumped to her feet. *"You've checked on her. Now you need t'go away."*

I had come to wake her up as I had promised. She hadn't wanted to go to sleep in the first place, so she was no doubt going to be groggy when she realized she'd nodded off, but I guess the crying had wiped out the last bit of energy she had.

"How do you know she was crying?"

I arched an eyebrow at the teen. "Duh, Vampire hearing."

114 | Cross My Heart

Ignoring the fact that I could hear her soft sobs from down the hallway and behind a closed door, the fact that her perfect skin looked blotchy was a bit of a clue. I couldn't say I blamed her. It had been a long and very weird night, and she seemed uncomfortable being in her cousin's house.

She currently looked peaceful, relaxed for the first time since I had found her at the cemetery talking to her dead aunt.

"She's as weird as you."

"It's not weird t'talk to your deceased loved ones."

"That explains why she's talking t'you."

I grabbed my waist. "Oh, my sides, they're splitting. You should be a comedian."

She stuck her tongue out at me.

I was torn between waking Elle up and leaving her to rest. She clearly needed the sleep, and after watching her aunt's insane beyond the grave message, well, she needed all the rest she could get because it sounded like we were going on a goose chase to find a needle in a gigantic haystack.

Besides, the sooner I woke her meant we would be back to her being distant and snappy and constantly looking at me as if she didn't know who I was.

It was nice to just look at her, take her in for a moment. Her auburn hair was fanned out on the pillow, her features softer, making the angry, guarded woman I had met last night seem a million miles away.

Adult Elle. "She's certainly aged well."

"Is that your way of saying that you find her pretty?"

"She's not … not pretty."

"Jeez. Full of compliments, aren't you?" She climbed on to the bed, waving her hand in front of real Elle's face. *"Well, she's definitely out of it because she can't even hear you talking t'yourself."*

"I'm not talking to myself. I'm talking t'you."

"She doesn't know that. Any minute now, she's going t'open those big, beautiful, green eyes of hers and see you standing at

the side of the bed, perving over her."

"Is there a reason you're still here?"

She shrugged. *"You tell me. I mean you're with the real Elle now, so you don't need t'keep dragging me out. Maybe it's t'do with the fact that you know she doesn't trust you, so, you want t'keep me around because it's safer."*

And didn't that just sound extremely pathetic and sad?

"Well, you're a very sad man."

"You're a lot meaner than you use t'be."

She gave me a wide smile before leaning over sleeping Elle to pull a succession of stupid faces.

I knew I should wake her up, because even though I didn't want to admit it, the little figment of my imagination was right—Elle didn't trust me, at all. And I had no idea how to change that, but watching her sleep was probably not the best way to go about it.

Uncrossing my arms, I closed the last couple of steps to the bed. Teen Elle sat back as I reluctantly leaned forward.

"Elle?" I said gently, not wanting to startle her. My hands clenched by my sides in anticipation as I remembered that she had hidden knives on her person. "Elle?"

No response.

I gave her arm a gentle nudge. "Elle, you need t'wake up."

"Maybe you should kiss her?"

I angled my head. Eyebrow arched. "What?"

"Maybe she will wake up if you kiss her."

"You mean in like a fairy-tale kinda way? What t'hell do you think this is?"

Young Elle shrugged. *"Nothing about her life falls under being normal."*

"This isn't a fairy-tale." I straightened and looked down at real Elle. She was far from being a princess, had never even wanted to be one when we use to play make-believe in our haven. "Besides, I'm no prince. I'm a monster, remember?"

"You're too daft t'be a monster."

"I feel like that was supposed to be a compliment?"

She hopped off the bed and walked over to the vanity table, skimming her fingers over the items there. *"You're more Jester material, if you ask me."*

"I didn't."

As tempting as the idea was, and part of me hated to admit that it was tempting, I'd never really thought of her being the type of girl I wanted to kiss. Even though I had meant what I had said, Elle wasn't ugly, but I mean, she was my friend. My best friend, once upon a time. Sure, she'd aged well. Like, really well, but …

"Do you want t'kiss her?" Teen Elle appeared at the other side of the bed, palms flat on the duvet cover, curiosity claiming her features.

My focus slid back to Elle's face, her mouth. They had been set in a firm line bordering on a frown for the entire duration I had spent with her. Now, they were still, relaxed. The bow of her lip was soft, subtle … yet again, words that didn't fit her.

"You do! You want t'kiss her!" Her comment came out in a lyrical fashion.

"It would be the worst idea in the world." My focus slipped to sleeping Elle's neck, to the delicate hollow where her shoulder and throat met. "Y'think its creepy me standing here while she sleeps?" Her skin looked soft … so exposed. "Well, it's going t'be more so if she catches me leaning over her."

Realization struck. *"Oh. Aye, she may think you're trying t'bite her?"*

And I really hated to admit that that idea was far more tempting than kissing her. "Exactly."

"And she has threatened t'kill you if you try."

"Multiple times."

"Yeah, the kiss is a bad idea." She straightened. *"Don't do it."*

"I wasn't goin' to." I pulled my focus away from the resting hunter. "It was your idea."

She tapped her index finger against her chin. *"Technically, it was yours since I'm just your conscious talking."*

My head dropped to my chest. "God, I hope when I get this Vampire thing under control, you go away."

"Only time will tell."

Resigning myself to the fact that I needed to get this over and done with—and to end this conversation with my imaginary friend—I leaned forward and gently gripped sleeping Elle's shoulders.

"Elle?" I shook her. "Elle, it's time t'wake up."

Her eyes snapped open, and the next thing I knew, I was falling forward and over. My back pressed into the bed I stared up at the wide-eyed Elle currently straddling me. Something cold and sharp pressed against my Adam's apple.

"Woah." My entire body was rigid, my palms flat and held at the side of my head in surrender. "Good morning, sleepy head."

"Than?" Her brow furrowed, realization slowly sparking in her eyes. "What the hell?"

"I told you I'd wake you up if you drifted off." I shifted beneath her as the knife against my skin grew hotter and that familiar sizzle started to burn my throat, automatically regretting it as the movement drew my attention to how warm and real she felt sitting on top of me. Between her and the softness of the bed at my back … well, a guy could get used to being trapped between such luxuries, especially after sleeping alone on steel for six weeks.

"Typical. You don't want t'kiss her, but you wouldn't mind f—"

"If I'd have known this would have been your reaction, I'd have woken you up sooner." The blade at my neck dug a little deeper. A hiss escaped me, a hint of something burning slithering up my nostrils. "I'm kidding. I'm kidding, grumpy. Sheesh."

Her gaze darted around the room. "What time is it?"

"After nine." I pointed at my smoking skin. "Do you think we could maybe have this conversation without you trying t'slice my throat?"

She snapped her hand away as if she hadn't even realized she was holding a blade there. Her focus remained on my throat; a small line formed at the bridge of her nose. I felt the skin across my larynx tightening.

"Healing," Teen Elle reminded me as her amused gaze flitted between me and her older self. *"Well, this isn't awkward in the slightest."*

"Erm, you hungry?"

"Hungry?"

"Yes. When did you last eat?"

She met my gaze, concern crinkling the corners. "What have you been up to?"

"Watching TV. Catching up on world events." I propped myself up on my elbows. "Listen, why don't you go get a shower and I will make some breakfast."

She stared at me as if I'd just grown another head. "You're going t'make me breakfast?"

"It's the least I can do." I pushed up a little further, until I was resting on my hands, The new position meaning I was practically on level with her … in every way. "Although, if you'd just prefer to stay like this …?"

Her gaze finally left my face, falling lower to where her thighs cradled my hips. Her eyes widened, and if it weren't for the speed with which she scrambled off of me, I could have sworn I saw her cheeks growing red.

"Real smooth, Than."

"Okay." I tried to cough away my amusement as I pushed myself up and off the bed. "Breakfast it is."

"Is that my bag?" She pointed the knife still in her grasp at the purple duffle on the vanity table.

"Yeah, I got it from the car before the sun came up." I pulled the duvet straight, using the opportunity to glance at my jeans, relieved that the hoodie I had borrowed was covering my unexpected reaction. "I thought you'd want t'change."

She stared at me, following my movements as I fluffed the pillows. "What?"

"Nothing."

Bed straightened and Slayer awake, I made my way to the door, pausing on the threshold. "Just for the record … do you always sleep with a blade?"

She glanced down at the dagger in her hand and nodded. "Always."

"Bet you're glad she didn't wake up and find you looking at her, otherwise, it wouldn't have been your throat under that knife, but your little tent pole."

"It's not little." I scowled at the grinning teen who casually made her way round the bed and passed a very confused-looking Elle whose attention flitted between me and the empty room. "I will see you downstairs."

I briskly made my way down to the kitchen. After my shower, I had made sure that all the blinds were closed. Luckily, today was a typical gloomy English day, but I still wasn't a hundred percent sure how the whole being in daylight worked. Luckily, the black hoodie I had dug out of the Werewolf's sports bag was two sizes too big for me. Meaning it was a great extra layer of protection.

"A Vampire making breakfast." Teen Elle sat on one of the stools at the breakfast counter. *"Isn't this what single women fantasize about, superhuman men doing super normal everyday tasks?"*

I opened the overhead cupboards until I found a pan, bowl, and mug. "How am I supposed t'know what women fantasize about?"

"Hey, I'm only saying what you're thinking."

"Well, what am I supposed t'be thinking about?" I placed them on the counter and made my way over to the fridge. "This entire situation seems ridiculous."

"Oh, it is." Pushing against the counter, she spun on the stool; once, twice. *"How about you think about how much you wanted t'kiss Elle just then?"*

"No." The reply rushed from my lips, earning a giggled reply. "I mean, no because I didn't want t'kiss her."

"You can't lie t'me, lover boy. I'm in your head."

"Oh, god, don't ever call me that again." It was gross enough, but coming from the mouth of a teenager … yuk.

"Fine. I'm not going to push. Yet." She spun around on the stool again. *"Maybe start thinking about what you're planning on doing next?"*

And wasn't that a good question. "The plan is t'find Heather who will hopefully make some sense of my situation."

"And if that doesn't work?"

I didn't reply because I had honestly not thought that far ahead. Instead, I opened the fridge and collected the pack of eggs from inside, happy to see they were still in date. The options for breakfast were straightforward as there wasn't much food there, just the odd essentials that were close to going off date. Not to mention Heather's odd little mixture, which I had already helped myself to. Despite the clear scent of blood contained in the glass bottles, the bitter tang of cranberries sure helped dull the iron taste. Even though I thought my thirst was quenched since I'd had no urge to drink since escaping my prison, I'd still found myself downing three litres of this odd little vocktail.

"What t'hell is a vocktail?"

I closed the fridge door. "A mocktail for Vampires?"

She starred at me blankly.

"A mocktail is a non-alcoholic version of a cocktail."

"I know. I just—" Her head fell into her hands. *"You're such a nerd."*

My focus lifted to the ceiling at the sound of running water … followed by the slide of a lock.

"She thinks you're weird too, y'know?" The teen lifted her head. *"Did you see the way she looked at you for straightening the bedsheets?"*

"She's always thought I was weird." I wandered back to the stove and got to work on cracking the remaining three eggs into the pan. "And last time I checked, it was just good manners to tidy up when you make a mess in someone else's home."

"Aren't you a gent? Here I was thinking you were doing it t'get

some brownie points?"

Running out of the room after our awkward little encounter and my surprising reaction to being so close to her didn't seem right. It would make me look like an idiot or a perv, or worse, like I was scared of her.

"Aren't you?"

"No." I snorted. However, she doesn't trust me, and acting as human as possible seemed to be the only logical thing to do. "You saw her reaction to my healing throat?"

It was yet again another reminder that I wasn't human. Meaning she shouldn't trust me, or that I couldn't be trusted. And although somewhere deep inside me I knew she wouldn't hurt me … I wasn't yet willing to see if I was right.

Grabbing a fork and spoon from the drawer, I slid a spoonful of butter into the pan and switched on the hob.

"Does she even like eggs?"

"She used to." I filled the nearby kettle and switched it on before turning my attention back to the pan. "Besides, it's not like there's a lot of options. Something t'eat is better than nothing t'eat."

"By the smell, I think she will opt for nothing at this rate."

I didn't think it was possible for me to gag at food, but she was right.

"They can't be off. I checked the date." I continued whisking the yellow liquid, watching as it slowly became solid.

"Maybe it's your sensitive nose?"

I turned the hob off as soon as the eggs had taken their scrambled form. Moving to the kitchen window, I cracked it open, allowing the cool air to sweep in and waft away the putrid smell.

"Do you think it is?"

"I know as much as you do." She continued spinning around on the bar stool. *"If Elle thinks they smell funky, then it might just be the butter."*

Taking hold of the pan, I scooped the eggs into the bowl. "Well,

122 | Cross My Heart

the butter's in date so there's no reasonable explanation as t'why they would smell so bad."

"Well, that really sells breakfast for me."

I jumped as Elle appeared in the kitchen. Her hair was damp and scrapped back in a messy bun. Dressed in dark denim jeans, a black vest, and an unbuttoned green checked shirt, she stood in the open space, scanning the dining room and kitchen. Her fingers wrapped around the hilt of the blade resting in its holder at her hip. "Who are you talking to?"

"No one." I laughed, putting the pan in the sink. "Just myself."

"Yeah, because that doesn't make you sound any less weird."

I threw a pointed look at the teen and picked up the bowl of scrambled eggs and placed the fork inside. "Here. There isn't much in."

Her focus slipped to the bowl and then moved to the kettle.

"I'm good." She skirted past me and collected the mug from the side and set to making herself a coffee.

"Told you they didn't smell right."

"You should try and eat something. It's been ages." I placed the bowl on the breakfast bar. "They're fresh."

She glanced over her shoulder at me.

"The eggs." I nodded at the bowl. "They just don't smell great to me."

Her left eyebrow arched. "They smell fine."

"Then it's definitely me." I looked at the teen triumphantly. "Must be another Vampire perk."

Surely, Vampires couldn't be that turned off by food. It was a strange idea, but then again, it wasn't like I had an opportunity to figure it out as they'd had no food at the facility. Plus, I had been travelling late at night and through the early hours of the morning, no takeaways open. No homecooked meals tainting the air of the homes I had walked past. I guess time would tell if this was a one-off or definitely a Vampire thing.

Black coffee in hand, Elle turned and headed to the pantry door, which was situated next to the fridge. "Have you drunk?"

"Yup. Quite a bit of your cousin's odd mixture."

She stepped inside and flicked on the light. Placing her mug on one of the shelves, she knelt down and began to run her hands across the floor.

"What's she doing?" Teen Elle asked, hopping off the stool.

"Erm, Elle?" I picked the bowl of scrambled eggs up and wandered over to the doorway, pausing when I heard a click.

Elle straightened, and part of the floorboards lifted. Leaning down, she pulled the wood to one side.

"Is that a secret door?" I found myself asking as she collected her drink and headed down into the darkness.

"Of course it is, eejit. We're in the home of a Vampire hunter." Teen Elle pushed past me and followed her real self.

I stared at the dark hole, hesitant to follow. Why would I want to go back underground in a dark dank space? Was it a trap? Had she lied about wanting to help me? Would Elle lock me up down there?

Beeping met my ears, followed by a clunk and a whine as something heavy was made to move. A rhythmic clap and pale light illuminated the secret doorway.

"There's only one way t'find out." The teen popped her head through the hole. *"Well, don't just stand there like a ninny."*

Reluctantly, I headed down. The stepladders led to a small type of hallway. An open door lay to my right, and as I stepped through into the light, I suddenly felt as though I were in a spy film.

"Is this what I think it is?"

Elle stood by a desk near the far wall, her attention fixed to a large frame hanging there. "What do you think it is?"

"Is this Heather's training room?" I stepped farther into the room, wandering around the gym equipment that took up the middle of the space. "Like the one you said you have at home?"

"Aye, but ours is bigger." Elle turned to evaluate the room. "And not as depressing."

"This is awesome." Teen Elle stood next to the red punch bag,

ducking and weaving, throwing punches that never connected with the heavy sack.

The room was grey and dull, but it was basically a home gym. "I guess it's a good use of space."

Real Elle snorted. "Only you would find this normal."

"Well, its normal for you, isn't it?" I asked, stopping beside her.

She moved around me and took a seat at the desk. "Yeah, I guess."

My focus stayed on the large frame she had been staring at. The parchment inside was old, worn. It was huge. The lines of what looked to be the shape of an oak tree were fading, along with many scribbled names. As my eyes travelled lower toward the trunk, the names were a little easier to read. Danielle's name rested beneath her parents, parallel to her cousin Alexis', Heather's name scribbled neatly below.

"Holy shit, is this-is this your family tree?" I looked over at her. "It's gigantic."

"Tell me about it," she mumbled, switching the computer on.

"Have you met any of your relatives?" There were a few names situated a little higher than Elle's and Alexis', but it almost looked as if the last three generations hadn't had children.

"Not really. I can recall my parents talking to the odd one on the phone." She cradled her mug between her hands and took a mouthful of coffee. "Most of our family stopped this bullshit years ago."

"What do you mean?" I walked over to the desk.

"Some refused to have children. A few were disowned from refusing to follow this lifestyle. And y'know, a lot were killed."

"Did you ever consider walkin' away?"

She stared into space for a long time, before finally replying.

"Once I saw what they had done to Alexis …" She put her mug on the table. "It would have been easy to say, 'this isn't worth it.' Watching loved ones get killed or go crazy, or paralyzed like my Da." She crossed her arms and rested them on the table. "It would be easy t'be scared, but the truth is seeing what they did t'my Da, t'my cousins … It made me angry. No way was I going t'let Leeches get away with hurting the ones I loved."

She lifted her gaze to mine, suddenly seeming defeated. "I'm- I'm sorry this happened t'you." The words were quiet as they left her lips.

"Did she just apologize?"

"Elle, I—?"

Her attention moved to the computer. "But this is what they do. They attack and turn people and ruin their lives and the lives of their families. I will admit that since Heather and Sofia left, since most of the Leeches followed them, well, there hasn't been much to slay the last few years. These last few months, well, the decision was pretty much made for me, until Sofia died. Until Heather never checked in. So, it was either I come and help my cousin with this insane legacy that has been placed on both of us, or I hang up my sword."

Her gaze moved across the room.

"Being here has reminded me of what has been taken from my family. Something that was so easy to ignore hiding away in my parents' house in peaceful little Wicklow." Her eyes found me once more, determination now burning there. "So, the short answer is no. Even though I have had my doubts, I have never truly thought about running away from this life. It's not really ever been an option."

The light of the computer screen highlighted her face. I could see the glisten of unshed tears resting in her tired eyes.

All the years I had laughed at her—this was no joke. In their own way, her family saved people's lives. *She* saved people's lives. If she had been there the night Freddie and I were attacked … I'd still be human, and Freddie would be alive. Our families wouldn't be worried about us. We would have been able to see them again.

If Elle or Heather or someone like them had been there, my life wouldn't have turned into a horror film.

"You also wouldn't have reconnected with Elle."

I glanced over my shoulder at the teen who was still having a ball playing with all the gym equipment. I could feel the protest on the edge of my tongue, but who was I kidding? She was right. If Freddie and I had gone on our merry way, the chances of me seeing Elle again would've been very low.

"You weren't even a hundred percent sure about dropping in on her when you both ventured across to the Emerald Isle."

I wasn't sure if she would have wanted to see me. If she would have agreed to. If she had, it would have no doubt been awkward —well, minus the sword in my face kind of awkward. Part of me felt it was easier to not let her know that I was home.

The teen stopped her fake-lifting of weights and pinned me with a stern look. *"And that's just shite, Than. Its cowardice t'not have even tried. You really have been a shite friend for not contacting her, but more so for crawling back t'her now."*

These were unusual circumstances.

"It doesn't matter. You're lucky you know a Vampire Hunter. You're lucky you were once friends with one, otherwise you would have been severely screwed."

I felt heavy, ashamed. Truth was I was lucky to be standing here. I was lucky to have her to help me, because without her, I would have lost my mind weeks ago. I really would have been gone.

"Isn't it funny how being crazy enough to create yourself an imaginary version of your childhood friend has actually kept you sane?" the teen pointed out as she set to running on the treadmill.

"Yeah, it's hilarious." With a roll of my eyes, I turned back to find Elle staring at the gym equipment. That little crinkle at the bridge of her nose had formed.

"Thanks."

Her cautious gaze turned back to me.

"Y'know? For not killing me."

"Yet."

A laugh escaped me, and I was pleased to see the twitch at the corner of her lips. Her attention moved back to the room. She slowly scanned the space as though looking for something.

"She wants t'know who you keep talking to," the teen commented. *"Eventually, you're going t'have to admit that you did lose your mind back there."*

I placed the bowl on the desk and shoved my hands in the pockets of the hoodie. "So, why are we down here?"

"Well, there's nothing in the house to indicate where Heather may have gone other than the DVD which was near useless."

"And really creepy."

I would have freaked out if a family member had left me some beyond the grave message. It was definitely one of the strangest things I had ever seen in my life. How was someone supposed to deal with that?

"So, this is basically our last hope." She picked up her mug and took another swig. "Hopefully, there will be something down here that may give me a clue to where Heather is or maybe where I can find the Werewolf's Pack."

"Pack?"

"Like a wolf Pack. Werewolves have similar traits to normal wolves the way they function." She held her hand up. "Don't ask because I don't know a great deal about it."

With another swig of her coffee, she placed the mug on the desk and began clicking away at the computer.

"I'm sure there will be something here," I commented, trying to sound positive, and moved over to the large bookshelf jammed full of big, old-looking books all squeezed in with other books resting on top and bits of paper sticking out from between various pages.

"Your breakfast will be cold."

"Not hungry." Her stomach grumbled.

"Liar liar." My focus fell to a large trunk. "Is that an actual chest?"

"Don't. Touch. It."

If it hadn't been for the modern computer and gym equipment, it would have been really easy to believe that this was a Vampire

Hunter lair. I was just disappointed there was no medieval cage down here.

"Shouldn't you be thankful?" Teen Elle hopped on to the computer desk, legs swinging back and forth. *"If there was a cage here, you might end up in it."*

I ran my hand across the wooden lid. "Are there stakes in it?"

"Than," Elle warned.

"Spoilsport." I stopped beside her, ignoring the teen who watched us both intently. "I haven't poisoned it. What good would it do me?" I pushed the bowl closer to her. "I need you, remember?"

A sigh escaped her. "Fine. Leave it there."

"If you don't want it, I spied some beans and other canned goods in the pantry. I can make you something else?"

"No, I'm fine."

"Okay, but make sure you eat something today. I'm sure Vampire Hunters need their protein and fibre."

"What are you, her mother?" Teen Elle chimed.

"If I eat the eggs, will you shut up?"

I folded my arms across my chest. "Aye."

Picking up the fork, she skewered a chunk and popped it in her mouth. "Happy?"

"Eggstatic."

Teen Elle fell back on the desk. *"I'd say kill me, but I can't die."*

"Is there anything I can do t'help?"

"Not really." She dropped the fork back into the bowl and returned to the computer.

"Well, I guess I will go and carry on catching up with world events."

"Okay."

"Yeah, I don't think you're going to get much out of her, Than." The teen rolled off the desk and bounced to her feet.

"Me neither."

"What?"

"Nothing. Shout if you find that you do need a hand."

A grunt was my reply.

Chapter Seven

~ Danielle ~

Friday 16th October, 2015

I woke at the sound of a smash. Jolting upright, I immediately regretted it as all the muscles in my neck went into a spasm.

"Shit," I hissed, cupping the back of my neck, working my fingers into the muscles at the junction where my collarbone and shoulder met.

Nathan appeared beside the desk, collecting the pieces of the mug I had obviously knocked off the surface.

The computer screen before me was black, the orange light indicating it had gone in to sleep mode. My head was killing, and my eyes were heavy.

Damn it, I had fallen asleep.

"What time is it?"

"A little after ten-fifteen." He placed the ceramic shards on the desk and walked back into the centre of the room.

"What day is it?"

A chuckle escaped him. "It's Friday night."

I stretched my neck side to side listening to the muscles popping, the tension easing as I rolled my shoulders. Something slid down my back. Twisting, I noticed a beige blanket crumbled up between myself and the chair.

He'd put a blanket around me while I slept.

Second time you have fallen to sleep while there is a Vampire in the house with you.

God, my father would have had a heart attack if he knew.

Reaching down to my hip, my fingertips skimmed the hilt of my dagger. The feel of the blade always reassured me, but more so because I knew Nathan knew it was there.

You can't seriously trust him?

He had had ample opportunity to hurt me, but instead, he had turned into a nanny, trying to make sure I was eating and getting rest. It was somehow worse than him trying to hurt me, because I didn't understand why he was doing it.

Guilt?

Guilt would have made the most sense. He had been a rubbish friend. Maybe he was trying to apologize without having to say the words. As long as it wasn't pity. Pity because I was worried about Heather. Pity because I was obviously still pissed about his absence in my life, which he no doubt found childish, maybe even pathetic. I didn't need his pity.

"How long—"

"A few hours." He sat cross-legged on the floor, the hoodie he had borrowed reaching over his knees and making him almost look like one of those toys that rocked back and forth; a weeble. "You've barely slept the last two days. I thought it was best t'just leave you be."

What had he been up to while I was sleeping? Had he left the house?

I patted my left jeans pocket. The house keys were there. Not that it really meant anything. He could have taken them and unlocked the door and then put them back. In the meantime, he could have killed the neighbours.

Pulling the blanket up and around my shoulders, I stood, ignoring the protest of my cramped-up legs. I stepped toward Nathan, studying him. I couldn't say I was surprised to see that he had found something to style his hair. The brown mess that had original symbolized a mop had been swept and moved into a style that would make a boy band member proud.

I think he had taken half a dozen showers over the last two days. I wasn't sure why exactly. Other than removing the dirt, grime, and dried blood the first morning we'd arrived here, it wasn't like he was dirty or even stank. His skin was pale and smooth but looked much healthier than the first time I had seen him at the graveyard.

Apart from the ill-fitting clothes, he could almost pass for a human.

"You okay?"

He was looking at me; the blue in his eyes had come back, along with that mischievous twinkle that remained hidden in the depths regardless of his mood. He had been a cheeky lad, a joker always pushing his luck. Thinking about him as that young boy, I would go as far as saying he had the spirit of a leprechaun. A spirit I could still see now in eyes that should have held no life at all.

"Elle?"

Shaking myself from my thoughts, I nodded to the piles of books that surrounded him. "A little light reading?"

He smirked.

"Well, I figured I might as well learn something while I have the chance to." He shrugged. "I guessed that your family would have a reasonable amount of information on the general working of Vampires and whatnot." He lowered his head back to his current page. "You weren't joking. They really hate my kind."

I flinched. It was the first time he had unconsciously admitted his predicament. The first time he had referred to himself as a Vampire and not 'still him,' still human.

Even though I knew what he was, the evidence was constantly in my face, from his complexion to the small indents of his fangs that constantly caught on his bottom lip. Watching him drink Heather's mixture to watching his skin sizzle under my silver blade, seeing his skin heal in a second … looking at him now, crossed-legged, surrounded by books as if he were a student studying for an exam, it was a lot harder to see him as anyone but Nathan. My best friend.

"Well, they've had good cause to." I moved around him and glanced down. The pages were worn, the original text faded, but in between the sentences penned in ancient Romanian were the small, bolder English translations.

The diary of Marko Pavel's father. The man who had doomed us all to this lifestyle.

"Neculai Pavel had good reason."

"Wife, daughter, and twelve-year-old grandson slaughtered by your own son right in front of your eyes? Hell yeah, it's enough reason t'go on a revenge spree."

"A failed one." I sighed. "Which is why Marko is still out there and why everyone who came after Neculai has been tasked with finding him."

He looked up at me. "Have you just spoilt the end of the book for me?"

Typical Than, able to make light of something that was so far from being funny. And he did it in such a way that you still never doubted his belief in you.

I moved past him. "Believe me, there's no happy ending."

"The stories not finished yet, is it?"

The question stopped me in my tracks. The way we had been brought up and trained, the story of my family had always seemed finished regardless of what we did. But we, Heather and I, we were still writing it. Every member of our family ... they were like chapters in that book that Nathan currently held. They were parts of one ongoing story which had been told to us as if the ending was inevitable, and although it felt that way ... it was nowhere near over.

For the first time in my life, I felt unsure. For the first time, it actually felt like there was the smallest speck of light at the end of this dark path I walked. Yes, everyone died and one day I would, but maybe, just maybe, it wouldn't be at the hand of a Vampire as I had been led to believe.

You're clearly going loopy if you believe that.

"I guess not." I wandered to the wall, pressing my back against the brick in the hope of releasing some of the bunched-up tension. My muscles clicked and popped as I pushed into the brick.

"Did you need me t'get you anything?"

I couldn't help the tired laugh that escaped me. "You know you're not my maid, right?"

"I'd have a sexier uniform if I was."

I scrunched my face and shook my head dramatically. "Oh, that so isn't an image I want in my head."

Such a strange boy.

His laughter filled the space, bringing memories of our childhood rushing back to me. Of adventures and times when I was able to be anything but a Vampire Slayer. I didn't have to train or learn the history of it all, to listen to my parents arguing with Alexis or Sofia. A time when the responsibilities I now had just seemed like distant worries.

You shouldn't let your guard down. He's still a Vampire no matter what. He could still turn on you, betray you ... leave you.

My chest clenched. I opened my eyes and watched as his focus was lost in the pages of the ancient journal.

The only reason he was here was because his world had been tipped upside down and I was the only one who would believe him. He was only here because he needed my help. If he hadn't been captured, he wouldn't have been here with me right now. I'd be here on my own.

The thought hurt, but then, it was the truth. He was back in my life because he had no one else he could turn to. Once he had his answers, he would leave again … and I hated how much the idea annoyed me.

My focus roamed around the room for what felt like the tenth time in the two days I had been down here. Yet again, I wondered if Dorian and Alexis had trained together in this room. Wondered what it was like to have someone who fought alongside you, who had your back. Someone who would follow you anywhere even if it led to their death.

It was a dramatic thought, but considering our lifestyle, everything was all or nothing. It was a nice thought, having such a strong connection with someone. Having someone who would always take your side; someone you could always rely on. My mother and father had found it. Alexis and Dorian. Heather had

Sofia … Not anymore, though. Now she was on her own, like me.

I gave myself a mental shake, tearing my focus off Nathan. Such thoughts were irrelevant. I was here to find Heather. Not to wonder about life and what limited options I had, or the overall outcomes.

Two days of searching through the computer's archive. Flicking through every book on the shelf. Looking through drawers and every nook and cranny to see if I could find something, anything that would give me a lead.

There was no information on where the Pack was located. I could only presume it was a privacy issue or that my aunt didn't want anyone else in the family to know.

No indication as to where the UK Nest was. Alexis and Dorian must have known so it should have been in with all the other information about the Colony, but it was missing. Had the Nest moved after Dorian's death? Or had Sofia removed the details, so Heather didn't go there?

I was willing to bet it was the latter, but it sure as hell didn't help me.

I scrubbed my hands over my face, hoping to get rid of my jumbled thoughts. "I'm going t'get a shower. See if I can wake myself up."

"Maybe you should just go and get some rest, y'know, in an actual bed?"

He really wants you to go back to sleep. Why?

"I can't sleep until I have a starting point." I wandered over to the desk and collected the broken mug.

"If I knew what we are looking for—?"

"I don't even know, Than." I pulled the blanket tighter around my shoulders. "I will be down shortly."

"No problem. I will just be here, learning."

I wandered to the door, pausing at the threshold. My previous thoughts about his doings during my naps resurfacing. "Have you had enough t'drink today? Is there still plenty of mixture available for you?"

"Yes, to both." He angled a look at me. "And there's still a few slices of pizza left from earlier, if you're hungry."

Strangest Vampire I had ever met. He really wasn't grabbing the concept of what a Leech was, but then again, he was the strangest boy that I had ever known.

"Great." I made my way up the stepladders. "I won't be long."

"I'm not going anywhere."

Making my way through the pantry, I stopped in the kitchen, looking for the bin. "There has to be one somewhere."

"In the cupboard near the backdoor," Than called up.

I flicked the kitchen light on and made my way over to the backdoor. "I'm not sure if I should be freaked out at how well y'know your way around this house?"

"I'm nosey, remember," came the reply.

Opening the cupboard, I saw a bin attached to the inside of the door. I dropped the shards inside, the heavy ceramic knocking the uneaten scrambled egg down the side of the black bag, revealing a crumbled envelope with the letters 'er' visible.

I reached inside, pulling the small manilla envelope, and straightened it out on the counter. Heather's name rested in dark pen on the front, written in my aunt's handwriting.

Reaching back into the bin, I batted away the odd bits of garbage until my fingers skimmed paper. I pulled the scrunched ball in the same shade and straightened it. Relief and fear collided in my stomach as I read the short note.

Heather. The Sphinx. Right, back corner. Small group. Luca Mancinelli. September 25th, 2015. 11.30p.m. It's your only chance.

"Well, shite."

My mother had mentioned that Heather had stated Sofia had seen Luca in London, but well, my aunt hadn't simply mentioned it. She had told Heather exactly where he was going to be, and knowing my cousin, she would have gone for him, guardian Werewolf in tow.

I closed the cupboard door, my hip hitting the side as I stared at the note in my hand.

Luca was a Second Generation who would have had an entourage with him. I could only presume The Sphinx was a bar or nightclub of some sort, which meant my cousin would have held the advantage of them not wanting to cause a scene, but if she had gone … if they had fought … had she survived? If so, surely, she would have checked in with my mother?

Did that mean she hadn't made it?

Yet again, my mind started to spin with all the possibilities. Throwing in the mystery of Nathan being able to cross the threshold and enter this house … I suddenly felt dizzy at the thought that my cousin could be dead.

Despite being slightly stronger than a human and with the ability to heal a little quicker, being an Infected didn't mean that she would necessarily survive. But then again, if Luca had killed Heather Ryan, the only born Infected, we would have heard, wouldn't we? The Vampires would be gloating. They would be laughing at us. They wouldn't simply keep it to themselves.

I hated the idea, but it gave me hope that my cousin was still alive.

I took a few deep breaths, calming myself, focusing on the sick knowledge that the Leeches would have made sure we knew if they had succeeded in killing Heather.

If she was indeed alive, I then had to presume she was unable to check in with us. I knew she didn't own a mobile, which I had always found strange, but there was still the odd phone box scattered around the place. And I'm sure the Werewolf would have had a phone?

Whatever the reason, I could only presume that neither of them was able to check in. So, the big question was, what would stop Heather from calling my mother?

"You look deep in thought?" Nathan stood by the fridge. "You okay?"

"I think I found a lead."

"That's great. Isn't it?"

"Yeah, we're just three weeks too late t'follow it."

"I don't understand."

I walked over and handed him the note. "Instructions from Sofia."

He accepted the paper, his brow furrowing as he read. "So, Heather would have definitely gone after this guy?"

"For sure." I took a seat at the breakfast bar. "If she had died—"

"I'm sure she's fine."

"Well, we would know if she had."

"How?"

"Heather is special, remember. I'm sure the Vampires would be screaming about killing the born Infected. They've been after her for years, so I can only presume they'd want us t'know."

"So, she's alive?" His expression lightened. "That's good."

"Of course it is."

"You might want t'tell your face."

"Why hasn't she checked in? Why hasn't she told us what happened with Luca, what she found out?"

"Maybe she hasn't had the chance to?"

That would be an easy solution, but considering it had been three weeks since the date on the note … how can someone go three weeks without getting to a phone?

"Or she can't."

"Okay." He placed the note on the end of the breakfast bar. "So, she's alive and unable to tell her loved ones she's okay because she can't get to a phone."

My temples began to throb. I pressed my fingertips against the pulsing points and rubbed. "Who can't get to a phone nowadays?"

He was silent for a long moment. "People who are lost in remote areas with no connections. Jungles, mountains … forests."

"I hardly think they will be up a mountain or in a jungle, Than."

"A forest, then? I had to run through one." He moved back to the fridge, opening the door. "Prisoners!"

I dropped my hands to my lap. "What?"

"Prisoners can't use phones. Well, normal prisoners get at least one phone call, but Vampire prisoners don't. I would have loved t'have called t'check in with my mum, tell her I'm fine, knowing it would be the last time I ever spoke to her, but it would have been easier than what she must be going through now."

Time stopped, Nathan's voice fading into the background as my tired brain fought to process everything he had just said.

Nathan had been kidnapped in London and taken to a facility where he was turned and experimented on. That facility was hidden in a forest which was located somewhere in Scotland which he'd discovered after escaping and making it to the nearest town. It was all still very confusing, but Heather was out in London hunting Luca. She was the only born Infected and the Leeches had wanted to kill or change her for years…

"Some will want to use you." Sofia's voice echoed in my mind.

There are no coincidences. That's what my aunt had always said. No matter how shit things were and how much you hated hearing it, she believed that everything in life happened for a reason. That life had a pattern and reason to it. That fate was real.

I jumped off the stool, throwing the blanket on the counter. "You're a freaking genius."

"Uh, thanks. I mean—" His expression turned smug. "—obviously."

"They must have taken her. Think about what Sofia said. "Some will want t'kill you."

"And as you said, if they had done that … well, after three weeks, you'd probably know by now." Bottle of mixture in hand, he shut the fridge door. "But Sofia also said, "some will want t'change you."

"Heather would rather die than be turned into a Leech."

"Which we know isn't the case because of point one, but say she did get changed, would she tell you, considering how you've been brought up and what your family believe?"

Honestly, I wasn't sure. Maybe she would feel ashamed. Like she had failed Sofia, her mother and father. Well, everyone. Could I tell my parents if I'd been turned? How would they react? I knew how they would. My father would be ready to kill me while my mother tried to talk him out of it in the hope that I would be different or that I could be cured.

No, I wouldn't blame Heather if she had been changed and hadn't told us.

"Okay." I turned and began to walk the stretch of the kitchen. "She could have possibly been changed, and if so, there's the smallest chance she would have contacted us."

"Very small chance." He unscrewed the lid of the bottle. "Leaving the "some will want t'use you" comment."

"If you want to use someone, someone who wouldn't want to help you, you'd take them, right?"

"Which explains why she wouldn't have contacted you, because she would technically be a prisoner of sorts," he agreed, before taking a mouthful of the mixture.

"Okay. So, Heather and Brendan go and find Luca and whatever happens, one way or another, they get taken."

"Taken where?"

"The UK Colony Nest?"

"In Scotland?"

"What? No." I moved back to the counter and leant against it. "No, the Nest is in London, or at least it should still be in London. There's no information on its location in any of the archive files, but I had to presume that she would be taken to the Colony Leader."

He moved to the opposite counter and leant against the sink, facing me. "Then why was I held hostage and experimented on in Scotland?"

Yet again, that was a great question. Why did the Vampires have a very important facility so far away from their Nest? It was a question that Nathan needed answering more than I did, and unfortunately, I had no answer for him.

"I-I'm not sure, but I think the best bet we have t'find Heather is t'find the UK Nest."

What would the Vampires do with her? Would the Leader, Michael, contact Marko? Would Marko come to the UK for Heather, or wasn't he bothered about a trivial little Infected who happened to be born that way and be a Vampire Slayer?

Shit, what if Marko was in the UK?

My mind was racing. Marko was an Ancient. The only one we knew of and the only one who really mattered to my family. He would slaughter Heather.

"Where do we start?"

Nathan's question pulled me from my thoughts.

"I have no idea."

"Right." He took another swig. "Well then, I propose you go and get some rest and then we will—"

Again with the rest.

"I can't," I ground out, irritation creeping up my back as he yet again stated that I needed to rest, to get out of the way.

There was too much to figure out. Too much to do. Why did he keep trying to get me out of the way?

"Elle, it's been three weeks since the note. Three weeks you haven't heard from her. One more night won't make a difference."

Wouldn't it? A second could mean the difference between life and death, and it had been three weeks. That was a hell of a lot of seconds that had been and gone.

My hands began shaking as the weight of time and the guilt of not being here with Heather began to crush down on me.

"You don't know that," I snapped, walking to the fridge and collecting the pizza box. "Why are you so eager for me t'go t'sleep all the time?" I threw the box on the counter and batted the door shut. "What are you up to while I'm out of the way?"

He almost choked on another mouthful of mixture. "Woah, Little

Miss Paranoid."

"Seriously, I—?"

"Apart from watching the news—" He placed the bottle on the counter. "—I've been reading all those big scary books that are down in your cousin's little lair."

I itched to grab my dagger, to stab something. I had been sat on my arse for three weeks, and my cousin was on a suicide mission. I'd been working at a stupid pub when the Vampire who had destroyed my family could be swanning around the UK … could be torturing my cousin. Three weeks of me doing nothing, and I now stood in a kitchen arguing with a new-born Vampire.

"I'm supposed t'believe that?"

"It's the truth, Elle. Jesus." He moved over to the breakfast bar and took a seat.

I gripped the edge of the counter to stop myself from reaching for the comforting weight at my hip. I shouldn't stab him. He'd not done anything wrong.

He's a Vampire. No other reason is needed.

I couldn't stab him. It wasn't his fault.

How do you know? He just happens to show up back in your life as a Vampire in the same time frame as Heather goes missing. Is that a coincidence?

"Who sent you?"

"What?" His eyebrows crashed at the bridge of his nose. "No one sent me. Look, I get that you don't trust me, and you have so many reasons not to, but I'm really trying here."

"Trying what, exactly?" My nails bit into the underside of the counter. "Lull me into believing you're harmless so you can kill me when your Master gives you permission?"

"What the— Are you jokin'?" His left fist landed on the countertop, index finger jabbing the marble. "I'm trying hard t'show you that you *can* trust me. That I have no interest in hurting you or sucking your blood."

"Actions speak louder than words."

"Have I tried to hurt you?" He stared at me, wide-eyed. "Well, have I?"

Despite the occasions I had drifted off, I still remained in one piece, unbitten. The weight of the blanket hanging from my arms was another reminder that the weirdo had even tucked me up while I slept on the computer chair downstairs.

"All I want t'do is figure out what's happened t'me and what I'm going t'do next."

"What d'you mean, do next?"

"Well, what am I supposed t'do?" His shoulders slouched as he counted his problems on his fingers. "I can't see my family. I can't go home. I can't go out during the day ... I highly doubt there is a rehab for getting over being human."

"You go to the Colony."

His eyes widened, back straightened. "You want me to go and live with the monsters that did this t'me? The monsters you hate so much?"

The level of hurt that rippled across his face caused me to wince. He was genuinely offended at the suggestion.

The tension eased from my shoulders. I relaxed my grip.

"I don't know what you're supposed t'do." I slumped against the counter. "This is all new t'me."

"New t'you?" He laughed.

"New t'both of us." My limps suddenly felt heavy as my frayed nerves tangoed with my ongoing exhaustion. "You're a Vampire—"

"I know." He pushed off the seat and moved away from me. "Jesus, I know. You keep reminding me. Every damn day, you point it out as if this was a decision I made and should now be punished for."

"I just mean—" I sighed, reaching inside of the pizza box. needing fuel. "I kill Vampires, so I don't know what the alternative is."

Where did good Vampires go?

Presuming he is good.

Does he look bad?

He looked so far from what a Vampire was supposed to look like. Nothing about him matched any of the Vampires I had ever fought. Nothing about him matched what we were taught or what we read.

He kept his back to me. Hands pressed on the counter tops, his voice was soft. "All I thought about for those six weeks was … you."

The air caught in my throat, along with the chunk of pizza I had just swallowed, his whispered confession catching me off guard.

I coughed, patting my chest.

"What?" The word was strained as I tried to dislodge the bread from my gullet.

"I was alone, tied up in the darkness for hours on end with nothing but my thoughts t'distract me. So, I thought about everything you had ever told me about Vampires and how I always laughed. I thought about how you were the only one I could trust t'believe me when I told you that the craziest thing in the world has happened t'me."

He turned, lower back resting against the counter, arms folded, though his head remained down.

"All I did was think of you, of us, our childhood. Talking out loud t'you—" He looked up at me, thick, black blood crawling from the corner of his eyes. "—you are the only thing that kept me sane in that place. Thinking about how I owed you an apology. A million apologies. How you would no doubt say, 'I told you so'."

He laughed, hugging himself tighter. "Thinking about the fact that I needed t'get out of there and find you because you're the only one who could tell me what t'do … you're the only reason I'm still here, Elle."

My heart was pounding so hard in my chest. I felt so conflicted, so confused. I couldn't breathe. I didn't know what to say or do. I'd had no training for this. No training on what to do with an emotional Vampire.

Vampire equalled kill. Vampire didn't equal friendship, but the friendship came before the fangs.

Did he have an ulterior motive? Was this all just a trick?

The sight of him standing there crying, it was damn near heartbreaking. The fact he was admitting he was lost and scared and confused …

He's a Vampire.

Yes, Nathan was a Vampire, but he was the softest most pathetic and useless Vampire I had ever met. He was clueless, and he was all alone. He no longer had anyone, family or Colony. The fact that he was created rather than turned, I wasn't sure if he had a Master or Mistress, and if he did, well, they had currently abandoned him. And although his ignorance and rejection had hurt all these years, my duty was to protect people from Vampires even if that person was a Vampire themselves.

My training had never covered this, and although I had been trained to distrust all Vampires, somewhere deep inside, I believed he was telling the truth, about everything. He didn't know what was going on, and he didn't know what to do. He wasn't going to hurt me. I could see it in his eyes, the despair. It was what had stopped me from killing him back in Wicklow.

He was still Nathan, and he needed my help. I was the only one who could help him. What kind of Vampire Slayer would I be if I ignored what had happened to him, what his survival and existence stood for? What kind of friend would I be?

After everything, I couldn't turn my back on him. It would make me as bad a friend as he had been, and I wasn't going to give him the satisfaction of us being equally bad.

I dropped the slice of pizza on the top of the box and slid off the stool. "Is this your way of apologising for being the worst friend in the world?"

A laugh scraped his throat. He wiped his eyes, smearing the black blood all over his pale skin, making him look like a panda.

"And for breaking your promise of keeping in touch?" I held my hand up, cutting him off. "Happy Birthday and Merry Christmas aren't keeping in contact."

"You're right." He folded his arms once more. "I have been a bollocks friend. I don't deserve your help."

"You don't." Taking hold of the nearby kitchen roll, I pulled off a few sheets and walked to the sink. "And you would have remained a stranger if you hadn't been turned and therefore desperate."

It was both a question and a statement that I needed him to confirm.

"I'm so sorry, Elle."

I turned the tap on in order to wet the paper towel. "Sorry isn't good enough."

"I know."

Moving closer to him so we stood face to face, I lifted his chin and began to dab the blood from his eyes. "But it's a start."

The relief that washed over him almost broke me. He was like a helpless child.

"Elle—"

"I'm going t'trust you, for old times' sake."

His skin was cool as his fingertips slid across my palm and he took my left hand in his. "I know that goes against everything you believe."

"You're the most clueless Vampire I've ever met."

He laughed, shoulders bobbing as his head dropped. "Yeah, guess it serves me right for never paying attention t'you."

"I trust that you won't hurt me, or my family."

"I'd *never* hurt you, Elle." He squeezed my hand and glanced at me from under his ridiculously long eyelashes. "I cross my heart."

And hope to die. He didn't speak the words, but they were a whispered understanding between us.

"You should be careful what you wish for." At the feel of tears gathering in my own eyes, I moved my attention back to the task. "And I believe you won't drink or hurt innocent people."

"I swear it."

Untangling my hand from his, I threw the bloodied damp paper in the sink and grabbed a couple of dry sheets. "I'm going to help you figure this out, okay?"

"I believe you."

His hands found my hips as I moved back in front of him, the gesture causing me to freeze on the spot. I was torn between making a joke and scolding him, asking him what he was doing, but the way he was looking at me made me bite my tongue. His blue eyes were full of questions as they wandered over my face, so focused, as if he were reading something of great importance on my skin.

Ignoring the rapid beat of my heart and the fact that heat was pulsing through my clothes in the places his hands rested, I continued wiping at his cheeks, trying my hardest to clean away his dark tears, ignoring the flush I could feel crawling up my neck and the fact that I appeared momentarily dumbstruck by his closeness.

"I'm going t'help you find Heather."

I moved the towel down his cheek, following the trail that stopped at the corner of his lips. "I know."

Unlike that night in the graveyard, he looked healthy, his features still boyish, but in an appealing way. My focus fixated on the tips of his fangs that rested on his lower lip. "Your fangs are so small."

So unlike normal Vampires. Vampires' fangs only appeared when they transformed, and even then, they were long and sharp. So similar to the fangs of a snake.

"It's because they're scared. You should see them when I get excited. They're huge."

An unexpected laugh bubbled up and broke free, his comment thankfully breaking this strange moment. "You're such an idiot."

"At least I make you laugh." He smiled, chuckling at my reaction. "Am I all cleaned up?"

Looking at his face only caused me to laugh harder. "You currently look like your zebra face paint has been spoilt by the rain."

He quipped an eyebrow. "So, sexy?"

I pushed myself away. "I think it would be best if you wash your own face."

"Well, considering you're so useless." He flinched as I threw the balled-up paper towel at his face. "Getting back to your earlier comment, I had thought about visiting you a few times and definitely recently, but I-I didn't think you'd want to see me."

"Well, I definitely wouldn't have made it an easy reunion," I confessed as I plonked down on the bar stool, picked up my slice of pizza, and continued eating.

"I wouldn't have expected you to." Turning to the sink, he ran the tap, cupping water in his hands, and splashed it over his face. Taking a few sheets of the kitchen towel, he then wiped his face.

"Gone?" he asked, turning back to me.

"Pretty much."

He collected the wet, bloodied towels from the sink and threw the lot in the bin, before collecting the glass bottle of mixture and joining me once more at the breakfast bar.

"So, Little Miss Paranoid, t'answer your early question, the reason I keep telling you t'get some rest and even eat is because despite what you think, I can see that you're exhausted, and if we find what we're looking for, which I'm guessing will entail a shite load of Vampires, well, you aren't going t'be any good as a fight partner if you can barely keep your eyes open."

I swallowed the last chunk of my slice of pizza. "Oh, so now I've partially forgiven you, you're suddenly an expert on what's best for me?"

"You know I'm right." He took a swig of mixture.

"I'd never admit such a thing."

"I know," he replied with a huge grin. "But seriously, you have been stuck in the basement for two days straight, nodding off for short periods of time and only eating when I nag you enough."

I couldn't argue with the facts. I was tired. I could feel every cell in my body humming with exhaustion, but after forty-eight hours, we finally had a starting point.

"Look. Bed. Shower. Food. I will continue with Vampire 101, and come tomorrow morning, we will be ready t'take on the world. Okay?"

I grabbed another slice of pizza from the box. "Okay, but tomorrow—"

"We will be kicking butt twenty hours from now, if not sooner. I just—" His attention became lost on the red liquid sloshing in the bottle he was swirling. "—I need a little bit more time t'figure out what I can and can't do." He gave me a sheepish glance. "You know, so I actually stand a chance at surviving and not being a burden t'you."

I placed my hand on his knee. "I won't let them hurt you more than they already have."

A smile played across his lips, revealing the bottom of his little fangs.

"Careful, slayer." He placed his hand on top of mine. "It's starting t'sound like y'care about me."

I never stopped.

I swallowed the words before they could leave my mouth.

"Besides, if anyone is going t'kill you, it will be me." I slid my hand from under his and stood. "I've earned that right after more than forty-eight hours of having t'put up with your jokes."

Pizza in hand, I slipped off the stool.

"As if you never laugh."

"Laughing *at* you, Than. Not with you." I exited the kitchen and headed upstairs.

*****

~ Nathan ~

I slid the last book on the shelf and pressed my forehead against the old leather seams.

"Boy, that was a lot of reading."

"There's a lot of history between these creatures and Elle's family."

"So, do you feel y'know everything there is t'know?"

A vengeance pact that had been passed on for years, an entire family sacrificing their lives to keep complete strangers safe from creatures born of someone's nightmare.

"That sums it up."

Each member of her family had been raised from infancy to hate Vampires, and they all had very good reasons to, especially after the family stories. Not one mention of a decent Vampire. Did that mean there weren't any? Would I eventually lose my humanity and turn into one of these horrible Leeches, take my place as yet another villain in her family story books?

"I don't think there's an evil bone in your body, Than."

"Aww, Elle." I pushed myself from the bookshelf and turned to the teen who was resting in the computer chair. I placed my hand on my silent chest. "I think that has to be the nicest thing you've ever said to me."

"Must be. It would explain why there's a bit of sick in my mouth."

Elle was choosing to trust me—something that went against everything she had been taught to do. Everything that she believed.

"You and she were getting quite cosy up there."

The feel of her warm skin under my fingertips … God, nothing had ever felt so good. And the way she smelled, like honey and milk. She was warm and real and the first human contact I'd had in six weeks.

"She was cleaning blood off my face."

"Looked very intimate to me."

She had finally looked at me like she used to, like she knew me. It was such a relief.

"Plus, you apologized for being such a shit-head."

It had been easier than I'd thought it would have been, admitting I had been close to losing my mind. Admitting that she had been the only thing that had kept me going.

"You didn't mention me, though."

"I think explaining that I was talking to an imaginary teen Elle may have steered the conversation off in a different direction."

"True. I doubted she would have gotten that close t'you if she knew you were fantasizing about little girls."

I moved past her. "Don't say it like that."

"Like what?"

"Creepy-like. It's not like that."

"Oh, don't get your knickers in a twist."

"If I'd had known what Elle looked like now, then I would have thought of you as an adult."

"Yeah, somehow, I think imagining adult Elle would have driven you crazier."

I didn't want to admit she had a point. Fortunately, Elle didn't have social media so it wasn't like I could have even known from prior to my six weeks in Hell. I doubt I would have been able to do her justice anyway.

"So, you do want t'kiss her?"

Did I? Being so close to her. Being able to feel her breath on my face and the warmth of her skin …

"Okay, okay. I get the picture." She pushed off the seat. *"Plus, I think if you told her that you imagined her keeping you company …"*

"It would sound just as bad."

"Yup." She stopped next to me. *"So, what now?"*

"Well, I apparently have super cool senses and strength and all the other things that make Vampires fairly cool. So, I guess I better get t'grips with my new talents." I lay my hand flat against the red punch bag. "What d'you think? D'you think I will break it the first hit?"

"I think you're getting a head of yourself."

"I don't want t'be taken again."

I couldn't be. I knew I wouldn't survive if I was. They would either kill me, or I would lose myself completely.

"You can laugh all you want at that."

"I wouldn't laugh at that."

"I don't want t'make it easy for them, y'know." I unzipped the hoodie and shrugged it off. "Plus, I don't want t'stand there like a—"

"Dickless Vampire?"

"And leave Elle t'do all the fighting. They've made me a monster." I threw the hoodie on the ground and turned back to the bag. "I want t'make them pay."

A wide smile broke across the teen's face as she moved into my peripheral vision. *"Well then, let's make sure they know it was a mistake t'turn this Irish lad."*

Chapter Eight

~ Danielle ~

Saturday 17th October, 2015
2:11pm

The scent of coffee and pizza assaulted me as I trudged down the stairs.

"I can't believe you let me sleep this long," I stated while walking into the kitchen, stopping at the sight of Nathan standing at the breakfast bar, his left arm outstretched, a hot mug of coffee cradled in his grasp, the handle pointing to me.

"You obviously needed it."

"Erm, thanks." I accepted the mug off him and moved to the opposite side of the counter.

"Besides, roughly two hours and the sun will have set, so we can be on our way. I remember how impatient you are, so it seemed easier t'just leave you be."

Well, I couldn't fault him there.

"What's this?"

Made up of sheets of white A4, the colourful print outs were stapled together to form a map of London.

I looked at him quizzically. "You made a map?"

"Say what you want, but it's very difficult to see everything on a computer." He placed his finger on a black dot he had drawn. "This is where The Sphinx is located."

Taking a swig of my coffee, I looked at the map following his index finger as he moved it to a red dot a little lower down.

"This is roughly where Freddie and I were when we were attacked."

I didn't miss the catch in his voice at the mention of his dead travel buddy. He hadn't spoken much about his friend, and in all fairness, I hadn't even asked about the guy.

With guilt niggling at me and the understanding that Nathan and I were now on friendly terms once more, I decided it was only right to try and offer some comfort. "How long did you two know each other?"

"Since I moved t'Switzerland. He was the first kid that spoke t'me at High School." He folded his arms across his chest. "He was really interested in forensics. Loved learning about Jack the Ripper and other historical murders. The idiot liked t'read Sherlock Holmes." He glanced at me. "He kinda reminded me of you."

My brow furrowed. "He did?"

"Yeah, he wasn't a normal kid."

"Gee, thanks." I took another mouthful of coffee.

"I mean, he was interesting. That stuff didn't freak him out." He laughed. "He was the reason we stopped off in London. He wanted to visit Whitechapel and do the Ripper tour and even booked us in to a cheap hostel near the Sherlock Holmes museum."

"He sounds … interesting."

"Yeah." He placed his hands on the counter, his fingers curling around the edges. "He didn't deserve to die."

I ducked my head to catch his gaze. "Neither of you deserved to."

"He sure as shit would have known what all the crap in that file would have meant." He nodded to the manilla folder that sat to his right.

"He an expert in Vampires and Werewolves, as well?"

"No, but he was smart, y'know. Smarter than me. He would have had a better clue."

I reached across and squeezed his shoulder. "I know. It's hard when everyone is smarter than you."

A grin curled the corner of his mouth. He angled a look at me.

"Thanks."

"Happy t'help." I dropped my arm and took another swig of coffee. "So, at a glance, the two locations aren't far from one another."

He straightened and took hold of two pencils and an elastic band. "It's roughly one-point-four miles between the two locations, which got me wondering if the Vampires kept things close t'home."

"They have the whole of London t'hunt in."

"Yeah, but think about it. All the Ripper murders were in Whitechapel. He had a hunting ground. Predators tend t'have an area they like t'hunt in, and you said this Luca guy was pretty important, so they definitely don't want him t'stray too far from their crib?"

"Nest."

He placed one pencil on the black dot and pulled the elastic band, placing the second pencil on the red dot. "So, with all that in mind, it would make sense that they hunt in an area where it's easy for them to take their victims back with them and so forth."

I watched as he drew a perfect circle starting and ending on the red dot.

"There's more nightclubs in this area, for one, so more vulnerable drunk human." He placed the pencils and band on the counter and pointed at the circle he had drawn. "So, would it make sense t'check this radius, especially because these two locations are so close together?"

I stared at the map, the hot mug cradled in my hands. "Y'know, you're smarter than y'think."

With only the knowledge that Heather had been directed to a nightclub, The Sphinx would have been our starting point, but with no hint of indication in which direction the Nest was, we would have been pretty stuck once we go there. Sure, the idea was to search the area and widen the search, but knowing that the spot where Nathan and Freddie had been taken was so close by suddenly made this task a little more hopeful.

156 | Cross My Heart

No such thing as coincidences.

We could go in the wrong direction, or maybe the Nest had moved, or maybe the Vampires lived way on the other side of the city, but I couldn't fault his logic. The Leeches stayed around Dublin when they followed my aunt and cousins over. Sure, they fanned out a little, wandered into town and such, but they were never too far from us. So, it would make sense they would hunt around their safe haven. Animals did it all the time.

I suddenly felt dumb. It all seemed so obvious, but I was only ever following orders, my father telling me which areas to hunt or check.

"Thanks," he replied to my previous compliment.

"Not Freddie smart, but—" I flinched as the band weakly hit my forehead.

"I just figure it was a starting point. London is huge, and with only the note t'go off …"

"This is-it's great." I raised my mug to him in a salute. "I think you might be on t'something."

He seemed genuinely pleased with himself, like a schoolboy who had answered a question correctly.

"So, what's the plan?"

He moved over to the oven, opening the door and collecting the tray. The remaining three slices of Hawaiian pizza lay on the black metal, the cheese bubbling slightly. My stomach rumbled.

"We patrol the area, and we find a Vampire, and then we get it t'take us to the Nest."

"That easy, huh?" He slid the pizza off the baking tray and onto a large plate which he put down in front of me.

"They won't willingly take us to the Nest. They will need some persuading." I patted the blade on my hip.

"So, let's say they take us." He placed the tray on top of the stove. "Then what? I imagine there's going t'be more than a couple of Vampires in there."

"We sneak in and look for Heather. Kill any Vampires that attack us."

"That still doesn't answer the part about there being a load of Vampires in there."

I placed my mug on the counter and picked up a slice of pizza, blowing across the surface. "They won't all be in. They will be out hunting. We will be fine."

"Easy for you t'say. You've been doing this for years."

"And you have all their strength and speed. All you have t'do is react and defend yourself." I took a bite of my pizza. "Besides, I heard you going t'town on the punch bag last night. So don't tell me you don't have a decent right hook."

A sheepish look crossed his face. "Yeah, we may need to replace it."

***

In theory, the radius idea had been great, but practically, it wasn't working as well. We had spent hours looping the perimeter of Nathan's pencil border, which happened to be the heart of central London. A place I had never been to, which was yet another slap in the face at how isolated my life had been. I lived like an hour or so away by plane, and I had never travelled to London before. It seemed crazy. Wasn't that an unwritten must-do on the bucket list of anyone who lived in the UK or Ireland?

Regardless of the fact, I didn't have longer than a few seconds to take in the sight of Big Ben, Number 10, Downing Street, or even Buckingham Palace as I circled round and round the selected area, closing the circle until Nathan and I once again met across the road from the Sphinx.

He looked deflated as we came to a halt. "Elle, we've be doing this for hours."

"We just need t'find a Vampire."

"It's proving rather hard."

"They should find you easily."

He looked confused. "They should?"

"You're—" I gave him an apologetic smile. "—one of them. Or rather, you're a different type of them, and you escaped them. If they get a whiff of you, they should take notice."

"You may have explained this as we left the house."

"I didn't want you t'stress."

"Me, stress?"

We had done the first sweep together, which had taken just under two hours. I had then suggested we split to cover more ground, which would have been far easier for him considering Vampires could be rather fast. That's if he even knew how to be fast.

Splitting up had made more sense, but after almost six hours, my hope was running dry.

"I just don't understand." I glanced across at the nightclub Heather was last known to have visited. "Logistically, we should have at least come across one by now. This is London, for God's sake. The UK Colony is apparently rather large, and there's so many people out."

London nightlife had a pulse, and it was easy to see why the Vampires would have chosen to remain in the capital. The place was like a buffet with tons of quiet streets and dark alleyways and backroads. Perfect dining for a Leech.

The fact that my father expected us to have any in Ireland was almost laughable. Who would pick a salad over a steak?

"Maybe they're all on a diet?"

"Seriously? Jokes?"

He shrugged. "What now?"

"I just need a minute." I walked to a nearby alley and leant against the wall at the mouth. Nathan mirrored me.

"A penthouse," he commented, looking up at the buildings around us. "That's where I'd hide out."

"A penthouse wouldn't be big enough."

"The palace?"

"Get real."

"What? It *would* be big enough."

"Yeah, way too big. Besides, I think we would notice if the monarchy were Vampires."

"Well, where would you choose to Nest?" He rolled his eyes at my disgusted expression. "I know, dare you imagine yourself as one of the undead, but seriously, you become a Vampire and you can live anywhere, where would you live?"

"Well, it isn't that simple, t'start." I sagged against the wall. "When you're turned, you have t'stay with your Master or Mistress for a while, and then once they allow it, you can wander off and start creating your own Bloodlings."

"Those are the Vampires that are linked t'you, right?"

"You have been doing your research."

He grinned. "I'm a quick study."

"Well, say you start doing that, then yeah, you would need a Nest. It depends on which decade you're in and from, I suppose. And being the Leader of the main Nest, well, that's just a ton of politics—"

"Oy, country girl, just answer the question."

"I don't know." I folded my arms. "I've never imagined being anywhere but home."

God, wasn't that sad. I couldn't imagine living anywhere else, even imagine having my own place. Well, there had never been a point thinking about such things as we were taught to see a constant and ever-changing expiry date depending on what type of day it was.

"Well, your parents' house and land are a perfect safe haven."

"Tell me about it."

"There's nothing wrong with keeping your family safe, Elle."

"Much good it does anyone."

He walked over to me and clasped my shoulders. "We're going to find her."

I managed a smile despite the lack of reassurance I currently felt.

Something wasn't right. Where were all the Vampires? Or were my expectations too high? Did I honestly think I'd walk into

London and all the Leeches would be walking around with blood oozing from their mouth as they stood on a pile of victims?

"Considering what y'know about the Leader, where would you guess he'd set up house?"

I scrubbed my hands across my face in an attempt to wake myself up. The night was still young. Maybe the Leeches didn't come out until later.

"Michael was born in the Elizabethan era but was turned around the Stuart Period."

"Yeah, that doesn't mean much t'me." He let go of my shoulders and moved to the opposite wall. "Was he rich or poor?"

"Born, bred, and turned in London. He came from a good family. I believe he worked his way up to the upper circles of society."

"When did he become Leader of the UK Nest?"

"Within a few decades?"

I'd actually read he was one of the youngest Vampires to have fought and won the right for leadership. He hadn't even been a Vampire for a hundred years, but having read his history and how he'd worked himself up to be someone, he didn't seem like the type of man that would lie back and take orders. I also knew what he did to Dorian … He was one sick bastard.

"So, needless to say, he has been brought up in a day and age where a person's class was a big deal, and if you were rich, you had a proper massive house with servants and nice things?"

"The Nest is not Buckingham Palace."

He rolled his eyes. "No, but rich folks are usually quite proud, so I imagine he still has a big house somewhere, and considering we are near the area in which the royals have lived for many years, which happens to be in proximity to our two locations, I'm willing t'bet the Nest will be some old, fancy building. Can I use your phone?"

I slid my mobile from my pocket and unlocked it, closing the space between us, and handed it to him. A few clicks, and he turned the phone to me. A Wiki page filled the screen.

"This is a list of Grade One and Two listed buildings in London.

All listed in alphabetical order of which county they are in."

"That will take forever."

"Not if we stick with the two-mile radius idea. Hunting ground, remember."

"Yeah, but their hunting ground could be bigger."

"Well, this is the best we have at the moment." He looked at the phone and began typing once more. "Bayswater is just outside of the perimeter, but Belgravia is within. Plus, it's not too far from here, and it's situated on the other side of the palace."

"Why have you suddenly got an obsession with Buckingham Palace?"

"I haven't. You're the one—" He shook his head. "Never mind. I say we start here. We have nothing else to go off, Elle. At least let's try and if we find a Vampire on the way, then we can ditch this plan and go back t'yours."

I was so aware of the time, of each second ticking by. We had come to London with no lead only to follow one that was three weeks old. We literally had nothing, no clue, no idea.

At least this was something. Checking old building. It kept us moving and made it feel like we might be on to something.

Who was I kidding? We were clueless and had no choice.

"Okay." I accepted my mobile back off him. "This is better than nothing."

"I'm not just a pretty face, y'know?"

With a roll of my eyes, I tapped on to the GPS to figure out the easiest and most public route that would take us to this fancy area. It would only take six minutes in the car which we had brought into the city with us and parked in a car park near by the nightclub, but I needed us to stay out in the open in the hopes that Nathan would lure a little bloodsucker in.

"Okay, roughly twenty-five minutes from here to there." I shoved the phone in my pocket. "If you sense or smell anything, just say so."

"Like what?"

"Fresh blood, for one, or that musky scent that Leeches always stink of."

"Musky scent?" He pinched and lifted the oversized black T-shirt to his nose, inhaling deeply. "Is that what I smell like?"

"You stink of cologne, which in the long run is probably burning all the Leeches' nose hairs, which is no doubt why they haven't confronted you yet."

"I'd rather stink of Dolce than of death. Especially since these aren't even my clothes."

"Well, congrats. You nailed it. Now come on." I set off at a swift pace down the high street, Nathan on my heels.

Luckily, it was a straight route. My focus flitted between the people I was passing and any turning or entry way. Poised. Listening for arguments or screams, which wasn't easy considering how nosey London roads were, but Nathan's hearing would hopefully be able to filter anything out.

Once we hit the perimeter of Hyde Park, I stopped to take out my phone and double check the GPS. "We just have t'walk round this corner and then cross the road in a few feet. You heard anything suspicious over the racket?"

"Other than drunks arguing about stupid things?" He shook his head.

I shoved my phone back into my pocket as we continued en route. "How are you so good at this?"

"At what?"

"Figuring all this out? The map, where t'look?"

"I guess because I'm not emotionally involved?"

I stopped and turned to him. "What is that supposed to mean?"

"Well, think about it, Elle. You've grown up with this. It's been your entire life. It's personal. For me … it's all new. I want answers, so I'm looking at the facts and making the links." He shrugged. "Plus your ancestors kinda pointed out a lot of stuff in their journals and findings."

"It's been a long time since I read them."

"Well, I get why you wouldn't want t'read them again." He playfully punched my shoulder. "Plus, you're forgetting I had t'put up with a crime and mystery fanatic for years. I guess I kinda just picked up on looking at the bigger picture."

"You seem to have picked up on a lot."

It was helpful, but I found myself wondering yet again if Nathan knew more than he was letting on. Did he know where the Nest was? Was he leading me into a trap?

"My head isn't as empty as it appears."

Trap or not, I still didn't have much of a choice but to go along with all of this. I needed to find Heather, and whether she was at the Nest or not, it was the only place I could go for answers. Especially because I didn't have a damn clue were Brendan's Pack would be. Were they looking for him? Could they be trusted? Come to think about it, could Brendan be trusted? What if Heather was missing because of him?

"Earth to Elle."

I blinked. Nathan was standing in front of me waving his hand in front of my face.

"You okay? You blanked out."

"Thinking," I replied, brushing past him and continuing down the road.

What if I had all of this wrong? What if Werewolves had kidnapped Heather? But then, why would they? And why would my aunt ask one to help if that was the case? She would have seen if they couldn't be trusted, wouldn't she?

My aunt wouldn't put Heather's life in danger, would she?

God, Auntie S, it would have been so helpful if you had been a little more detailed in your goodbye video.

Watching the road, I indicated to Nathan that we needed to cross. Sprinting between the vehicles, ignoring the abrupt honking of horns, we made it to the other side. My phone bleeped in my pocket to indicate we had reached our destination.

I retrieved it and showed Nathan the area on the map. "Mainly residential. So, it should be slightly quieter. So, keep your eyes open, and say if you smell of see anything that's … odd."

A long road lay ahead of us. After the shop and hotel that sat at the top of the street, the remainder was lined with what I could only presume were town houses as they towered well above the size of a terrace.

We set off at a steady pace, pausing once the line morphed into a semi-circle. A triangular private park lay in the centre, parking spaces situated before the black iron fence. The houses were the same on both sides of the curved, quiet road. The smooth white stone just kept going, each house only made visible by the sight of a front door and steps leading up to them.

My focus travelled the length, noting the windows. Five floors in total. All windows had small balconies either made of stone or black iron.

"Jesus, it's pristine." Nathan shook his head. "Even the pavement looks white."

"Let's split up. Both take a side, and whistle if you find anything. Okay?"

"You're the boss."

I stayed on the left side while Nathan headed down the right. I took my time as I passed each house, listening out for noises, scanning the doorsteps for signs of blood drops. They would be easy to see considering how clean the street was, but would Vampires be stupid enough to leave marks on such a clean surface?

A sharp whistle broke my concentration. I crossed the road, moving past the parked cars. Turning the sharp corner of the private park, I found Nathan frozen to the spot outside one of the houses.

I stopped in front of him and placed my hands on his shoulders with the pretence of making it look like we were in a deep discussion in case we had any curtain twitchers or passer-by.

"What is it?"

"Can't you smell that?"

I inhaled, getting a good load of his cologne. "Not over your Dolce, I can't."

"I can't explain it." His focus didn't leave the house. "There's blood, but not loads. I just—" He finally looked at me. "It smells wrong. Does that make sense?"

"It makes enough sense."

"Are there lights on?"

He glanced. "I can see a faint glow in the windows next to the door."

"Okay. So, the black iron fence that's behind me, there's a gate. We're going down and in."

"Isn't that breaking and entering?"

"Only if it isn't the UK Colony Nest." I cupped his chin and brough his focus to me, locking eyes. "Are you willing t'bet my life that there are Vampires in there?"

"Elle—"

"Yes or no, Than?"

His eyes flicked to the building, nostrils flaring. "Yeah, something is definitely in there."

"Good enough for me." Hands falling to his T-shirt, I pulled him until my back hit the iron.

His eyes widened. "What are you—?"

"Reach down and open the gate."

I heard the click and the slight whine of metal as he opened it. Letting go over his T-shirt, I turned and hastily made my way down the stone steps, my gaze snagging on a patch of black at the bottom. The space was wider than I had expected, and a metal door lay to my left, a security pad sitting at the heart of it.

But it was the door in front of us that held my attention, or should I say the giant hole where I presumed the handle would have been. I glanced over the railing into the corner past the security door—the splintered chunk of wood had been discarded, the brass doorknob crushed.

Unfortunately, I'd had to leave my sword in the Rover as there was no way I could get away with walking around central London with it on my back. And I was starting to get a sneaking suspicion that it would have been the weapon of choice for this evening.

I slid my dagger from my holster and glanced back at Nathan who had stopped behind me, his nostrils flaring.

"Keep quiet," I whispered.

He nodded, uncertainty flashing across his face.

"We got this?"

Shoulders back, he balled his fists and gave a curt nod.

I moved to the wall. Back pressed against the brick, I splayed my left hand on the black wood and slowly pushed it open.

Chapter Nine

~ Nathan ~

I was pretty sure that if my heart was still working, it would have punched a hole right through my rib cage. I had never been so freaked out in, well, my life even though it had technically ended.

There was something off with this building. Sure, it was a 'house' on the outside, but so far from homely. Not that I could actually imagine a Vampire's Nest being homely. I couldn't put my finger on it, and in all honesty, I didn't want to, but we were here to find Heather. Finding Heather meant that I would get a better understanding of my predicament, or at least I hoped I would.

So regardless of the icy chill sweeping over my already cold skin, I had to suck it up and go into this strange foreboding building.

I could smell blood, and boy did I hate how easy it was for me to pick up regardless of the fact that the air around me was tainted with a number of scents, from remnants of exhaust fumes to rubber on asphalt, a number of dishes that had been made and consumed in the homes surrounding us, the trees and damp grass of the nearby park. All of that, and yet, my new super nose had zoned in on blood—some human, but the rest … There was a familiar tinge to it that I had smelled before but couldn't remember where.

All I could do was watch as Elle pushed open the secret little door at the bottom of the outdoor stairs. Once upon a time, it was probably the servant's entrance, where deliveries and such would have been received. I would have thought that someone would have sealed it nowadays, but as my focus dropped to the gaping hole in the wood, I realized that it probably could have been.

"Shouldn't we be concerned that someone else had the same idea and broke in?" I whispered.

She didn't look at me, but the ripple of concern that crossed her face was answer enough. Someone had broken into a Vampire Nest. Why the hell would you, unless you were a Hunter like Elle and her family? Unless they thought this was a normal home? God, they were in for a shock. Perhaps that's why I could smell blood? Had a thief broken in and ended up being supper?

Poor thieving bastard. I would say it served them right, but that would be way too harsh. Although, karma was a bitch.

"Well, they should scout their properties better, like the burglars from Home Alone." A shimmer of a silhouette rippled behind real Elle.

Yeah, that didn't work out well for them either. I looked at the space where the teen was starting to form. *I can't have you here right now. This is serious. I need t'have my wits about me.*

"Don't tell me that. Tell yourself. Just relax."

Relax? I had to contain a snort. *I'm about t'walk into a building full of Vampires ... And this time willingly.*

"Elle won't let anything happen t'you."

Yeah, and that didn't make me feel any better. What if something happened to her?

Oh, shit, what if something does happen to her?

Would I be able to defend her? Escape with her?

"You're overthinking, Ninny."

Shut up.

Elle slipped inside. I followed her in, mimicking as she kept her back pressed against the wall to the right of the door. I slowly closed the useless stretch of wood, revealing a stone archway to our left. Through the opening, I could see that the room was lined with what I could presume were fridges and freezers.

A nudge to my ribcage brought my attention to Elle who nodded in that direction.

"I think that means she wants you t'check no one's in there."

Ignoring the growing form of Teen Elle who stood in the archway, I moved across and peered into the room. It wasn't huge, but the industrial appliances sure as hell made the room a heck of a lot smaller.

I turned back to Elle and gave her a thumbs up to say the room was clear. With a nod, she slipped into the next open archway only to return a second later with a nod.

The lights in the hallway were a warm yellow, which suited the fact that the walls were bare brick. It was kinda rustic and didn't really suit the exterior of the building, but who was I to judge?

I followed Elle down the hallway, past the stairs that led to the ground floor, watching as she moved through the next archway. I paused at the sight of tipped over tables and broken chairs. She slowly made her way round the space, her gaze tripping over the wreck of a room.

"Well, clearly someone is a sore loser," the teen said pointing at the scattered playing cards.

Elle stopped at the left, where the French glass doors lay open. I stopped beside her, glancing out onto the wide courtyard mainly made up of flag stones and potted plants. Across the way was a three-story building, a set of black iron stairs leading up to a door, similar to the set just to the side of the doors we currently stood at.

"Jesus, this place is huge," I whispered.

Her focus moved back to the room, gaze falling to the wooden floor, which I now noticed had the same black marks that rested at the bottom of the door we had come through.

"Is that what I think it is?"

She met my gaze. "That depends. What d'you think it is?"

"I saw similar markings at the facility after it had apparently been attacked." I glanced back down at the markings, which could have passed for burn marks apart from the ash texture. "They're Vampires, aren't they?"

"They were." She made her way back to the large archway, glancing to either side before she slipped into the last room that had been situated at the very end of the hallway.

"Well, at least we don't have to worry about hiding Vampire bodies once they're really dead."

Silver lining, I guess.

Elle appeared. "All clear. Storage that leads to a kitchen, and it looks like the bottom of that building could be a garage of some kind."

She shrugged and made her way back down the hallway.

I followed as she made her way upstairs. She kept her back against the wall and a tight grip on her blade. As she reached the landing, her eyes widened. Turning to me, she placed her index finger on her lips and then pulled her ear.

Quiet and listen out.

She headed through the door at the top of the stairs. I waited on the landing. The walls were white wooden panels with golden trimmings. As my gaze moved higher, I noticed that the top border were carvings of what looked like vines and flowers, all painted gold. The ceiling was high, and two intricate crystal and gold light fittings hung down, casting the same warm white light. The old beauty of this place was ruined by the odd indents in the walls and the fact that the wide gilded mirror across the way was cracked, as if a heavy weight had been thrown against it. A few shards had fallen to the floor and had been crushed into pieces.

I tried to count the markings of extinguished Vampires dotted about the rich wood floor, but I couldn't be sure—they seemed to collide into one another as I doubted a Vampire could be that large on only a liquid diet.

Elle exited the room, concern and confusion masking her face. She glanced at the open glass door to her left before descending into the hall. The front door lay ahead of us, two large arches in the walls at either side. Elle glanced to the left at what I could only presume was the sitting room. A grand marble fireplace took centre stage, another gilded mirror sitting high above the mantel piece reflecting the chandelier that hung down into the room … which was more of a mess then downstairs had been.

Even though the fancy furniture now lay in pieces, it was easy to see that the room hadn't been heavily furnished. The mess was comprised of two red chaise lounges and armchairs, end tables, vases, and the odd ornament. The same scorched markings splattered across the place.

"Okay, I'm starting t'think this isn't someone having a hissy fit over a hand of cards." Teen Elle stood among the mess with her hands on her hips.

I turned to the archway on my right and stepped through into another sitting room, the décor almost matching apart from a grandfather clock and one of those fancy drinking globes. I stepped over the mess, glancing to my right to see that the room extended a little further.

Elle stopped beside me.

"This is exactly the same as the room across the way." Her brow furrowed as she walked over to the next archway that led to another hallway. "This is the house next door."

"What?" I walked over to where she stood and looked at another front door. A glance to my right confirmed that there was another set of stairs and a door leading out back.

We both looked at the archway in front of us to see one more sitting room, but no other archway beyond the third hallway.

"Are you telling me that the Vampires own three of these houses?"

"And they've knocked the walls through in the centre house to open them up to each other."

"Jesus, they're filthy rich."

"They've had time to get filthy rich."

She took a deep breath and circled back to the centre living room.

"Okay. Safe to say something happened—" She glanced at the floor. "—There are a lot of vanquished Leeches here."

"That's good, isn't it?"

"That depends on who did the vanquishing."

"Heather and Brendan?"

A small pop of hope entered her eyes. "Maybe, but ... I don't know. This is a lot of Vampires."

"Your cousin's special."

"Yeah, but this is just ..." She threw her hands to the ground. "*A lot.*"

"Michael killed her father. Poisoned her mother and therefore her. Safe t'say this would kinda make sense."

She closed her eyes and pinched the bridge of her nose. "Okay. We need t'finish checking everywhere t'see if any Leech is left alive and can tell us what t'hell happened."

"And if Heather isn't here?"

Her shoulders sagged, arms dropping to her sides as she stared off into the room.

"Or whoever may have done this?"

"Then we hope that we can find something t'give us an idea of where t'hell we go next." She pointed at the hallway of the first house. "Would you mind checking the top levels while I start checking this house?"

"Sure. I will shout if I find anything or anyone."

"Ditto."

***

~ Danielle ~

I rolled my neck in a full circle and then side to side, forcing the built-up tension in my muscles to crack and pop.

This wasn't good, and I wasn't even sure what this was. Why were there a ton of disposed Vampires littered everywhere? Why was the UK Colony Nest smashed to pieces? Sure, I hadn't finished searching, but I was willing to bet my life that every other room would be broken or at least contain charred Leeches.

Who would do this? Nathan was right—Heather had a million

reasons to destroy the Colony, but this was crazy. There were different generations in this Colony, and although I knew my cousin was strong and had her Werewolf with her, I highly doubted they could have caused this much damage, especially to the number of Vampires who Nested here and while there were civilians living on either side of it all.

And destroying an entire Nest? I know killing Vamps is what we did, but surely, there would be some sort of consequence to slaughtering a Colony?

With Nathan searching the first house, I began my exploration of the second, moving further through the sitting room and trying hard not to trip over the remains of expensive furniture that littered the floor.

I moved into the study at the end of the corridor. It pretty much matched the one in the first house. Nothing of any interest jumped out, so I decided to head upstairs before descending back down into the basement.

The mahogany banister was cracked in the centre; two of the wooden poles lay discarded on the wide stairway. The walls were the same fancy white and gold patterns all the way through, every room giving off the same elegant and regal feel. Crystal light fittings and chandlers. Artwork and sculpture. Beautiful antique furniture and large mirrors. Long, thick curtains hung at all the large, long panelled windows, which I had noticed had UV-tinted glass.

The houses were classy. It was easy to see why they had been selected for the Colony Nest. Each house had six floors and ample rooms and plenty of ways in and out. It was elaborate and deceiving, and quite perfect from what I had read about Michael.

The first floor was smaller, the hallway recognisably shorter. The glass door at the top of the stairs led out onto a rooftop terrace, the hallway only having two other doors lining the walls. I moved to the first one, peering round the wood as it lay open. Surprisingly, the mahogany dining table still stood upright with the chairs all neatly pushed under. I walked around the room, past the fireplace and through the open archway into another sitting room. This one seemed a little fuller. A little more personal.

The red sofas had been tipped over, and the coffee table in the centre lay flat, the fancy legs collapsed beneath. The fire still blazed in the fireplace. Trinkets and photographs lined the mantel, but it was the huge portrait hanging above that caused me to stop and stare. A man stood by a large window, the countryside visible on the other side of the glass. I couldn't name his clothing, but the top was puffy and vibrant. It looked like he wore leggings and a dress, with a high white frilled collar that looked heavy and tight enough to choke you, which might explain his pale complexion. Narrow, black eyes starred down at me under thick black eyebrows. His hair was raven black and curled at the ends, stopping beneath his ears.

My gaze fell to the gold plaque at the base of the intricate frame. "Lord Michael John Kirk."

So, this was the Colony Leader back in his hay day? The stories and information I had heard and read started to make sense.

"So, you're the bastard that fucked so much up?" I asked the portrait.

The planes of his face were sharp and harsh, his lips thin and unforgiving. Maybe it was just the way the artist had painted him, but I could see the cold brutality burning in his dark eyes. Yeah, it was easy to see how this young Vampire had become Colony leader.

"Well, I hope she killed you. I hope you suffered," I said, before making my way back out to the hallway and ascending the next flight of stairs.

The remaining three floors were smaller in length. The master bedroom on the second floor was clearly Michael's. I was sure I would have guessed right regardless, but the fact that he had at least four more portraits of himself hanging up was a big clue. His walk-in wardrobe was impressive and filled with top design suits and the odd casual item. Not one sign of jeans or T-shirts in sight.

The smaller rooms on the last two floors were nice, the décor not matching the flow of the house, but then, most of the Vampires here would be younger than Michael and naturally wouldn't share his rich tastes. Apart from the rooms being a tad messy, nothing was broken. There was no sign of a struggle or any indication that any Leeches had been slaughtered up here.

As I descended the stairs, making my way down to the basement level, it dawned on me that any Vampires who had been on the uppers level would have made their way downstairs at the sound of intruders and fighting. Still, checking every floor and room was the smart thing to do.

Needless to say, I wasn't surprised to find that the lower doorway which was similar to the one Nathan and I had used had also been broken open, the difference being that someone had barged into this one, knocking it off its hinges. The black painted wood lay on the floor before another small end room filled with fridges and freezers. A sneak look confirmed that they were filled with blood.

"Elle?" Nathan's voice echoed throughout the house.

Every hair on my body stood on end. I sprinted up the stairway, the hilt of my dagger still resting firmly in my hand.

As I reached the landing of the centre house, a loud snarl met my ears, pulling my attention to the right. The air caught in my throat at the sight of the black Werewolf standing amongst the ruined furniture in the sitting room of the third house.

"I asked you a question," came an unfamiliar male voice. "Where did you get these clothes?"

I moved into the room to find Nathan pinned halfway up the wall situated next to the fireplace, held by his T-shirt which was balled up in the fist of an athletic, shirtless, blond man.

"Let him go." I sank as much lead into my voice as I could muster, my focus flickering between the two and the very large Werewolf whose piercing ice-blue gaze had turned on me.

"Found someone," Nathan said dryly. His eyes were trained on the Werewolf, his face a mixture of disbelief and wonder. The hold he had on the male's wrist was pointless as he didn't even seem fazed by the fact that his feet had left the floor.

The blond's attention turned to me. A strong jaw line

accompanied by high cheekbones and a roman nose. He could pass for a businessman, and at the look of his lean biceps and flexing six-pack, one that took care of himself. But it was his eyes that ruined his calm, collected appearance. And those dark, swirling grey irises were narrowed on me.

His nostrils flared. "You're human."

It was stated as a fact and not a question, but still, I nodded.

"You know this Leech?" His attention moved back to Than, his fist tightened in the black material.

"He's with me."

The Werewolf snorted. Not a reaction that seemed fitting with such creatures. It was almost too human.

"He's a friend."

The male's head snapped back to me, anger, confusion, and disgust fighting for dominance on his face.

"Friend?" He spat the word.

"Aye, has been since childhood." The reply seemed stupid considering the circumstances, but the need to point the fact out seemed important.

That caused the male's brow to furrow further. "He's a Vampire."

"Only has been for a few weeks. He's useless."

"Hey!" That snapped Nathan out of his daydream and earned me a scowl.

The Werewolf growled, a hint of white fang thrown in my direction.

"I swear it. He's as dangerous as a bee." I slid my blade back in my holster and held my hands up to show them I meant no harm. "Please, let him go."

"Not until he tells me where he got these clothes from."

Nathan looked down at me. "I tried to tell him I borrowed them —"

"Liar." The man snarled, shoving Nathan further up the wall. The biceps in his left arms bulged, but he didn't even break a sweat.

"It's the truth." I took a step forward, pausing when the Werewolf mimicked me.

The blond's nostrils flared again. "They smell like a member of our Pack."

Despite the tension that embraced my spine and shoulders, a slight flutter of relief passed through me. "Brendan?"

His attention back on me, the colour in his eyes began to soften, flecks of blue filtering through. "You know Brendan?"

"My cousin does." I lowered my arms. "Her name is Heather."

The Werewolf whined. The male glanced over his shoulder at the creature.

"My aunt Sofia knew Brendan. She was Heather's grandmother. She asked him to help Heather with something." I took another step forward. "I haven't heard from her in three weeks. That's why I'm—I mean why we're here. We're looking for her."

"That doesn't explain how—"

"Brendan has left a bag at Heather's house, a travel bag," I cut in quickly. "Nathan needed a change of clothes after escaping a facility where he was held captive. Brendan's clothes were the only male clothes in the house." I took another step toward the man. "The Vampires kidnapped him and his friend while they were in London. They experimented on them, changed them."

The Werewolf made a low grumbling noise in its throat.

"A facility?" The male's eyes met mine, tired, ash-blue eyes.

"Aye, if you let him go, we will explain."

The Werewolf stepped toward us. My hand automatically dropped to the hilt of my blade, but the Werewolf's large hand landed on the male's shoulder. Its large fingers flexed, claws dinting into his taut skin, but not enough to pierce it. It was then I noticed the blue flecks running through its fur. It was only inches taller than the male. Bowing its head, it pressed its nose to the side of the man's face, and I watched the tension ease from the male, watched as he lowered Nathan to his feet. He untangled his hand from the borrowed T-shirt and backed away from us. The Werewolf let go of his shoulder and remained behind him.

With a sigh, the male folded his arms over his chest. "Start explaining."

"First." I stepped in front of Nathan. "Where is Heather?"

He stared at me silently for what seemed like an eternity before confirming, "She's alive, and with our Pack."

Relief washed over me like a tidal wave. "Oh, thank God."

"Now, I believe you owe us an explanation as to why I shouldn't kill this Leech along with the rest of his Colony."

"This isn't my Colony," Nathan stated, straightening out the oversized T-shirt.

I stepped in front of Nathan. "He isn't a part of this Nest let alone this Colony. He and his friend were captured in London and were held captive for six weeks in a facility in Scotland. They sedated him—"

"Castrated me." Nathan stepped beside me.

"The Vampires experimented on him."

"And I didn't ask for any of it. Nor did Freddie." His voice hitched at mentioning his friend. "Only difference is he wasn't lucky enough to survive this shite." He indicated to himself.

The Werewolf did another whine. The male's jaw flexed. Something flickered in his eyes as he stared at Nathan.

"Why haven't you killed him?" His focus moved back to me. "Isn't that what your family does, kill Leeches?"

He made it sound so simple, and up to a few days ago, it had been. Part of me wanted to point out that I nearly had when I first realized what he was, but it had also been the first time I had ever been face to face with a Vampire who had once been someone I knew and cared about.

"Aye, but Nathan isn't a normal Leech."

"You really can't go a minute without insulting me, can you?" Nathan mumbled, folding his arms across his chest.

"Nathan was created. Not turned. Whatever they did isn't normal for them."

"You expect that to mean something to us?" The blond arched his left eyebrow.

"No, but Nathan found a folder that he brought with him. It mentions the Were-gene, which makes me wonder" I took a step forward. "Have any of your Pack gone missing in the last two months?"

The Werewolf headbutted the man's shoulder, and he sighed, suddenly looking defeated.

"When was all this?"

"He was held in a facility for six weeks."

"They were going to move me somewhere, but I managed to escape into the forest," Nathan continued. "That was about ten days ago."

"That coincides with the fire." An Irish lilt met my ears.

I glanced over my left shoulder as a middle-aged male walked into the room, paying us no attention he walked straight past us, stopping when he stood in front of our interrogator. "Everything clear?"

The blond lowered his eyes slightly. "No signs of any other Leeches."

"Good. The others have set off back t'Carter with the Colony Leader."

"You have Michael?"

The older male ignored my question. "Would you go and help Al and Chris with maintenance?"

"Sure." The blond's focus moved to Nathan one last time. "Shout if you need any assistance." He strolled out of the room, the Werewolf at his heels.

"You're Heather's cousin?"

The Irish man finally turned to us. He was broad-shouldered, dressed in a black T-shirt and jogging bottoms. Blood marked his skin, but I couldn't see the wounds it had wept from.

"Danielle, and this is my friend Nathan."

His gaze briefly flicked to Nathan before returning to me. "I'm Graham. Pack doctor."

I could see it. He had an empathetic face, but with an edge of 'didn't-take-no-shite' mixed in. It had to be the warm brown eyes paired with such a serious brow and broad nose. Stubble coated his jaw, making his cheekbones sharper. His hair was a wave of dark brown that gave him a casual air, as did the fact he was currently bare-footed and clearly not bothered about the fact he had walked through charred Vampire remains. The black ash coated his tanned skin.

I glanced around the room. "What are you all doing here? What's going on?"

He crossed his arms over his chest and took a deep, thoughtful breath. It reminded me of the doctors you saw on TV when they were about to explain something to the patient's family or give them bad news.

"Your cousin and Brendan were kidnapped while they were out looking for a Vampire in London. They were taken to the same facility that your—" His jaw flexed as if he had a bitter taste in his mouth. "—friend here was held at."

"Heather was—?"

He held his hand up. "They ran tests on her and on Brendan, who as you know, is a member of our Pack and as you stated earlier was asked t'help Heather by your relative. The Pack rescued them, but your cousin wanted t'go back as she had discovered a large room of … I've forgotten what you call them." His brow furrowed. "Before a victim fully turns?"

My eyes widened. "They had a room full of Infecteds?"

"I believe that was the term. I think she wanted t'put them out of their misery." He shrugged. "Anyway, it was a trap, and the Leeches set the facility on fire. They all managed to escape only t'come back and find that the Vampires had also set fire to the Pack keep and kidnapped three Pack members, one of which is our Alpha's daughter. The other is my nephew." His eyes darkened, shoulders tensing. "The Pack has been hunting for them since that night, and this Nest was the final place we needed to search."

Yeah, he was a doctor. Facts delivered calm and emotionless until he mentioned his only family member had been taken.

"Shit," Nathan exclaimed.

Heather had been kidnapped and experimented on. The Vampires had a room full of Infecteds. The Vampires had set fire to the facility. A facility that both Heather and Nathan had been kept at. Werewolves had been taken. Werewolves had hunted down all the Vampires in the United Kingdom, which at least explains why we hadn't run in to any in the last few hours.

The world felt as though it had been tilted on its axis as I ran the details around and around in my head. My focus moved around the destroyed room we currently stood in for the fifth time, noting the piles of ash.

"You've slaughtered them all?" The words were quiet as they left my lips in stunned belief, but the doctor seemed to hear me just fine.

"Not all." His dark focus moved to Nathan once more.

"Nathan isn't like them."

"He's a Vampire."

"Yeah, but not by choice," Nathan replied, a hint of frustration tainting his words.

"He came t'me for help." I scrubbed my hands across my face. "He wants t'find out what they did t'him."

"It's one of the reasons we are looking for Heather," Nathan continued. "She will have a better understand of why they were experimenting on me. What they were trying t'achieve."

"They're trying t'recreate themselves," he answered flatly. "Or rather, create more superior versions."

Some will want to use you. Sofia's voice flittered through my mind.

"That's why they took Heather." I turned to Nathan, my fingers pressed against my throbbing temples. "They want t'figure out how she's survived so long as an Infected."

He turned toward me and lowered his voice. "They're the crazy ones, right?"

"Aye." Dropping my arms to my side, I stepped closer to Graham. "Can you take me t'her?"

The warmth had filtered back into his eyes, which evaluated me. Finally, he replied. "I can take *you*."

"Nathan comes with me."

A dry laugh left him. "Not possible. If my Alpha sees him, he will kill him."

"He had nothing t'do with any of this. He didn't ask for this. He and his friend were taken and turned against their will."

"Isn't that what Vampires do?"

"No. They feed or kill. If they create an Infected, they give them the option. Nathan wasn't given that option."

"I wouldn't have chosen this."

Nathan's voice cracked with unshed tears, and I felt a piece of my heart breaking.

"Maybe he can help Heather and you all figure out what the Vampires are up to. You said they experimented on Brendan, and Nathan's file says Were-gene, and you just admitted that three of your Pack have been taken, which means they have already been targeting Werewolves."

No such thing as coincidences. Sofia always said that.

This all couldn't be a coincidence. It just couldn't.

A muscle ticked in the side of Graham's neck.

"Look, Than is just as mixed up in all of this as you and I are. He means no harm t'you or your Pack. If he tries anything, I will kill him myself." I held my hand out. "I promise."

"She will. Trust me." Nathan sighed. "She's nearly done so twice already."

"You're not helping," I mumbled under my breath as I glanced over my right shoulder.

Graham's large hand wrapped around mine. His skin was boiling, his grip bone crushing. "I *will* hold you t'that."

I gave him a curt nod. With one swift shake, he freed my hand from his grasp.

"We have things t'do here. If you stay and help us get it done, then I will take you both t'Carter, but I warn you he won't be welcoming to a Vampire regardless of how he came t'be or how long you have been friends for. His truce with them is over. All Leeches are fair game."

I glanced at Nathan and then back at Graham. "We understand."

***

So, when Graham said that they had things to do, it was basically cleaning up all the Leeches' charred remains and moving the broken furniture down to the basement. I found this strange and asked why they bothered if they hated the creatures so much. It earned me a laugh.

"We're only tidying up what we need to in order to hide the existence of their kind and therefore ours."

Okay, I suppose that made sense.

He had said that all Vampires were fair game and that the 'understanding' that the Leeches and Werewolves had was over —that understanding being that they kept to their territories and out of each other's way as best as possible.

Did that mean they had killed every Vampire in the UK? He said they had been hunting for a week straight and any Vampire that stood in their path would have met their end. It was justice for what had been done to their Keep and for who they had taken.

I could understand their reasoning, but surely, that was going to cause a shitload of trouble in the long run. Had they even considered what would happen if there were no more Leeches in the UK?

It was the early hours of the morning by the time we had all finished the 'maintenance.' The four other Werewolves who had been present left in pairs, taking different exits out of one of the three houses.

Graham agreed to meet us at Heather's house in a couple of

hours so we could set off to meet the Alpha who lived in Scotland. Should we have been surprised by the location? No. Nothing was ever a coincidence, especially if it needed to be convenient. After a short explanation from Graham about trouble that they had had with the Vampires themselves back in the summer, it now made sense why the Leeches had a facility in Scotland—it was Werewolf territory. Easier access to the Were-gene? Easier to stay under the radar and away from Sofia and Heather's attention? Also, another reason why the Pack would be so pissed at the Vampires, they had breached the heart of Werewolf territory.

He confirmed that everything Nathan and I had been wondering matched up with the conclusions that both he and his Pack had come to after hearing what Heather and Brendan had been put through.

The blood suckers were hoping to recreate the fluke luck that had made Heather the only born Infected. And somehow, they thought they could achieve something by adding the Were-gene to the cocktail.

If I was honest, my head was pounding as Nathan and I made our way back to Heather's. I was relieved my cousin was alive and safe, relieved I now knew where The Pack were located, but in my three weeks of wondering where she was and the forty-eight hours of scouring through everything to find a lead on where she could be … well, I never would have guessed any of this. It was crazy, and considering my family and our lives, that was saying an awful lot.

The only thing I was still confused about was the question of whether Sofia had seen all of this? And if she had, how could she put her own granddaughter through it all?

God, my parents were going to freak when I updated them.

Chapter Ten

Sunday 18th October, 2015

With Nathan tucked away and settled in the backseat under storage and set with a couple of bottles of mixture, we left London around eleven. I had the feeling that Graham had wanted to leave earlier, but my understanding was that it had been a long week, and the rest he had managed to catch up on was much needed.

He had chosen to sit in the back. I never liked feeling like a taxi driver, but something told me it was more to do with the resting Vampire travelling with us. By sitting in the back, his weight kept the lid to Nathan's makeshift coffin shut, so he couldn't get out even if he asked politely.

Or maybe it was because I had a dagger? Maybe it was because we were strangers and he could keep an eye on me from his position? Whatever the reason, I didn't care. I was in my car, and we were on our way to Heather. That was all that mattered right now.

I was just pleased that there was no traffic. The drive was long enough without some idiot doing something stupid and causing a pile-up on the M6. The last thing I wanted was to be stuck on the motorway with a strange Werewolf who had hardly said a word since we'd set off. Usually, silence didn't bother me, but my travel buddy sure knew how to make a quiet drive feel super awkward.

After a couple of hours, I finally decided to break the ice. "So, you're a doctor?"

"I am."

A glance through my overhead mirror confirmed he hadn't moved a muscle since we had set off. He sat slap bang in the middle of the back seat, his head leaning on the headrest, eyes closed, arms folded over his navy sweater-covered chest.

"That must be pretty helpful, but I thought you guys heal quickly?"

"It depends on the wound and what was used to inflict it."

That made sense. "You seemed t'be unscathed from yesterday's slaughter."

"You seem very unsettled by all of it considering you slaughter Vampires on a daily basis?"

Was I unsettled? Shocked, perhaps. I certainly didn't expect to walk into the UK Colony Nest and find no Vampires but stumble upon a handful of Werewolves instead. And I admit I was a little unsettled at being told that the Werewolves had been on a week-long rampage, hunting down Vampires and killing them. The fact that they'd hit the Nest ... Jesus, they were a new level of pissed off and had clearly been out for blood.

I guess what unsettled me the most was the realization of what it meant if there were no Vampires left in the UK. Home had been different. Ireland had never had a high level of activity except for the years that Alexis, Sofia, and Heather had lived there. When they'd left, so had the bulk of the Vampires, and yet, that had never seemed worrying. Perhaps it was because I knew that the Colony was situated in London, that Leech activity would naturally be higher in England.

No Vampires in Ireland didn't mean much, but none in the UK, that was a completely different matter.

"I guess I'm just intrigued at your lack of concern of the consequences."

"What consequences?"

It had been the question that had kept me awake for a few hours. What would the consequences be now there were no Vampires in the United Kingdom?

"Well, you're almost certain that you have rid the UK of Vampires."

"I'm sure there are a few strays."

"Maybe, but you do know that if you kill a Vampire who has

Bloodlings, their Bloodlings die, too?"

"Cure an infection, and it will wipe everything clean."

But how long would it stay clean before a new infection appeared? There were more Vampires in this world than anyone would like to imagine.

"If you have wiped out a Colony, there will be retaliation."

"Do y'think we care?"

Well, it definitely doesn't seem like they do. "You should. Any remaining Vampires will be pissed. You have basically done what they have done t'your Pack."

"Nothing can compare to what they have done." His voice dropped to a rich timbre, a growl vibrating in his chest. "Let them retaliate."

"What I mean is they came on t'your Alpha's land, they kidnapped three of your Pack, and they burnt down the Keep. So you slaughter them all as payback." I risked a glance in the mirror. "They will want payback for the slaughter of a ton of their kind. And if there is anyone left, and they call for help from other Colonies across the world?"

Eyes open, his attention was fixed on the right window, though I doubted he was paying attention to the scenery. Or the light rain that had started to fall. His jaw had tensed, and uncertainty had claimed his features.

"Acting on the spot isn't always the sensible thing t'do, even though your reasons were understandable."

He remained quiet. Perhaps it wasn't sensible of me to prod the sleeping bear, or wolf, rather.

"You said Michael had been taken?" But then, being sensible wasn't all it was cracked up to be.

"T'Carter. Aye."

"He will kill him?"

"Is that a serious question?"

Yes. Just possibly a very stupid one. "Which will also mean there is no Leader."

"There are no Vampires left t'lead." A hint of uncertainty rang in his tone.

He wasn't a hundred percent sure if they had gotten them all, and how could he be?

I met his gaze in the mirror. "But there is now a defenceless territory for others t'claim."

"This territory is not defenceless."

At the flash in his eyes and the growl that edged his voice, I decided it was time to stop pointing out how unbelievably stupid it had been for his Pack to wipe out the Colony. Realistically, I should be happy. He was right—this is what I was trained to do, slay Vampires. The Pack had possibly done me and my family a favour. I mean, all we did was kill the odd one when needed, but that was because we knew that the only safe way to wipe out a species was to kill the source. And that was Marko. Were there other ancients out in the world? Maybe, but Marko was the only one we knew of for sure, and naturally, the only one my family had an issue with.

Destroying Marko Pavel was how we planned to rid the world of Leeches, and if there were stragglers, it would be easy to discard of them. What the Pack had done was just create an opening for trouble, and although I wasn't sure what form it would come in, I knew deep in my gut that destroying the UK Colony had been the mother of all bad moves.

***

Being autumn, the sun had set shortly after six, which was around the time we had finally decided to stop at a junction and stretch our legs. We still had a couple hours to go, and at the sound of the doc's rumbling stomach, it was clear he wouldn't make it without some food, plus, I had to use the little girl's room.

Leaving the car unlocked, I told Nathan that we would be back shortly and that the sun had set if he wished to sit shotgun.

Something Graham hadn't been too pleased about, but seven hours was far too long to be cooped up in such a small space.

Half an hour later, we were back in the car. The doc remained in the centre of the back seat, McDonalds bags piled up on his left.

At the scent of cheeseburgers and fries, my stomach rumbled, and the ham salad baguette I had purchased no longer seemed appealing. To my surprise, a brown bag appeared at the side of my face as Graham offered it me.

"You sure?"

"Aye."

I wasn't the type to argue when someone handed me free grub. So I accepted the bag and dived in. Food had never tasted so good.

The passenger door opened, and Nathan climbed in.

"You okay?" I asked after swallowing a mouthful of my burger.

"Fine. Just need t'stretch my legs."

A snort sounded in the back.

"Something funny?" Nathan glanced through the overhead mirror.

"Leeches don't get cramp."

"Fine. I needed air."

"Leeches don't breathe."

A soft growl vibrated in Nathan's chest as he turned his attention out the passenger window. "I wanted t'be outside before being stuck in here with you for another few hours."

His comment was that of a child who didn't want to be around his annoying siblings. I had to muffle a giggle.

"That makes more sense," Graham remarked before taking a huge bite of his Big Mac.

Well, the remainder of this trip was going to be interesting, to say the least.

"Do you need anything?" I asked as I scrunched up the burger wrapping and dropped it into the bag.

"No, I'm fine."

He seemed tense. Maybe uncomfortable, but then, I couldn't imagine he was looking forward to our destination. Truth be told, I hadn't thought much about the fact there would be more Werewolves waiting at the end of this trip. Just that I would see Heather. See she was safe. Despite the fact I probably should really think this through, I didn't have the energy. I just needed to know what the hell was going on.

Placing the fries in the cupholder, I scrunched the brown bag up and shoved it into the side of my door.

Fed, watered, and no longer needing the toilet, I turned on the ignition, and we set back out on the road after I had checked the route that my GPS was dictating. Graham confirmed and assured me he would point me in the right direction once we hit the long winding roads of the Scottish Highlands.

And Jesus, it was eerie. I knew Scotland was rural, and Graham had explained the Pack Keep was at the top of the Highlands, but the higher we got, the roads seemed to get thinner and had more bends. Not to mention there were no streetlights. I was literally driving in the pitch black with a Werewolf and a Vampire as passengers. It felt like the start of a dark comedy film.

Three hours after our pit stop, I manoeuvred the car into a crawl as Graham pointed out we were there. My floodlights highlighted the dirt road before me. Large, open fields lined the roads, unfenced and flat. The light weaved over the rough trunks of the line of trees to our left, but there was no sign of a residence or of life anywhere around us.

"Usually, there would have been lights filling the windows of the house and a spotlight at either side of the gate." Graham's voice held a hint of sadness in his tone. "There. Can you see the wall?"

A yard or so ahead, a high wall seemed to spring from behind a line of trees. "Aye."

"The gate will be open."

I watched carefully for the opening, turning left as soon as I caught sight of black iron. My lights streamed through the opening, the pale glow washing over the large, gravel courtyard.

"Shit." The gasp left my mouth as I came to an abrupt halt.

Blackened bricks and broken tall windows filled my windshield. Nathan and I unbuckled our belts and lent forwards so we could glance up at the destroyed building. The fire had consumed everything, and I could only guess that the main reason would have been that considering how far the residence was from the nearest town, it no doubt took the fire service forever to get here.

I had seen fires on the news and in films, but never up close. Even though there were no blazing flames in front of me, I swear I could almost see them, hear the hissing and crackling as they greedily went to town on this manor house, which I was sure would have been beautiful.

I knew Vampires were monsters. I had seen enough, but this seemed insane and so unnecessary. An act of simple destruction. And why? What purpose could setting fire to the Pack's Keep have? Surely, they would have known that it would only piss the Werewolves off. Cause retaliation? Was that what they had wanted? Or had they hoped to kill all the members? I just couldn't understand the reason behind this.

"This is what your kind have done t'our Alpha's home." Graham unclipped his belt. "This house has stood for generations—"

"This had nothing t'do with me," Nathan replied, straightening in his seat. "I didn't light the match."

"Regardless, you won't be welcome here." The handle of the door clicked, and the doctor slid out of my car, empty McDonalds bags in hand, then closed the door behind him.

"I'm not sure you should come in." I glanced at Nathan.

His jaw was tense. His lips pressed in a line, but his focus remained dead ahead. "I'm not scared of them."

"I never said you were." A sigh escaped me, and I flopped back in my seat. "I don't know how many Werewolves will be in there or how pissed they all are."

His brow was furrowed as he looked at me. "I didn't do this."

"I know that."

"I had no involvement in this." He jutted his left hand toward the building. "No say. No vote."

"Hey." I placed my hand on his right and gently squeezed. "*I know*, but this isn't like some turf war. These people will not hesitate t'kill you." My eyes widened as I stared at him. "Like, *really* kill you."

"Then I need t'give them a reason not to." He slid his hand from beneath mine, opened the door, and slid out.

"Like what?" I stared after him.

Christ, this wasn't going to go well.

I jumped out of the car and followed quickly. Gravel crunched beneath my boots, and I tightened my jacket around me. It was freezing and windy, and each small gust that rushed past me brought the faint scent of smoke. This fire had happened a week ago, and yet, the scent of the destruction lingered to the bones of the site.

A shiver ran up my spine as I looked up and saw that part of the house had caved in. The structure was broken, and we were about to step inside. *A double death trap, great.*

We followed Graham who had walked down the left side of the building. My feet met firm concrete as we strolled along a patio. A hint of flowers teased my nose, and I could just about make out a low hedge and flowers to my left. Moving round the back of the building, I saw that Graham had kindly waited for us. Regardless, my gaze darted around the area. The only noise was the shudder of leaves as the wind wandered through the treetops. Even in the darkness, I could see that the back garden was huge and ended where the forest began. Fields lined either side, both separated with what looked like fences. Did the Pack own all this land?

"Things are a mess in here, so be careful you don't trip," Graham explained as we stopped before him.

"Didn't know you cared," Nathan replied.

"I was talking t'her," came his reply as he held his phone out before him, allowing the white light to fill the blackened room.

"Is it safe with the building being in such a mess?" I glanced into what appeared to be the kitchen.

"The fire marshal gave the okay the other day. We're allowed t'enter and start collecting anything that hasn't been destroyed."

He stepped through the doorway and took a few steps, turning and pointing the light on the open doorway to his left.

I grabbed Nathan's wrist. "Stay behind me."

"Elle—"

"Seriously, I don't think they will hurt me, but I don't know what their reaction will be when they see you." I slipped my phone from my pocket and switched the torch on. "Graham and the others could have killed you on the spot. Luckily, the fact they could smell Brendan on your T-shirt caused them to pause. I don't know what's going to happen—"

"I get it." He cupped my chin. I was surprised to see him smirking. "You care about me. It's sweet."

"Can you go back t'being pissed off, please?" I batted his hand away. "It's so much easier t'deal with."

"It will be okay." The smirk remained.

"Christ." My chest clenched. God, I hoped it would be. I wasn't going to admit it, but yeah, I cared if he got slaughtered in front of me.

"I've got your back."

I stepped across the threshold, rotated my wrist allowing the light to sweep across the space. My gaze following, making note of the blackened walls and broken furniture. A charred door lay on top of the large breakfast counter. The door I could only presume should be attached to the splintered frame that Graham had just ducked under. The crack of glass met my ears, and I looked down to find shards beneath my boot.

"The stairs are steep."

I glanced up to see Graham disappear through an opening to our left. A quick perusal of the space showed broken jars, discarded cans, singed packets, and the odd mounds of ash. It was a pantry, and a decent-sized one. I glanced at the large panel of dark, solid wood that stood unscathed before us. No handle.

Letting go of Nathan's hand, I reached out and curled my fingers around the edge, pulling. It was heavy, but with another tug, it moved enough to reveal shelving on the other side.

"Werewolves must like secret doors leading t'super kitted-out basements, too," Nathan remarked.

Pushing the door back so it stayed wide open, I stepped over the threshold of the secret doorway. The torch of my phone seemed brighter in the narrow stairwell. Long stone stairs stretched out before us.

"Watch your step," I told Nathan before descending. With each step, the air seemed to change. Something rancid and regrettably familiar met my nose.

"Ugh, what t'hell?" Nathan retched behind me.

"Vampire blood," I replied as my feet hit the basement floor.

"So that's what it is." Recognition coated his tone. "Makes sense now. I could smell hints of it at the facility and at the Nest."

"You get used to it."

"I don't think you should. It's freakin' vile."

That was an understatement. "You want t'try being smothered in it."

"I will take a rain check."

Graham stood by a large iron door which was ajar. The dead bolt, though unlocked, was huge. Faint light teased the opening.

"I thought the electrics had been damaged?"

"We have a different generator down here for when we have … guests." The doctor glanced between me and Nathan. "Are you sure you want t'bring him in here?"

"I'm capable of making my own choices," Nathan replied. "I'm undead. Not a child."

"I beg to differ." Graham pressed his large hand on the iron and pushed the door wide open.

I don't know what I expected to see. I was personally used to stepping into a basement filled with gym equipment. Instead, I was greeted with a very long and wide stone room. Furniture and items you would expect to see in a basement were situated at the far end of the room, but it was the large iron cage that stood in the centre that caught my attention first. The bars were thick and menacing.

"I expected Heather t'have something like that in her basement," Nathan whispered in my ear.

Graham stepped into the large room. "Carter, I apologize for disturbing you, but I have someone here who wishes to see Heather."

"Oh, fuck."

Nathan's gasp and the grip in which he grabbed my upper arm broke my moment of wonder. Off in the right corner where the glow from the low hanging ceiling lights didn't quite touch the walls hung a naked, one-legged man.

Patches of skin had been cut from his torso and arms. Silver glinted from the thick blades imbedded in his rib cages. His head hung low. Black blood stained what remained of his pale flesh.

"Michael." His name left my mouth on a stunned whisper.

Was he still … with it?

"These guys really don't like Vampires." He'd stolen the words from my mouth.

"Nathan, maybe you—"

My words were cut off at the sound of a crash. Splinters of wood were scattered across the ground due to the wooden chair which was hurled against the wall.

Four sets of eyes suddenly pinned us to the spot. The air in the large room seemed to be evaporating with every beat of my heart. The four men stepped from the shadows and stood before the cage—two older, two younger, and only one still had his top on.

What is it with Werewolves and being topless?

"You brought a Leech here?" the stocky male snarled, his silver eyes locked on us.

Graham's head dropped to his chest. "He is with the girl."

The male's broad chest heaved, causing the two fierce scars that lay at the centre to expand. Even though they were partially hidden through a thatch of dark hair, the tissue was a pinkish colour, indicating that they were fresh. Unusual that the male wore any marks considering Werewolves were supposed to heal quickly, but clearly, something had stopped the process. Splatters of dry, black blood stained his tanned skin. Some had been caught by the nest of hairs on his chest and the thick beard he wore. The thick splodges of dead cells had caused his wiry hair to get matted. Exhaustion clung to those swirling eyes, his expression a pained scowl. Brown wavy hair which stopped just above his shoulders was dishevelled and sticking to his forehead and neck.

"He's a Leech," came another snarl, nostrils flaring. His fingers flexed. His entire body seemed to be vibrating as if he was fighting to stay stood on the spot.

"I guess that's Carter."

If it was possible for Nathan to become paler, well, he had just turned blue.

The stocky male stalked toward us, the skin rippling on his bones, teeth bared and nails turning into talons before us.

"Jesus." Nathan's grip tightened as he pulled me back and behind him.

It took me a second to realize what he was doing. My hand dropped to the hilt of my dagger which I slid out, and with a swift turn, manoeuvred myself back in front of Nathan.

Before I could open my mouth in warning, Graham had stepped in front of his Alpha and placed his hand on the male's heaving chest. His head remained bowed.

"This is *Heather's* cousin, Danielle and her … friend, Nathan."

At the mention of Heather, Carter's expression relaxed slightly. Something flashed in his eyes. His entire body was still poised, and his focus remained on Nathan.

"It's rather unusual for Slayers and Leeches to be friends," one of the younger males commented, folding his arms. His chest was smooth and chiselled, and though I wanted to gag as soon as the thought flitted through my mind, he reminded me of one of those perfect roman statues. He clearly took care of himself as every line of his physic was perfect, which made the angry scar beneath his left ribcage stand out.

"He was my friend before he was a Leech," I replied, before taking a deep, steadying breath.

"And it wasn't my choice," Nathan finished.

I fought the urge to close my eyes and hang my head, not wanting to take my focus from the pent-up men before me.

"The being turned into a Vampire," Nathan explained. "Being her friend was my choice."

Dear God, please let us survive this regardless of the idiocy that comes out of Nathan's mouth.

The younger male's eyebrow quipped. His face was even chiselled to perfection, a strong jawline and cheekbones. Smooth skin and perfectly styled hair. He could have been a model if it weren't for the matching scar that hugged the left side of his throat.

Clearly, something had gone down as the younger male's scars matched his Alpha's. Had there been a fight between the two? Or could it be linked to the attack on their house? Were these injuries sustained from fighting off Leeches? If so, why hadn't they healed?

Shaking myself from my evaluation of the males, I kindly asked, "So, I ask that you leave him be."

"Do you always let your girlfriend stick up for you, blood sucker?" the male continued, a smirk curling his mouth.

"I can never get a word in edge ways," Nathan replied. "And not that it's important, but she isn't my girlfriend. She is a friend who happens to be a girl and a Vampire Slayer. So, she's naturally wired to jump to anyone's defence."

I twisted and gave Nathan a 'what-the-fuck?' look. Eyes wide, he just shrugged. Chatting even more shite had always been a sign of his nerves.

"We're getting off subject here." I turned back to the males, relieved to see that all but the Alpha seemed to have relaxed slightly.

"Carter, they're just here for Heather." Graham removed his hand from his Alpha's chest and stepped aside.

"She's not here," Carter stated through clenched teeth.

It felt as though a boulder had dropped to the pit of my stomach. And just like that, we were back to Square One. "Do you know where she has gone?"

"Why should we tell you?" The younger male walked towards his Alpha, stopping a foot behind him. "You could be anyone. Simply claiming to be Heather's cousin and yet having a Vampire for a friend. Seems fishy to me. Considering how much you all hate Vampires."

The model was going to tell me how much my family hated Vampires. Cutting off a bemused laugh, I slid my dagger back into its holster and took a few steps into the room.

"My name is Danielle Renaud, and I am the niece of Sofia Renaud who recruited a guy called Brendan, who is a member of your Pack, t'help my cousin, Heather Ryan. Brendan helping her was the last bit of information we received from Heather. It's been over three weeks. I'm here—I mean, we're here looking for her."

"She is who she says she is." Graham reached into his pocket and retrieved a small card and held it out to Carter.

The Alpha didn't glance down. Instead, the younger man plucked the card from Graham's fingers and looked at the piece of plastic.

"Could be fake."

"It's not," Graham replied. "Plus, Heather's scent is on her, and Brendan's on him as they have been staying in her home."

"Using their stuff." The younger male moved past his Alpha.

"Heather's clothes are a little too tight for me," Nathan explained.

I mimicked the Werewolf's steps, wanting to keep as much distance between them all and Nathan. I stopped a breath away from him, only having to lift my head slightly to meet his gaze.

"Nice photo." He gave me a toothy grin. Flecks of silver danced in his brown eyes as he handed my driver's license back to me.

"Thanks." I slid the card into my jacket pocket, before angling a look at the doctor. "I would have given it t'you if you would have asked."

"My apologies." He didn't look very sorry.

"Now, would you kindly tell me where my cousin is?"

"Italy," the Alpha replied.

Shit. Italy? What? Why the hell would she go to Italy?

My brow furrowed. I took a few steps back, so I was able to look at the burly male. "Did she happen t'mention why?"

"Surely, you could call and ask her yourself?" The young male studied me.

"Heather doesn't own a mobile."

He snorted. "Who doesn't own a mobile nowadays?"

"It's the truth." The fully clothed male finally spoke. "She didn't have one, but considering the circumstances, we acquired one for her so she can keep in touch."

"Circumstances?" I quipped my eyebrow. "Is something wrong?"

"Other than the fact that you have a Leech for a friend?"

"Owen," the clothed male warned. "She received a letter from Sofia with a plane ticket inside."

I sighed. "So naturally, she is doing as she is told."

Great. I finally found her, and now, she was in another country following instructions to do what, exactly? God knows what my aunt had said to get her to go over there.

"She's gone to look for Marie." The clothed male seemed to have read my mind. "She believes our taken Pack members may be on their way there."

"What?"

"Elle?"

Owen growled low in his throat, unfolding his arms.

I scowled at him before turning to Nathan who had stepped

further into the room.

"Marie is Luca's mother, right?"

"Aye, and one of Marko's Bloodlings."

His brow furrowed. "So, she's still hunting for Marko."

She was doing what she was told to do. What we had been trained to do.

"If your Pack have been taken there, then why haven't you gone after them?"

"None of your business."

"Owen," the clothed male warned again, stepping toward the model. "Pack politics."

"It's a hunch." Carter suddenly sounded somewhat defeated. "Heather isn't sure, but she believes the fact that Sofia sent a ticket… so on so forth."

"We don't know for sure."

"Hence your new punch bag?" I nodded toward Michael.

"And why Brendan has been allowed to go across and stay with her. Why we provided her with a phone."

The clothed male seemed so out of place in this room. Despite being dressed in jeans and a forest green sweater, he looked a little like the male who had caught Nathan the other night. That air of a businessman about him. Yet, he seemed reserved, not to mention a hell of a lot calmer than everyone else in this room. His hair was more of a chestnut brown, and like his Alpha's, fell to just under his ear. Light stubble covered his strong jawline, and his eyes, though tired, were a warm mix of hazel with dashes of gold.

"You're using her to—"

"We're not using her," Carter snapped. "She was going regardless, and she offered to keep her eyes and ears open."

So not only was my cousin hunting for Marko, but she was trying to rescue kidnapped Werewolves. What the hell was going on?

"Dante, you need t'see something." Graham reached behind his back and pulled a manila folder out of the back of his trousers.

"Hey, that's mine." Nathan stopped by my side, unable to go any further when Owen stepped in his path. "I thought I'd lost it."

This time, a dry laugh did escape me. "You certainly have some hidden talents, Doctor."

He ignored my comment and handed Nathan's folder to Dante, the clothed, guy, who opened it immediately and began reading.

"Is it a souvenir folder from all your victims?" Liquid silver pooled into Owen's eyes now that he and Nathan stood toe to toe.

The comment caused Nathan's spine to go rigid. His face now back to the shade of white I was accustomed to, he locked eyes with the Werewolf, any sign of his earlier nerves gone.

"It's my autopsy." The words were punctuated slowly through clenched teeth. "And every little detail on what the Leeches did t'turn me into one of them."

"He wasn't turned," I stated, not even sure if they would understand what I meant, but hopefully, and considering everything they had been through recently and having Heather around, they'd get it.

"No, he was very carefully created," Dante commented and looked up at me. "This isn't normal even for them."

He said it as a fact, but the slight crease at the top of his nose was indication enough he wasn't sure.

"No. That's another reason why we needed Heather. She would be the only one who could explain this, and what it might mean." Taking Nathan's hand, I tugged him away from Owen. "Graham explained what happened, the Leeches taking Brendan and Heather, the Infecteds—"

"The fire."

"I'm so sorry."

"It's not your fault." Owen sneered as he started to circle me and Nathan.

"I had nothing to do with that." Nathan directed the comment at Dante.

"You expect us to believe you, Leech?"

"Do you judge every individual for the mistakes of their species?" He let go of my hand and turned to face Owen once more. "For example, I could easily stand here and judge Werewolves. Make them all out t'be an arse like you, but then this gent over here—" he indicated to Dante who continued to read the file in his hand. "—is calm and reasonable, and although I can see he doesn't trust me, he is at least being courteous enough to keep his thoughts and impulses to himself."

Owen's neck twitched, his jaw tense as their eyes remained locked.

"I don't want t'be this way."

"Kill yourself, then."

"And let them win? They took my life and therefore my family and my dreams. There is no way in Hell they are having my death as well."

"How eloquent of you."

"Fuck off."

An unexpected laugh bubbled up and spilled from Owen's lips.

"Okay, that's it." I stepped between them. "Can we please just try and discuss this?"

"I agree." Dante walked over to Owen and placed his hand on his shoulder. "There will be no more killing today." He dropped his voice ever so slightly. "Go and take Scott for a run. He needs some air."

My focus shifted to the other younger male who hadn't said a word or even reacted since we'd stepped into the room. Instead, he sat in front of the cage, back pressed to the bars, eyes closed, but his face was contorted as if he were in some kind of pain. Unlike Owen and Carter, his skin bared no scars, and like the others, he was yet another physically fit male. A fine layer of hair covered his chest, and his muscle mass was somewhere in between Carter and Owen's. He was clearly taller, his features more rugged, his black hair sweat-slicked and swept back.

"Danielle, I'm afraid it has been a very long and stressful week for us all, and well, we don't entertain Vampires under normal circumstances, let alone recently." Dante's attention moved to Nathan as he said that last part, and it was pretty clear that was as much of a welcome Nathan would be receiving. "We won't hurt you as yours is a strange circumstance."

"And we're currently too exhausted to do a decent job," Carter mumbled as he followed Graham to the far corner where Michael still hung.

Nathan gave a curt nod. "Thank you."

Dante looked back at me.

"I'm sorry you have come all this way to find your cousin isn't here, but I assure you she is fine and that she is in good hands with Brendan." He indicated to some chairs near the cage. "I can tell you what we have discovered, but I don't know if it will explain the contents of this folder."

"I just want t'know why they did this t'me."

I gave him a thankful smile. "Anything you can tell us would be great."

Chapter Eleven

Owen and Scott had left about twenty minutes ago. Graham and Dante sat on either side of Carter as they explained what had happened to my cousin and her Werewolf.

The Vampires had tried giving Infecteds the Werewolf gene by injecting them and feeding them a Werewolf's blood, but they'd had no luck. It just proved to exhilarate their energy and then leave them flat. So, Heather had been starved and Brendan had been kept weak, and they had been shoved in a room together in the hope of attacking one another and somehow exchanging curses.

"Hybrids," Dante explained. "They want to create better versions of themselves."

"But how do I fit in with that?" Nathan's focus had been fixed to the stone floor throughout Dante's explanation, his elbows braced on his knees as he listened intently.

"From what I can understand, they injected you with the Vampyrric Virus, which killed and 'turned' you."

"Which cuts out the 'traditional' way of feeding from their victims and then baptizing them."

"So what?" Nathan glanced at me. "It's t'save time?"

A raspy laugh met our ears.

"You poor fools." Chains rattled as Michael struggled to lift his head. "So clueless."

Carter growled, but the sound only caused the Colony Leader to laugh more.

"Why castrate him?" I asked, pulling focus back to the conversation at hand. "That … that is so far from what they do, I don't even understand how it fits in. Vampires can't conceive, so what good would neutering do?"

A shadow passed over Carter's face. "Eve."

My brow furrowed. "I'm sorry, who is Eve?"

"My daughter. She is Loup-garou."

He looked at me, and all I could see was a tired old man who was worried sick about his daughter. His eyes were a sad brown, and that proud physique that had stood poised and ready to attack now seemed to slump on the wooden chair facing me.

Nathan and I exchanged a look.

"Able to conceive," Dante stated as realization lit his features. "They put the virus into your sperm." He reached for the folder that lay open in the centre of us all. "And froze them."

I suddenly felt stupid. "I'm sorry, I'm not following."

"Heather was right." Carter's words were filled with dread.

"Breeding a new species is far easier than creating one." Michael's voice grated against his throat, exhaustion filling his tone, but the amusement that tickled the words was obvious.

Carter lunged to his feet and stalked toward the dangling Leech. His foot connected with the silver dagger in the Vampire's torso, and a God-awful screech filled the room.

Despite the horrid noise, the light in my head finally clicked. "They injected the virus into you so it would mingle with your blood stream quicker, and then they took your scrotum."

His face scrunched. "Please don't say that ever again."

"Living cells with the virus, which they removed and froze. That's why they castrated you."

He fell back into his chair. "They turned me because they wanted my sperm."

Dante nodded. "Because they want to impregnate the females of our kind who are able to conceive."

"Taking a leaf out of Heather's book." I shook my head in disbelief. "Born Hybrids. Like she was a born Infected."

"So, you're telling me that I'm now one of the undead, unable t'see my family, have a life, or grow old just because these stupid bastards were too lazy t'break into a sperm bank?" Nathan glanced between Graham, Dante, and me.

"Highly unlikely that it wouldn't have worked even if they had."

I twisted to face him. My mouth opened with the need to give a better reason for what had been done to him, but the only words that escaped me were, "I'm sorry."

"Fucking sorry?"

Another raspy gurgle left Michael. Black blood oozed from his mouth, but still, he laughed.

"And fuck you." Nathan jumped out of his chair, and within a second stood before Michael. Tension cradled his back and shoulder. He flexed his hands by his sides as he stared the Colony Leader dead in the eyes. "Fuck you and all your fucking kind."

"You mean … Our kind?"

Wrapping his fist in the Vampire's hair, he yanked the Vampire's head back, his face a mere breath away from the once sophisticated Michael who now looked like a battered drab of dead meat.

"I am not part of your kind." Nathan punched the words out.

"You might want to look in a mirror." A sickly, blood-filled smile stretched across Michael's chapped lips.

I saw the tension ripple through Nathan's body, but the way in which he snapped the Vampire's head to one side took me by surprise. A distinct crunch followed, and I realized that Nathan has just broken Michael's neck.

Carter remained a foot to his side, simply studying Nathan who wasn't moving, his feet rooted to the spot and his fist still in Michael's hair. He looked like a statue. Frozen and lost in the moment.

Getting out of my seat, I forced myself to walk toward him. "Than?"

"What the fuck?" The words escaped him on a whisper of disbelief.

I reached out and touched his right shoulder. "Than, it's okay."

He looked at me, black eyes staring in confusion, his jaw tense, blood trickling down his chin due to the puncture marks on his bottom lips.

I watched in amazement as his extended fangs shrank, as that blackness in his irises swirled like ink in water. "It's alright."

"No. No, it's so far from being alright." The words were broken, his voice strained.

"You should kill him." Carter's voice was low. "Put him out of his misery."

Nathan's gaze darted to the Alpha. "Both my life and death were taken from me. I will be damned if I allow anyone t'take my misery from me as well."

I glanced at the Alpha. "He's as much a victim as Brendan and Heather have been."

"And I'm bloody going to make sure no one else ever is."

My brow furrowed. I squeezed his shoulder to bring his focus back to me. "What d'you mean?"

He relaxed his fingers, sliding them from between the corpse's hair. Rubbing his hand on his borrowed jeans, he stared at Michael.

"I'm going to make sure that this never happens again. No one is ever going to end up like me or Freddie." He looked at me. Determination blazing in his blue eyes. "I'm going to take over the Colony."

***

~ Nathan ~

"What the actual hell?" the teen said in awe as she circled Michael, peering up at his face which had dropped back to his chest. *"You actually killed a Vampire and the big cheese. Shit, Than, you've really grown a set."*

I stared at the top of the Vampire's head, thinking about all the things I had read about him. He had been a bastard, and despite the fact that the Werewolves were still wanting to kill me, he had wronged them. Killing him had felt right, and I wasn't sure how I felt about that.

"It's in your nature now."

I don't want it t'be. I don't want t'go around killing people.

"He's a Vampire, not a person."

Once upon a time, he was a person.

"He was still a bad person."

"Than?" Elle shook me. "What are you on about? Are you crazy?"

Was I crazy? Yeah, I probably was, but I hadn't wanted this, and after the rundown of everything that had happened over the last couple of weeks, a lot of people didn't want to be involved in this.

"You said it yourself, no Vampires in the UK and no Leader means that this territory is vulnerable t'Vampires from other countries stepping in."

"That was a private conversation," Graham stated.

I glared over at the doctor. "I was present."

"You were in the boot."

"I was in storage, and I don't sleep. Just because I didn't partake in the conversation didn't mean I wasn't paying attention." I looked back at Elle. "You said there could be consequences?"

"Yeah, for the Pack. The Vampires will no doubt want t'get payback."

"Not if someone steps up and keeps them away. Not if the UK Colony and Pack have an understanding."

Carter barked a laugh as he moved past us. "You want us to form an alliance?"

"Aye, why not?"

"Because we don't work with Leeches."

"You *haven't* worked with Leeches because they're all selfish arseholes. That's not me."

Elle arched an eyebrow at my remark.

"Hush, you." I moved back to the three males. "Look, I've been thinking about this all day. I take place as Leader, and I make sure that innocent people aren't getting attacked and changed against their will, and I will make sure no one starts trouble or tries to kidnap and experiment on Werewolves."

Carter only laughed more. "The Pack doesn't need your help, little boy."

"No, but I need yours, and I think we can all agree that none of us wants any more of these bastards coming over and making decisions over our lives."

"I don't really think that Vampires decide what these guys do, Than."

I ignored the teenager who had wedged herself between Graham and Carter.

I'm sure that the Werewolves hadn't guessed that their own would be taken. That is having no control. They never thought it would happen. They won't want it happening again.

"I think it is a reasonable solution," Dante agreed.

Carter snorted. "And you're clearly too bloody tired to think straight, brother."

"These two are brothers?" The teen stared at their faces. *"I don't see it. Do you?"*

"We're all too tired." Dante sat back in his chair and folded his arms across his chest. "The last thing we need is more Vampires at our door. We have enough to deal with at this moment in time, and we're going to have a lot more on our plates real soon." He gave his brother a pointed look. "This ... Nathan doesn't exactly fit the profile of those who have created him, and the way Danielle trusts him ... I personally would feel better knowing that a decent individual has taken charge of any Leeches that might remain."

"Think that was a compliment."

"Thanks, Dante." I looked at Carter. "Do we have a deal?"

"Hang on." Elle grabbed my hand and dragged me past Michael to the dark corner. "What t'hell are you thinking? Do you have any idea what it would mean if you did this?"

"Aye. It means no one else will end up like me."

Her eyes were wide. She threw her hands in the air. "You think Leeches are just going to accept you as their Leader? No. You will have t'fight them and win. Prove you are worthy t'lead them."

"God, I didn't realize we lived in the barbarian age."

"Well, they do. They're still creatures, and it's all about dominance."

I folded my arms across my chest. "You don't think I can be dominant?"

"I don't think you realize what you're doing."

"What's new?"

"Than." She grabbed my shoulders. "*This* isn't a joke."

The sight of moisture clouding her eyes took me by surprise. I knew she wouldn't be thrilled at the idea, but the sight of concern etched on her face brough reality crashing down once more. The bit of adrenalin, or whatever the heck it was, that had filled me since we'd stepped into this basement seemed to disappear.

"Elle, I've just found out that I was changed just so they could have my sperm so that they can inject it into some female wolves and create little monsters." My head was spinning again. "This is all fucking insane. I'm unwillingly going t'father a ton of bastards with women who have no say over it. Who are being violated t'make something a million times worse than Vampire or Werewolves or whatever the hell else is out there. From the moment I was changed, I no longer had a purpose. I have no life. I have nothing."

"Things you already knew."

Perhaps, but it was still hard to hear, to digest. Even after seven weeks of being one of the undead.

"What were you expecting to learn?"

I didn't know. Would there have been an explanation that would have made me feel … better? Would I have felt better knowing that they were just goofing around and me and Freddie had just been the unlucky pick of the draw?

No explanation would have been okay. No explanation would have made me feel better. Listening to the worry in Elle's voice as she told Graham what a dumb idea it had been for them to kill all the Vampires—even though they deserved it—had been the only thing that had made sense over these last few weeks.

The Pack had gone and done something that would affect Elle's life. Not just her life, but her entire family's, and that wasn't okay with me. Her life was ridiculous to begin with. Ridiculous and fucking dangerous, and these idiots had gone and caused bigger problems. Shit was going to get political, and although I wasn't exactly one who knew the ins and outs of politics, I had watched enough gangster films to know that another crew moving in on someone else's turf was no better.

"Except for the knowledge that I have been used to harm so many. I can't deal with that, Elle. I can't stand here and do nothing. Remain fucking useless."

"You're not useless." Her arms fell to her side. "And you're wrong."

A dry laugh escaped me. "What's new?"

Her attention moved to the floor. "You have me."

I almost missed the words.

"No, I don't." I unfolded my arms and took hold of her hands. "This is your world, and you have your purpose. You have a job to be getting on with." I shrugged. "I need to find my purpose as this is my … life now. Maybe it isn't being Colony Leader. Maybe I should do what Lestat did in Queen of the Damned and become a rock star."

"Be serious."

I gave her a smile.

"This is the only way I can help correct all this shite that's being inflicted on innocent people." I squeezed her hands. "The only way I see myself being useful to you."

A line formed at the bridge of her nose. "You don't need to—"

"And them." I nodded toward the Werewolves. "There's got to be a reason I'm here, right?"

Even if it wasn't, it would do for now. If it would help keep her just that extra bit safer, it was all the reason I needed.

"God, I'm going t'throw up."

She took a deep breath and exhaled. "I get it, but I don't like this."

"Join the club." I let go of her hands. "This is the least I can do for you, Elle. So let me." I wandered back to Carter and Dante. "So, what do you say, frenemies?"

Carter stared at me blankly. "What the hell is a frenemy?"

"Friend slash enemy."

"I think acquaintance is better." Graham held the same blank look on his face.

I shrugged. "Acquaintance it is."

"We need to discuss this further." Carter glanced at Dante.

"Agreed. I think it is important we sit and figure out what is best for our Pack and what this could mean."

"I think we need to figure out how this can be beneficial to us all," I stated.

"Agreed. However, now is not the time." Carter stood and glanced in the direction of Michael. "We still have business to wrap up."

"Fair enough. When's best to continue this chat?"

"Are you available to meet here tomorrow evening to cement this agreement?" Dante stood and handed me the folder.

"Yeah, we will be."

I arched an eyebrow as Elle stopped beside me.

"I can't even think about going home until Heather gets back. So, I guess the least I can do is go back to London with you and make sure you don't get killed in the first five minutes of you being challenged by a ton of Leeches."

I wrapped my arm around her shoulders. "You're the bestest best friend a Vampire could have."

She shook her head. "Jesus, give me strength."

"Tomorrow it is, then." I took hold of Carter's outstretched hand. His grip was bone crushing as we shook. My entire arm had grown tense under the pressure, but I kept a smile on my face.

"Well, dickless, it looks like you're playing with the big boys now."

Chapter Twelve

Dante had actually drafted a contract. This guy was definitely the brains behind the Pack. The one who made sure everything was done properly.

The agreement was simple.

No attacking, murdering of changing victims, unless they asked to be turned.

No kidnapping or experimenting on humans or Werewolves, or well, any living creature.

Any information that may affect the Pack would be passed on and vice versa.

If any Vampire from other Colonies came to claim the UK, I was to fight them off.

If any Vampires came to seek revenge on the Werewolves, I was to find a diplomatic solution that was agreeable to the Pack, and if that failed, I and whoever I had with me was to help chase them away.

It was pretty simple and straightforward as contracts went. We just needed to be civil with one another. Something that would be easy for me, but only time would tell where the Wolves were concerned.

Alcander—who I had briefly met at the Colony Nest during 'maintenance'—was to be my first point of contact for the Pack as he lived in London, and he would have full permission to come into the Nest. He was a quiet fellow with long black hair, dark eyes, and olive skin. He didn't speak much, but the bits that I caught were tainted with an accent.

The one thing that did surprise me was that Elle requested that her family be made a part of the agreement with her being their first point of contact.

"Therefore, we all have an alliance." She shrugged when we had all looked at her. "Therefore, if Heather or anyone goes missing again, one if not all of us will have more of a clue with what is going on, and we know we can come straight to one another without an invite or fear of being ripped to shreds."

Her gaze had drifted at that point to Owen who had simply rolled his eyes.

I had a sneaking suspicion she wanted to be the neutral party. I wasn't sure yet if it was because she didn't trust the Pack, or that she was just overly concerned about my leadership skills. Either way, having her involved—and confirmed in writing—meant we definitely couldn't lose touch again. We had a commitment to one another. That word in regards to Elle shouldn't have felt right, but it did. It somehow tied us to one another on a whole other level. A reassurance that no matter what, we would never not be apart and in fact part of each other's life. It seemed to make her feel better knowing that she would never be in such a position again, having a family member go off radar, and although I'm sure Carter and the others wouldn't admit it, but having a Slayer involved in this agreement no doubt made the whole thing seem more appealing since Vampires and Werewolves were mortal enemies.

Slayers in Ireland, Vampires in London, and Werewolves in Scotland—we seemed to have the UK and that part of the English seas covered.

Now I just needed to figure out how to be a Leader of a Vampire Colony, and it would be clear sailing.

***

After our early evening meeting, Elle and I had hit the road once more. She hadn't been too happy about being stuck in the Scottish Highlands all day just to wait to sign papers, but while the Pack weighed up their options on whether I was crazy or not, it had given her and me time to come up with a plan.

We would go straight to the Colony Nest and see if any Vampires had crawled out of the woodwork and clarify that they were part of the UK Colony. Once we had figured that out, I would announce I was the new Leader, having snapped Michael's neck. Sure, I wasn't the one who drove the final blow that turned him into ash, but the Leeches didn't need to know that.

I'd fight anyone who challenged me, and with a bit of luck, I'd win. Once all that territorial bullshit was done, the ground rules would be laid out, all Vampires would be given an option to remain or leave, and then we would get to work and re-building.

It seemed straightforward, but Elle was right—the Leeches wouldn't be happy. Not with me, a newbie experiment being their Leader. Not at the fact a Vampire Slayer would be acting as a bodyguard, or the fact that a Werewolf would be paying regular house calls, but that was why they had the option to leave in the first place.

Despite our half an hour pit stop for food and to pick up some decent clothes for me, the journey back to London felt like it lasted an eternity. Elle was all talked out and only mumbled the odd word in reply to anything I said. She was worried. The fact that she was lost in thought for most of the long car journey was a big indication, but despite putting her name to the agreement, despite deciding to stay until there was word from Heather, she still thought that all of this was a bad idea.

By the early hours of Tuesday morning, we were once again standing outside the Colony Nest. Only this time, we had the keys to let ourselves in.

Elle stood on the threshold of the front door to the middle house as if her feet were stuck to the marble. Shoving the keys into my jeans pocket, I took hold of her hands and brought her inside.

Her gaze darted around the darkness. "This feels weird."

I closed the door behind her and then switched the light on. The warm light bounced against the crystal chandeliers, highlighting the enormous space which now looked very different without broken furniture and decomposed Vampires littering the floor.

"I know." I went to her side. "But one way or another, we have t'make this work, for all our sakes."

"Can you smell anything? Hear anything?"

The trio of houses were quiet with it being the early hours. Neighbours would be asleep. There were no cars on the roads. It was deadly silent so I should have been able to pick up on a mouse running around.

"It smells less like death than it did last time."

"It was a good idea to tidy up. If any Leeches did come calling, it would no doubt be obvious what had happened, but at least a human would just think someone had moved in or out, with the lack of furniture."

"I think a human would be preoccupied with the fact that this is a trio of houses that are all opened up to one another."

Somewhere above us, a floorboard whined. I concentrated, and after a moment, could make out soft footfall. "Someone's here."

"Which house?"

"The right one."

Removing her dagger, she moved past me into the living room of the right house. "Hopefully, it's not a squatter."

"Well, if it is, they're lucky it's just us here." I went to follow her but paused as another noise caught my attention. "Make that two visitors."

Glancing over her shoulder, she arched an eyebrow.

"This house." I pointed to the floor to indicate the noise came from downstairs.

She nodded and continued in the direction of the first noise, tiptoeing up the stairs.

Once she had vanished from view, I made my way quietly down to the basement. The light from the ground floor hallway only reached the base of the stairway to the lower level.

Darkness stretched out before me in all directions, but my eyes adjusted, turning the blackness into solid shadows. I remained at the bottom of the stairs, listening. Something shuffled. A crackle followed by a guzzling sound. As I focused on the small noises, my sight seemed to become sharper as if having a focus made the space around me more solid. It was crazy, but now wasn't the time to analyse how insane my senses were.

Rounding the stairs, I made my way down the hall. I could see the archway dead ahead, which I remembered led into the room with all the fridges. Someone was possibly having a late snack.

I noticed a cold, pale light slicing through the blackness as I stopped at the opening and risked a glance into the room. One of the doors to a fridge on the left of the room was wide open, the white light moulding to the silhouette of a hunched-over figure kneeling on the stone floor. I could just make out the plastic drawers which were stacked in the industrial fridge. Each one was packed with bags and bags of blood. A wet, suckling noise met my ears, and that's when I noticed a dozen or so drained blood bags scattered on the stone floor around the figure.

I reached up, trying to feel for the light switch, not wanting to take my focus from the hungry Vampire, but a loud bang from somewhere upstairs made its head jolt up. I froze on the spot, or maybe time seemed to slow down, because in a fashion which would have fit a horror film, its head slowly lowered and turned to me. Blood-red eyes starred at me from behind a curtain of dark hair. Trails of red blood marked the creature's white skin, dripping from its fangs.

And that's when it dawned on me—this was the first time I'd actually seen a Vampire feeding, and well, being a Vampire and not a scientist.

But then, confusion kicked in as I focused on the creature. Hadn't Elle said that their hair slithered out when they transformed? That they were bald and looked more like the Master from Salem's Lot? Weren't their jaws meant to dislocate and their fangs—?

My head hit the wall before I had even realized the Leech had moved. Bone cracked against stone, and my body slumped like a sack of potatoes to the hard floor. A heavy weight sat on me, something sharp digging into my chest.

Shaking off the momentary shock, my gaze found those red eyes, which were a mere few inches from mine. Despite its face being so close to me, I couldn't make anything else out but those eyes.

Hungry, angry, and well, just fucked. A gurgling hiss reverberated in the Vampire's chest as it dug its claws into mine through its balled-up fists.

"Fuck." The word left me on a whoosh as I was hauled up and flipped over the creature's head. I landed on my back, my legs flat against the basement's main door. Tilting my head to the left, I caught the end of the Vampire's legs as it high-tailed it up the stairs.

"Shit. Elle," I mumbled, rolling awkwardly onto my side.

"Jesus, you got your arsed handed t'you." The Teen popped into view as I made it to the stairs.

"That's the first time I've ever been face to face with an actual Vampire that isn't looking normal." I stumbled up the steps.

"They're not pretty."

Despite everything, at least Elle had been right about that. Hollywood definitely had their Vampires wrong. There was nothing sexy about them at all.

I circled into the living room and study of the middle house first only to find the rooms empty.

A rhythmic thud sounded, and I rounded the corner to see two Vampires lying at the bottom of the steps to the right house. Danielle hopped over the unconscious bodies.

"Only two of them over here." She looked at me. "You okay?"

"There was one downstairs," I said, heading to the living room of the left house.

"What happened?"

"It took me by surprise. Looked nothing like how I expected."

"I told you they weren't pretty."

"It didn't look how you said, though."

Her brow furrowed. "What d'you mean?"

A thud sounded somewhere upstairs.

"You search the left house."

I glanced at the female and male who lay in a clumsy heap at the bottom of the stairs.

"They'll be fine. All tied up." She legged it up the stairs of the middle house.

I quickly searched the basement of the right house before making my way to the first floor. A thud followed by a crash sounded, indicating that Elle had obviously found another Vampire. Possibly the one that had freaked out and jumped me, but as I hit the stairs to the next floor in the left house, the hint of blood teased my nostrils. I found the light switch.

"Y'know you don't need the lights on, right?"

Force of habit, I guess. Plus, I had spent enough time trapped in the dark. It wasn't a place I wanted to live in.

Warm light flooded the hallway, and my focus stopped on the closed door of the first room. A smudge of blood marked the brass doorknob.

"Be ready this time." The Teen stood by the door.

Duh.

Steeling my shoulders, I pushed the door open wide. The light flooded the room, highlighting the young lad sat on the floor in the left corner, legs pulled to his chest and arms circling his knees. He was wedged between the wall and a waist-high cabinet.

I moved into the room. A large bay window sat to the left, thick, long black satin curtains hanging at either side. A large black faux corner sofa took up the centre of the room, facing the flat screen television situated above the fireplace. Like most rooms in the triple living space that was the Nest, the walls were white and dotted with artwork. Apart from another cabinet which sat symmetrical to the first, and a long hallway table flat against the wall behind the sofa, the room was fairly empty for its size.

"Have you come to kill me?"

The words were said softly, and it took me a moment to realize they had come from the balled-up creature in the corner.

"What?"

He lifted his head. Startling bright brown eyes looked up at me with confusion. Fear marred his smooth pale skin, and despite the fact that dry blood stained his chin, he looked like a freaking Disney character. His black hair was a tangled mess that stopped at his shoulders.

"Have you come to kill me?" he repeated.

God, he was only a lad. This couldn't be the creature from the basement.

"Looks can be deceiving," The Teen sang beside me, her arms crossed as she gave the baby-faced Vamp the dead eye.

"No."

Another thud sounded.

"What's that?" The young Vampire looked around the room, hugging his legs closer.

"Nothing you need t'worry about." I moved over to the bay window. "What's your name?"

"Mark." He eyed me suspiciously. His nostrils flared. "You're a Vampire?"

"Yeah." I leant against the windowsill.

"I've never seen you before."

"I'm … new."

"You smell funny."

"I'm *very* new."

"Well, you're too late to officially join our Colony." His focus became lost as he stared off into space. He suddenly looked exhausted. "They've been slaughtered."

"I know."

Those tired eyes found me once more. "How do you know?"

"Because I killed Michael."

He snorted, relaxing his hold on his knees. "Werewolves killed Michael."

"No, Werewolves *tortured* Michael." I crossed my arms over my chest in an attempt to look relaxed. I was foolishly telling a Vampire who had already attacked me that I had killed his Leader. Probably not the best idea in the world.

"That's if he is the Vampire who attacked you. You didn't get a good look at him."

"*I* killed Michael."

He stared at me for a long time. There was something very off putting about the way he studied me.

"Like he's stripping you with his eyes, but skin and all."

Not helpful, Elle. I bit my tongue and held his gaze.

"Why were you with the Werewolves?"

"To make a deal."

"We don't make deals with Werewolves."

And boy, didn't I know it.

"Maybe Michael didn't, but I do, and it was just the one."

"What kind of deal?"

I would get to that, but I also didn't want to have to explain the vast details on a one-to-one basis. Especially if any of the remaining Leeches wanted to challenge me for Leadership.

"Is there anyone else here?" I glanced at the closed double door at the other side of the room, aware of the fact that I hadn't checked it or the other two levels above us.

"Only a few. There's not many of us left now." Anger tinged the end of his words.

Understandable. No creature in their right mind would be happy about having their kind hunted and killed, but the way the young Vampire said those words almost sounded like the Pack had actually wiped them all out. The Pack sure would be pleased with themselves.

"You didn't answer my question." His tone changed, a lick of irritation coating his words. "What type of deal?"

My gaze met his again, and he suddenly looked older, less fearful. More …

"Like a predator?"

A flash of red eyes filled my mind, and an unsettling chill crept up my spine. I'd spent enough alone time with my new friend. I pushed myself off the windowsill.

"I'm rounding everyone up to discuss the new arrangements. So, if you could come downstairs?"

His features suddenly softened, and he rested his chin against his knees. "How do you know you can trust the Wolves after what they've done?"

The action seemed odd. Almost forced.

"Instincts." I stopped in front of him and held my hand out. "Why don't you come downstairs, and I will tell you and the others all about it."

He slid his hand into mine without hesitation. His slender fingers wrapped around my wrist, clasping firmly. "You haven not told me your name."

I pulled him to his feet. He stood at the same height as me. His frame and build were almost identical to mine, but as we stood eye to eye, I could see by his posture that he knew how to hold himself.

Prizing my hand from his, I took a step back and forced a smile. "Nathan. I'm the new Colony Leader."

***

"You expect us to believe you killed Michael when we know for a fact the Pack took him and have been slaughtering our kind across the country?" The burly, blond Vampire sneered.

"I just told you I did."

The seven Vampires we had found hiding out in the Nest burst into another fit of laughter. We had brought them all to the living room in the middle house to break the news but hadn't quite made it past the part of Michael being dust and me taking over.

They stood haphazardly around the large room, glaring at me and Elle who had taken position with our backs to the open reception room. The room was void of furniture, which made the whole situation feel more vulnerable, but at least we could see them all clearly and could watch for any tell-tale signs of them getting ready to attack.

"It seems somewhat far-fetched." The female who stood by his side quirked an eyebrow at me.

I threw my manila folder on the mahogany floorboards.

"I have no idea what your Leaders told you or what they kept secret, but Vampires have been experimenting on humans and Infecteds." I pointed to my folder. "They have kidnapped Werewolves and burnt down the Pack Keep. *That* is the reason the Wolves have been out killing y'all."

"And why didn't they kill you?" a Hispanic-looking male asked.

"Because I'm not like you."

That remarked earned me another round of grumbles and sneers. My God, it was like talking to a room full of teenagers.

"Look, the bottom line is, I'm pissed off that this happened t'me, and I am damn well going t'make sure this stops."

"Pussy," the blond spat.

"Kick him in his face, Than. You don't have to take this shite." The Teen stopped in front of the Blond Vamp and attempted to punch him in the stomach, her phantom fingers passing through him.

I also don't want everything to be about violence.

"Laugh it up all you want. You may have been given the option to become an immortal blood sucker, but I wasn't." I placed my hands on my hips. "Now, your Masters and Mistress—"

"My Mistress is right next to me," the blond commented.

The dark-skinned beauty glared at me, her eyes an unusual mix of hazel and green. "And my Mistress is in America."

"So, the Vampires that sired you are not part of the UK Colony?" Elle looked at them all separately before glancing at me. "That makes sense why they're all still here."

"Some of us have lost Bloodlings." A brunette hissed.

"And I'm sure that hurts, but as of yesterday, this Colony and the Pack are now in an agreement to stay clear of each other," Elle explained.

The female snorted. "You expect them to honour such an

arrangement."

"Yeah, I do."

"This is a joke." The blond shook his head.

"You have a choice. You are free t'leave this Colony and go on your merry way, but I would highly advise you get out of the country because as soon as you leave this Nest, you are fair game for the Werewolves and Slayers of this world."

"So, you send us to our death?" the Hispanic male asked.

"No, *your* decision to refuse this new change will lead to your demise," I said with a smile. "If you stay here, you will be fed —"

"Blood bags are like piss. Nothing beats drinking from the source," the blond spat.

"Be that as it may, we no longer feed off humans, and if you are caught, you will be made an example of." I shrugged. "The choice is yours. All I can promise is you'll never be left in the dark, and you won't go thirsty."

"You sound like a school teacher." The Teen stopped beside me.

"I wish to stay." Mark spoke up for the first time. He had remained at the back of the room, huddled in the corner and out of everyone's way. "My Master abandoned me long ago, and I came here from Spain. I have no one."

"I don't trust him," the Teen mumbled.

"Glad to have you."

The six leeches sneered at him, causing the youngster to curl back into the corner.

"We will give you all a minute t'mull it over," Elle said, before pulling me into the reception room. The doors remained open so we could keep our eyes on what remained of the UK Colony. She lowered her voice. "You might want t'tone down the chipper attitude. This isn't a fraternity."

"How d'you think it's going?"

"As expected, I'm half waiting for Blond and Burly to challenge you. Half of them may not feel up to it if they've all had their Bloodlings slaughtered like the brunette said."

Honestly, I was hoping that they would all feel exhausted and defeated and would just accept the situation.

"Keep dreaming." The Teen snorted.

But naturally, I knew I wouldn't end up being so lucky. Still, a guy could hope, right?

"So, does it really affect them? Having the Vampires they sired disconnected from them?"

Elle folded her arms across her chest and stared at the small group. "Depending on how old their blood link is, yeah, it weakens them, but not for forever."

"And that link is formed—?"

"By being baptized with your Maker's blood."

I pulled out a chair from the small dining table and took a seat. "I don't know if I drank a Vampire's blood. I mean, I remember a lot of blood bags and injections, but I'm almost ninety percent sure it was always living blood. So, if I didn't drink a Vampire's blood, does that mean I don't have a Master or Mistress?" I slouched in the chair. "And if that's the case, what does it mean?"

"If a Master is killed, then their Bloodlings dies." She glanced at me. "So hopefully, it means your immortality isn't tied to anyone else."

"That's good, right?"

"Considering what's currently going on, yeah. I guess despite everything, the way you've been created has a small silver lining, after all."

"So, you will only die if someone kills you. Not if the Vampire who made you dies, because you don't have a sire?" The Teen, who now sat across from me, looked as confused as I felt.

"I guess that's a small relief."

I would never puff out of existence because of someone else. At least I knew that I had control over the circumstances and situations that could cause my immortality to be cut short. It was a small win, but a win nevertheless.

"Speaking of puffing out of existence, it looks like Blond and

Burly might want t'be the one t'make it happen."

I stood as the six Vampires crowded into the centre of the room. Mark remained huddled in the corner, quietly watching.

"Made a decision?" Elle asked the group.

"Shut it, whore," the blond snapped.

My spine went rigid at the insult. Hands balled into fists, I closed the distance between me and the group.

"Watch your mouth." I stopped a breath away from the vile male. "No one speaks to her that way."

A lewd grin curled his lips, and I watched as black began to creep into his grey eyes.

"I can handle myself, Than," She reminded me. "Besides, a Leech's insults aren't worth shite."

"We aren't taking no orders from an experiment and his whore." The Hispanic male sneered.

"And they clearly don't know any other insult." Elle barked a laugh.

"Fair enough. You know where the door is," I stated, not taking my gaze from the blond whose skin had started to ripple across his cheeks.

I wasn't sure if it was my intense staring playing tricks on me, but watching his skin roll like waves was just … I'd have probably gagged if I were still alive.

"We aren't leaving our home." His Mistress stood to his right. I glanced at her and watched the bright colours of her iris bleed black. "You don't belong here."

"And you certainly aren't the new Leader of this Colony," the Hispanic male said, standing to the blond's left.

My focus moved to him, and I watched his rich caramel flesh roll. Clearly, this is what Elle had meant by transforming. Funny, I didn't remember her mentioning Vampires' skin moving across their bones of its own free will.

"Says who?"

"Says us," the blond hissed.

"Shame." I took a couple steps back and rolled the sleeves of my light blue shirt up. "I didn't want it t'have to come t'this."

"Told you so."

"Not the time for that, Elle."

Their bodies grew tense. I watched as hair began to slither from their heads, the luscious locks falling in masses, strands disintegrating as they headed to the floor but never made it. The skin of their faces continued to ripple, bones crunching as their jaws disconnected.

"One at a time." Elle stopped at my side, pulling the sword from the sheath on her back. "You want t'fight him for leadership, then you will challenge him one at a time."

"You ready for this, Head Boy?" The Teen stopped on the other side of me.

As ready as I will ever be.

"Just remember, you're one of them despite what they say."

Not sure that's reassuring.

"Remember the forest. Remember how you snapped Michael's neck. I just mean you're strong and fast even if you don't know how you are."

I hope you're right.

I stepped forward. "If I beat you all one on one, then you will accept me as the new Colony Leader."

"If you can't accept that, then you walk," Elle finished. "Anyone butts in with a challenge or tries anything funny then this—" She swivelled her wrist. The light bounced of the silver blade. "—will be the last thing you see."

Without warning, the blond charged forward. Elle jumped out of the way and stayed with the group. The blond swung at me over and over. His nails had formed into long, thick talons. I kept jumping back, and without tripping over my own feet. A miracle even for me, but all I could concentrate on was getting away from his gaping mouth and giant viper fangs.

Definitely not like the Master from Salem's Lot.

My heel caught the leg of the chair I'd been sitting on, and I fell backward.

"Focus!" the Teen shouted.

The blond lunged. My right foot landed right in his junk. A wet gurgle vibrated in his throat, the impact causing him to stumble back. It was enough time for me to roll to my feet.

"Punch him," the Teen shouted.

Where?

He technically didn't have cheeks anymore, which were the usual target areas as well as the eyes, but it was pretty hard to hit anything above the cavern that was his mouth.

His snake-like tongue whipped around between his wet fangs.

"Fuck, you are one ugly—"

He charged.

I threw the door beside me wide open. He ran right into the panel, causing the wood to crack straight down the centre. I dashed into the hallway and legged it into the kitchen. The surfaces were clear, no electricals or ornaments. I yanked open cupboards and drawers to find them all empty.

"What are you looking for?" the Teen asked.

"A knife," I growled, moving around the island as the blond stormed into the kitchen.

"They don't eat, eejit. So why would they have utensils?"

"I don't know." I grabbed one of the stools at the end of the breakfast counter.

The Vampire ran at me. I swung the stool which broke on impact with his shoulder. Wood splintered, and the padded, grey top fell with a crack to the marble floor.

The four legs remained in my tight grip as I stumbled backward toward the kitchen door.

"Stakes."

"What?"

"You have four stakes in your hand. Use them."

"Where?"

230 | Cross My Heart

"Anywhere!"

I backed out into the hallway of the middle house and swung the legs at the wall. The two bottom legs dropped to the floor.

"His gut!"

The Vampire moved through the door, the Teen squeezing out behind him.

"Drop and ram them in his gut."

I glanced at the two stakes in my hand, still attached by a centre support. The ends were splintered, not exactly solid points, and the Vampire looked like he was made of muscle.

"Just bloody do it."

The Vampire charged. Without thinking, I dropped to the floor, my knees hitting the wood with a loud smack. My eyes fluttered shut as the Vampire drew close, and without thinking, I shoved the two stakes toward him as hard as I could. They hit something hard. A weight pressed upon me. Thick liquid coated my hands as something wet smacked against my forehead. The next thing I knew, I was tumbling back and being crushed.

The vile smell of Vampire blood met my nostrils.

Opening my eyes slowly, I looked up to see the Teen looking down at me. *"Nice work."*

The blond lay on top of me in a haphazard way, his body pinning me down, his head right next to my neck.

Releasing the death grip I had on the ends of my make-shift stakes, I wiggled them out from between us. Hands on the male's shoulder and side, I pushed him, ignoring the wet slide as the tip of his tongue slid down and over my left eye and cheek. A groan escaped the Vampire, causing me to squirm and kick until I was free of the lump.

Jumping to my feet, I looked down to find black blood smeared all over my new shirt and jeans. My hands ached where splinters had pierced my flesh, but as I looked at the indents, I could see the tiny shards wriggling out.

"Self-healing, remember," the Teen reminded me.

"Than!" Elle shouted, urgency ringing in her tone.

I turned around just in time to see the dark beauty, who sent both of us flying into the living room of the left house. We slid across the well-polished wood floor, stopping at the threshold of the landing.

I screamed out as her talons plunged into my ribs. I could actually feel the nasty claws scratching against my bones as she twisted her hands inside me. Something thick filled my mouth, oozing at the corners.

Rearing her head back, a guttural cry broke from her. Her fangs glinted, and before I could move, the razor-sharp points slid through my left shoulder.

"Fuck." The word was gargled, rasped through gritted teeth and the taste of my own dead blood.

"Fight, Than." I could hear the Teen shout. *"Fucking fight."*

Pain stung the end of my fingers, and as I lifted my hands to grab her bald head, I noticed my own talons had grown. I dug them into the taut skin of her scalp. The cry that left her vibrated through her and into me, but she remained latched on to me.

"Aim for her neck." I wasn't sure which version of Elle was instructing me. All I could hear was the panic in that all too familiar voice. The voice that had gotten me this far. The only voice I knew I could trust, even over my own.

Clutching the right side of her head, I stabbed my hand into the left side of her neck repeatedly.

I felt as though someone had poured acid down my shoulder, and every blow I made to her neck caused my own body to shudder. But despite the pain and the fact that my eyes suddenly felt heavy, I kept punching, kept listening to that voice guiding me out of this mess.

Eventually, the Leech's fangs and talons slid out of me, and then, her body grew slack.

My arm dropped like a deadweight to my side. Pain swam from my ribs to my shoulder and back again.

With the last bit of energy I could muster, I shoved her off me and pushed myself up to a sitting position. Elbows pressed into the wood, I glared at the remaining five Vampires, trying my best to hold myself up despite the fact I could feel my arms trembling. Or the fact that I could feel blood oozing out of the holes that now littered my torso and shoulder, the thick vile substance causing my shirt to stick to me.

I spat the blood that still filled my mouth onto the floor beside me and pinned them all with a look. "Who's next?"

Elle and the remaining five all stood in the built archway which connected the middle and left house. The Vampires were back to their human-looking self, genuine surprise highlighting their features. A mixed look crossed Elle's face, one that I couldn't read, but at the sight of the white-knuckled grip she had on the sword that pointed down at her side, it was easy to guess what she might currently be thinking.

Was she scared of me? Surprised? Concerned?

I glanced to my left and noticed that the female's body had started to melt and crumble, as was her head that was no longer connected to her shoulders.

"Jesus." I looked down at my right hand which was coated in her blood and then back at Elle who was suddenly looking a lot paler.

"Christ, Than, you just cut the woman's head off with your bare hand."

The idea that Elle could be freaking out or thinking something terrible snapped me out of my momentary shock, but a cry left me as I tried to push myself up. Searing pain spiralled through my torso and down my shoulder and left arm.

"No more challenges for today." Elle finally broke the stunned silence. "You want t'leave. Go. Otherwise, go to the right house and make yourself comfortable."

"He needs blood," I heard Mark state as I shuffled backward until my back hit the landing wall.

Elle stopped beside me, the odd expression still on her face. "You okay?"

"I've been better." I couldn't bring myself to meet her gaze, too nervous about what I might see in her eyes. "I'm sorry."

"For what?" She knelt down beside me, sword still in hand, but used as a leaning post.

"All the times I laughed at you. That was not easy, and my god, they're horrifying."

"I told you so."

"You just can't stop saying that, can you?" I laughed, regretting the action as it caused my abdomen to tense, caused more blood to ooze as pain pinched at me.

"I think I'm entitled to." She finally holstered her sword.

The sight made me feel a little better. I gave her a small grin, risking a look at her. The colour was coming back to her cheeks, but she suddenly looked tired. Then again, the last two days had been exhausting.

Mark stopped by my right, placing a drawer full of blood by my side. "This will help with your healing."

"Thanks." I eyed the red bags. I had the notion my stomach should be turning and I should be retching, but as I looked at the dark red liquid, my throat grew drier. Not helped by the fact that my own blood was clinging to the roof of my mouth like that horrid skin you got on the top of heated milk.

I glanced up at Elle. "Do you mind giving me some privacy?"

She looked genuinely stunned at the request. "Come on, Than. I've seen you drinking Heather's mixture."

"That's different." I pushed myself farther up the wall. "It looks and smells like cranberries. It's easy to pretend it's juice. This …" I deliberately turned away from her. "I don't want you t'see me drinking this."

"I know that you're a Vampire, Than. I've accepted that."

Hearing her say those words was all I had wanted since that night we had found each other again at the Monastery, but words weren't enough anymore. I couldn't bear to see that strange look on her face again. I didn't want her to be repulsed by me.

"I know, but there's knowing and then there's seeing, and you seem to be having trouble with the seeing."

She remained quiet. Her silence only confirmed what I had just seen in her eyes, on her face.

I risked a look at her. "It's okay. I'd have the same look on my face if I could see myself."

She had gone against everything she believed, everything her family stood for just to help me.

She sighed. "I just—"

"It's cool. I promise I understand."

"Okay." She straightened. "I will be in the other room if you need me."

"I know."

I waited until she had disappeared from view before picking up one of the blood bags. Mark sat cross-legged against the front door to my right, watching me with intense interest.

"Thanks again." I lifted the bag to my mouth and reluctantly tore the top off with my teeth.

"Piercing it would be easier and less messy," Mark stated.

A splash of blood spilled onto my shirt, mixing with my dry dead blood. "I will remember that."

I held the bag in front of my face. I hated how I knew the smell, hated that I could already taste it before it passed my lips. That now I held it in my hands, I was actually craving it. My thirst hadn't been an issue since I had left the facility. Despite the blood in Heather's mix being watered down, it had done the trick, but now, I could smell it, untainted …

"You do not like blood."

I glanced up at the young Vampire. "Guess I'm not a normal Leech."

"You certainly aren't." He looked over at the decomposed heap. "That was quite impressive."

"It was unnecessary."

"She would have killed you, which would have defeated your purpose."

Sure it would have, but I was a lover, not a fighter.

"Well, you're a decent fighter." The Teen sat down at the end of my feet. *"Or you're just dumb lucky.*

Definitely the latter. I have no idea what just happened.

"Neither do any of your Colony."

Shit. I'm the Leader now.

"Until someone else challenges you and wins."

Let's hope it doesn't come to that.

I glanced back at the Vampire. "I was hoping that we could have all come to an understanding without anyone getting hurt."

A laugh escaped him though I couldn't make out any humour.

"And yet, you have killed two Vampires in one go."

"Two?" I felt my brow furrow.

"Mistress." He nodded to the mound, and then turned to the space where I had left the unconscious blond. I followed his gaze to see another mound in his place. "And Bloodling."

So, it really did work, and fast. Kill a Mistress or Master, and their Bloodling would be dust. Made sense for how easy it would have been for the Pack. Each Vampire they killed would have destroyed a handful more.

Insane.

"At least you never have to worry about such things." He pushed himself up to stand. "You don't have one."

"How did—"

"Great hearing."

He'd overheard mine and Elle's conversation. Meaning they all had.

"Is that bad? That they know?"

Honestly, I have no idea.

Elle and I would just have to bear it all in mind for future conversations.

He nodded to the bag in my hand. "Drink up, or your healing will take longer."

Cupping the squishy bag as carefully as I could, I closed my eyes and knocked the contents back. The moment the copper liquid slid down my throat, I could feel the skin around my wounds tingling. No to mention a scratching sensation on my insides, almost like a needle threading my muscles.

"You really aren't a normal Vampire."

I opened my eyes to see Mark smirking.

"Interesting."

I gulped the liquid back and watched the young Vampire head through the sequence of archways toward the right house.

"He's an odd one." The Teen watched him over her shoulder.

"Yeah, but at least he's more accepting than the others." I threw the blood bag on the floor and grabbed another. I ran my tongue over my teeth, and sure enough, I could feel the sharp edge of my fangs as my gums pinched and they extended. I pierced the plastic and chugged.

"I'm not sure that's a good thing, Than."

Chapter Thirteen

~ Danielle ~

Saturday 24th October, 2015
Belgravia, London

"Carter, please can you just call or message and let me know if Heather has safely made it back to the UK?" I disconnected the call and threw my phone on the sofa.

I had been calling the Alpha for the last two days ever since I'd received a very short and to the point text from Dante stating that Heather and Brendan were due back any day now. It had been welcome news, but I hadn't heard anything since, and it was starting to feel like the Wolves were ignoring me.

I just needed to speak to my cousin, and then I could check in with my parents. The news would at least reassure them and cement the reason I needed to stay in the UK a little longer. God, my father would have a heart attack if he knew I was currently staying in the Colony Nest and sharing a bedroom with the new Leader.

Not that there was anything going on between us, far from it. It's just Nathan didn't like the idea of me being in my own room with strange Vampires in the same building, and as he didn't sleep, it meant I could use his new rooms and he would stay close by.

Truth be told, this had to be the only time in our history he was actually keeping me from losing my mind. I mean, I was living in a Nest. Sure, it wasn't for long, but the fact alone was madness.

Not that the remaining three members were anything to worry about. I had the feeling that the two females had taken a shining to the new Leader, and the boy, Mark, looked as though you could snap him with a simple tap. Not exactly a strong army for trouble, but it would do, for now.

The three of them had been sent out two days ago to search down any Leeches that might be hiding and give them the same choice that they had been given—follow the new Leader or get out of the UK.

I wasn't expecting an army to come back, especially as our survivors were only with us as their Masters and Mistresses didn't reside in this country. One way or another, our three members would either come back with some straddlers or empty-handed.

I guess the Pack would be pleased to hear that they had actually exterminated the entire UK Colony.

So, while I sat on my thumbs waiting to hear about Heather, Nathan got to work on tidying the place up and studying the businesses that Michael had, getting to grips with the wealth he had just laid his hands on and how he could somehow improve Vampires' way of life.

Jesus, my father would straight out die if he knew what I was involved in. I should be killing Vampires. Not helping them to adapt.

"You look deep in thought … again."

I looked up as Nathan stepped into the room, dressed in jogging bottoms, T-shirt, and trainers. He really didn't suit the look but wanted to wear something loose and comfortable while we trained. I had somehow been roped into teaching him to fight as he had won his first and only two challenges on sheer luck and savage instinct.

"Just trying t'get my head around things. I guess it's all finally catching up t'me."

This last fortnight had been the craziest of my life.

"Any word off Carter?"

"Are you serious? He seems t'have fallen off the face of the planet all of a sudden."

"Try Dante again?"

"I will." I hopped off the arm of the sofa. "Remind me again what the point of the agreement was?"

"So we could all live in peace and be on the same page." He brought his hands together in prayer.

"I feel like we got the short end of the stick."

"Yeah, I think we did."

"If I don't hear from them in the next few days, I'm going t'have t'go back up there."

The idea of making the nine-plus-hours journey was not appealing in the slightest, but if Carter and Dante continued to ignore my calls, it was looking like I wouldn't have much of a choice but to pay them a visit.

He dropped his arms to his sides. "I know."

"Are you going t'be okay on your own?"

I didn't like the idea of leaving him here on his own. Sure, we only knew of three Vampires that were still in the UK and they might not be back for another week, but that didn't mean he would be safe on his own.

"I'm not that helpless."

"Oh, I know you're not."

I still couldn't get the image of him punching the female Vampire's head off out of my mind. The way in which he'd repeatedly stabbed his talons through her flesh, muscle, and bone … The blood had actually drained from me as I'd watched. The rhythm in which he'd punctured her had reminded me of the shower scene in *Psycho* where Norman Bates' 'mother' stabs relentlessly until the victim is dead. Considering all the Vampires I had killed and the ways I had killed them … the ways in which I had witnessed them be killed … well, this was the first time I had actually wanted to throw up. I wasn't entirely sure it had anything to do with the way the Leech had been slaughtered. More to do with witnessing who was doing the hacking.

Nathan was far from helpless and most definitely far from being harmless, which is what I had repeatedly told the Pack and, I guess, myself. He was just as dangerous as any Vampire, if not more so as with every day that passed by, we were learning that he had all of their advantages and not many of their weakness. But that's what the Leches wanted, according to the Pack—a better, stronger species of Vampire, and my God, they were on their way to getting just that.

"It will be good for me t'have a few days here on my own."

I arched a brow at him.

"Besides, with all the new moves you're going t'teach me, I will be totally fine."

I stepped into the centre of the living room of the centre house which we had chosen to keep clear for meetings and training, etc. It just seemed easier than constantly having to replace furniture.

"This is my life now, Elle."

"T'be alone? Jesus, you're really getting into the iconic broody Vampire character, aren't you?"

"Get lost." He stretched his arms above his head. "I just meant, fights, challenges. These are part of my life now."

"You're right, but that means you're never going t'be on your own. There will always be Vampires around, and a lot of them will always be trying t'challenge you or just hurt you."

"I will be fine."

His focus shifted to the left of the room, and he shook his head.

I frowned. "You took this role on without fully realizing what it entailed."

"I took this role on so no one else has their life stolen from them." He looked back at me. "So that you didn't have something else t'worry about."

"Nathan, as you've even said yourself, this *is* my life. Whatever happens, whatever comes up, I just have to deal with it."

"Not this time." He finished stretching and gave me a wide smile. "From now on, you don't have t'worry about stray Vampires. You can concentrate on what's important—finding Marko, and saving your family."

He was right. With Nathan as Colony Leader making sure the Vampires behaved themselves, it meant that my family and I could concentrate on finding Marko and finishing this stupid family legacy once and for all. There wasn't enough Vampires left in the UK to cause any damage. They had been told they couldn't feed on humans anymore, and those that listened, well, it would cut down on deaths and the creation of Bloodlings. Those who did would be made an example of one way or another, and Nathan would deal with the victims by giving them a choice, with a full explanation on what it would entail—death or immortality.

By taking on this position which he still didn't fully understand regardless of his argument, he had just made mine and my family's life a lot easier.

The realization hit like a ton weight. I stared at him. "Please tell me you didn't do this for me."

He shrugged. "I told you I'm doing it so I'm of some use."

He'd put himself in danger to help me out.

"You're my family, too."

"A Vampire in the family?" He stated in a shocked tone, hand on his chest. "I'm sure your Da would love that."

"You were family to me before you were a Vampire, and I don't turn my back on family."

"You just almost slice their throats a couple of times."

"Hey, both times were a reaction due t'shock." I indicated to him. "I didn't expect to see you ever again, let alone in such a state."

"Yeah, I know. I know I'm a shite friend."

"No, just a shite human being, but that's been sorted." I gave him a smile and closed the distance between us. "I don't know what is going t'happen, but I will make sure you're equipped for anything. Having you turned t'dust is the last thing I want."

"The Slayer has once again admitted that she cares about the Vampire."

"The friend cares about her friend."

He slid a look to the left. I followed his gaze.

"What do you keep looking at?"

The space behind us was empty. The entire trio of houses were empty. We were once again alone.

"You." His reply was soft, almost a whisper.

I turned back to him, my brow furrowed.

A grin curled his mouth. "You are what's kept me going through all of this. After everything, the least I can do is make life a little smoother for you."

"That's not your responsibility."

"I want it t'be." He placed his hands on my shoulders and squeezed gently. "I want you to know that from now on, you can always depend on me." He rolled his eyes and glared at the empty room. "What I mean is I'm not going anywhere." His gaze met mine. "I'm immortal so I've literally got all the time in the world."

"You as an immortal." I shook my head. "I've only just realized what a terrible idea that is."

"And a very lonely one, but for now, I've got you."

I gave him a small smile. "And I swear as long as I'm around, you will never be left alone in this upside-down world of ours."

He moved his right hand down to my chest, placing his hand over my heart. His cool fingertips brushed across the skin at the top of my breast, and the air caught in my throat. I wanted to bat his hand away at the clear crossing of barriers, but the sad, serious question that left his mouth made me pause.

Those blue eyes locked on to mine, causing memories to rush back, of the last time we saw each other when we were both alive. "Cross your heart?"

I placed my hand on his chest and tried not to let stray tears fill my eyes as I met emptiness. I couldn't wrap my head around the fact that despite no longer having a beating heart, Nathan had somehow remained the big-hearted fool I had always known.

"And hope to die."

His hand slid up to cradle the back of my head. He ran the pad of his thumb across my cheek and pressed his forehead to mine. "Not if I have a say in the matter."

Epilogue

Tuesday 27th October, 2015
Farr, Scotland

I pulled up outside the ruined house of The Pack. Well, half a ruined house. The second storey had disappeared. Scaffolding surrounded what remained. Cement machines, diggers, trucks, and other building equipment were situated at the right hand of the courtyard.

I switched the engine of my Range Rover off and sat staring out at the half a structure.

Dante had messaged two days ago to say Heather was back and she was resting.

What did that mean? Was she tired? Was she ill? Had she been hurt? There were many reasons she could be resting, and not knowing was both worrying and irritating.

None of that was helped by the fact that trying to get in touch with the two males had proven useless yet again. Thankfully, after at least twenty-four hours of stress, Nathan had reminded me that Dante had given me Heather's new mobile number, which kept going to an automated voicemail. Not reassuring.

So, they had left me with no option but to get back up to Scotland. They couldn't ignore me if I was in their faces.

Still, I felt rude just showing up here without them knowing. Not that that had stopped me last time, but still, an invite would have made me feel less apprehensive.

Technically, it wasn't wrong of me to come here as we had all agreed to the part in the contract that stated we would be welcome no matter the time of day or day of the week.

I reached for my mobile and hit redial on Carter's number. At the very least, I could try one last time before I stormed in there demanding to know what the hell was going on. At least that way when he looked at me puzzled, I could tell him to finally check his phone and that I had tried to let him know I was planning on visiting.

Surprise, surprise, voicemail.

I hit Dante's number.

I couldn't understand why they were being so quiet. Sure, a lot was going on, which was made clear with the construction site outside my window, but surely, one of them could have picked up the phone just once over the last few days. Was it so much to ask?

Dante's voicemail rang in my ears.

Third time's the charm? I hit Heather's number … straight to voicemail.

Well, I'd tried to be civil and polite, and now I was just pissed off and confused. Not to mention tired. All I had wanted was some answers, and I had spent hours driving up here just to get them because two grown arse men couldn't answer their phones.

I took a deep, deep breath and exhaled slowly. I would make sure I pointed that out, but for now, all that mattered was I would see Heather.

Exiting the car, I made my way to the back of the house. As I walked past the empty spaces where the windows should have been, I could make out that the rooms had been emptied of all their furniture. The shape of three metal dumpsters met my gaze as I walked along the back of the house—items were piled up in the large metal containers which would eventually be taken to the dump.

I stopped at the back door which stood wide open, only this time, three camping lanterns had been placed around the kitchen which was now missing the island in the centre. The lights were pale and low, but it was a clear enough indication that someone was here …

A muffled cry met my ears. I turned to the pantry archway. The secret door was shut, but all the shelves in the storage room had been emptied. Grabbing hold of one of the shelves I knew was attached to the door, I tugged and tugged, and eventually, it opened.

As soon as my foot hit the stone stairs, the cry became more distinctive and more painful. The hushed timbre of male voices slid between the agonizing groans, and my stomach started to somersault.

What the hell was going on down there?

My heart hammered in my chest as I stood frozen at the iron door, which yet again stood ajar. Whispers floated around the large room, but all I could focus on was the panting and groaning of someone in severe pain.

I placed my hand on the warm metal, hesitant to push. I feared what I was about to see. What if something very personal and Pack-like was taking place and I was about to interrupt?

Then again, I wouldn't be interrupting if the Alpha had answered my calls. So clearly, he would be to blame, right?

Then again, what if it had something to do with Heather and why I hadn't been able to speak to her? The thought made me feel sick.

Taking a deep steadying breath, I steeled my spine and pushed the door open enough for me to slip through. At least fifteen people stood in the room, standing in a circle around the cage. I could see Carter kneeling on the floor in front of the bars along with another male who sat to his left.

"Just breathe," Carter said in a hushed, soothing tone. "Embrace it. Make it part of you."

Without thinking, I stepped closer, invisible to everyone in the room who I now noticed had their eyes closed as if they were meditating.

Another horrid cry echoed around the room, and I felt the hairs stand up on the back of my neck. The sound was more animalistic than it had been just a moment ago.

Perhaps this *was* something Pack-related? I suddenly felt uncomfortable.

I took a couple steps backward, keeping my focus on the room to make sure no one had noticed me sneak in.

"Come on, Heather."

My blood turned to ice at the sound of my cousin's name, and I halted. It wasn't Carter speaking. The male sounded northern, not Scottish. And although his tone was as calm as Carter's, there was something laced in the words that I couldn't quite make out.

I moved closer again, peering between the bodies that surrounded the cage. It was the blond who knelt on the floor before the cage. His voice was strained and filled with so much sadness.

"Kill … me." The words were strangled and inhuman.

"I'm sorry. I can't do that." Unshed tears filled the man's voice. He almost sounded like he was choking on the words.

An almighty growl was his answer, and my head snapped up as a body hit the bars of the cage. Disfigured hands wrapped around the thick iron. Skin crawled on the bones of the face that pressed against the metal. Bones which crunched and snapped. The body contorted. Hands spasming. The individual fell back on the floor, a groan tearing from them.

"I can't …" a wheezing, terrified voice cried.

Bile rose to my mouth as I rushed past the people who stood there ignoring what was taking place before them.

My knees hit the stone by the cage, eyes widening as a familiar, sweat-slicked face turned my way.

"Elle?" Ice-blue eyes stared at me under a furrowed brow.

"Heather?" My throat restricted around her name. She was a mess. Sweat and blood covered her skin; skin which was wriggling and splitting along her bones.

I looked across at the blond. His focus remained fixated on my cousin. "What have you done to her?"

A hand landed on my shoulder. I knocked it away and jumped to my feet, standing before Dante. My eyes were clouded with tears, chest heaving as shock wracked my body.

"You shouldn't be here—"

"I called," I growled between clenched teeth. "And I called, and called, and called."

"It's not safe."

"What have you done t'her?" Pain twisted around my jaw as I forced myself to stay calm and find out what had happened to my cousin.

He held his hands up. "Nothing."

"Nothing?" My laugh was hysterical as I side-stepped and pointed at her. "Sure doesn't look like nothing."

"We're trying to save her."

"Get her out." I pulled my dagger from its holster and placed it at his Adam's apple. "Let her out. Now."

"We can't do that, Lass." I looked over my shoulder at Carter who had risen to his feet. "Now calm yourself."

"Not until you tell me what's wrong with her and why you have her in this cage."

"She's changing," he stated simply, as if I knew what that meant.

"Changing? What do you mean, changing?"

"It's full moon, Lass, and it's her first. We're trying to ease her first change—"

"She doesn't look or sound at ease." I glanced at Dante who had taken hold of my wrist and stepped away from me.

"She's in the cage for *our* protection," Dante commented, his expression grim.

I snorted. Yanking my hand from his grip, I pointed my dagger at the Alpha. "You expect me t'believe that?"

"Lass, we don't have time to explain this." A growl laced in Carter's words. "She could die."

The words hit me like a ton of bricks, and I felt myself sway as the shock fully took over my body.

"We're all here to give her our energy to try and ease her change." Dante placed his hands gently on my shoulder, steadying me.

I shrugged him off.

"But she—I don't understand ..." I shook my head to try and focus myself. "How is she changing?"

"Because I gave her my blood to save her life," the blond replied solemnly. He didn't move from his spot on the floor or take his focus from Heather. "Which means she is now carrying the Were-gene."

"Which is currently altering and fussing with her genes, which her body is fighting against," Dante finished.

"She needs to give in, or the pain will kill her," Carter stated, once again kneeling on the stone floor.

"And if she survives, those bastards have finally gotten what they wanted." The blond's voice was strained. Green eyes filled with unshed tears looked up at me. "A Hybrid."

To be continued...

Soul's Blood

The final instalment in The Blood Series

Coming soon

Blood Series Glossary

Characters
Werewolves

The United Pack
(In order of dominance)

Carter MacLaren – *Alpha*
Owen MacLaren
Clare Walker
Dante MacLaren
Brendan Daniels
Scott Miller
Eve Miller
Solomon Whelan
Dabria Whelan
Graham Riley
Richard Jones
Thomas Walker
John MacLaren
May MacLaren
Philippe Bianchini
Alcander Linard
Christopher Jones
Flynn Riley
Katharine Jones

The Italian Pack

Maximo Valentini – *Alpha*
Rosa Valentini
Angelo Valentini
Rocco Valentini
Loretta Donati
Lorenzo Santoro

Rogues

Gideon McKeller +

Pack Unknown

Tina De Santos
Jennifer Assar

Vampires

Ancients
Marko Pavel

The Italian Colony
Marie Mancinelli – *Colony Leader* +
Luca Mancinelli +
Galen Rouphos
Leonardo Donati
Sorina Bouras
Kiya Suma
Carlos Avella
Emilio Bandoni +
Antonia (Toni) Santini +
Dmitri Carbone +
Julian Romano +
Cal Zangari +
Henri Fonda +

The United Colony
Nathan (Than) Kennedy – *Colony Leader/Experiment/Patient N*
Mark Nicholson
Michael Kirk +
Antonio Ferrari +
Carlson Archer +
Constance Lombardi +
Jackson Dean +

254 | Cross My Heart

Kane Enfield +
Katrina Cowan +
Lance Mason +
Jonathan +
Frederick (Freddie) Åström – Experiment/Patient F +

Slayers

Alexandra (Alexis) Ryan +
Bernard Renaud
Catherine Renaud
Danielle (Elle) Renaud
Dorian Ryan +
Heather Ryan – *First Born Infected/First Hybrid*
Jean-Louis Renaud +
Sofia Renaud – *Clairvoyant/Loup-Garou* +

+ = previously deceased characters or characters who have died/been killed during the series.

Terms

Alliance – *A union or association formed for mutual benefit, especially between countries or organizations*

Alpha - *Dominant Werewolf: Leader of the Pack*

Ancestor - *A person from whom one is descended*

Ancient – *The eldest known Vampires*

Baptize - *Term used by Vampires; Vampires baptize Infecteds with their blood in order to turn the Infecteds into Vampires*

Bad Blood - *Werewolf term for a Were who is deemed unstable for any number of reasons*

Blood Bonded - *Vampire connection through blood: Bond between Maker and Bloodling*

Blood House – *A Vampire Nest with human occupants*

Bloodlings – *A Makers term for the Vampires they create*

Bonded - *Werewolf connection through blood: Only between mates*

Bonding Ritual - *Werewolf ceremony: blood bond made between two mated Werewolves*

Clairvoyant - *An individual who is able to perceive events in the future (aka Psychic, etc)*

Colony - *Group of Vampires (aka Nest)*

Descendant - *A person that is descended from a particular ancestor*

Devampulating – *The emasculating of a male Vampire*

Fortune Teller - *A person who is supposedly able to predict a person's future by palmistry, or similar methods (aka Clairvoyant, etc)*

Generations – *The different ages of Vampires created after Marko Pavel*

Glamour - *Vampire trick; First Three Generations of Vampires* *are able to take hold of animals and humans minds and therefore control them*

Half-Breed - *A person of mixed descent/Any animal resulting from the crossing of different breeds or types*

Hybrid(s) - *The offspring of two animals of different species or varieties/ A thing created by combining two different elements*

Infected – *A human who has the Vampyrric Virus*

Initiation - *Blood ceremony to welcome new Werewolves/Loup-Garous to the Pack*

Leech(es) – *Term used by the Werewolves in regards to Vampires*

Legacy - *Something left or handed down by a predecessor*

Lingo - *(Latin) - A foreign language or local dielct*

Loup-Garou – *Female offspring of a male Werewolf*

Luna(r) - *(Latin name) - The Moon*

Maker – *The term for a Vampire who turns a human*

Master – *Male Maker*

Mate - *Werewolf term for Soul-mates/The One*

Mated - *Physical connection between two Werewolves*

Mating Process - *Werewolf version of dating; intense process which involves the couple having to challenge any other interested parties, announcing themselves as mates to the Pack, mating, and gaining permission off Alpha to be bonded*

Mistress – *Female Maker*

Monkshood - *Poisonous to Werewolves (aka. Wolfsbane)*

Nest - *Group of Vampires (aka. Colony)*

Offspring - *The product or result of something/ An animal's young/ A persons child or children*

Pack - *Group of Werewolves*

Pact - *A formal agreement between individuals or parties(aka Treaty)*

Premonition - *A strong feeling that something is about to happen, especially something unpleasant*

Prophet - *A person who will predict what happens in the future (aka Psychic, etc)*

Psychic - *A person considered or claiming to have psychic powers(aka Clairvoyant, etc)*

Pure Blood - *Term used for a born Werewolf or Loup-Garou*

Second-sight – *The ability to see future or distant events; clairvoyance*

Shift - *First Three Generations of Vampires are able to shift into an unknown form*

Shifter – *A human who is able to shift from their human form to an animal of their choice*

Silver - *Type of metal: Harmful to Vampires and Werewolves*

Slayer – *A person who hunts and kills Vampires*

Strigoii – *A Romanian Vampire*

Territory – *An area of land under the jurisdiction of a ruler or state*

Treaty - *A formally concluded and ratified agreement between states (aka Pact)*

Vamphood – *A twist on the term Manhood*

Vampire – *A species that is commonly known for drinking its victim's blood*

Vampyrric Virus – *The mutation that starts the first stage of being turned into a Vampire*

Vocktail – *A Vampire mock/cocktail*

Venom – *Poison contained in Vampires blood, which kills its victims*

Werewolf – *An individual who is able to shift in to a half-form; combination of woman/man and wolf*

Were-gene – *The Werewolf Gene*

Wolfsbane - *Poisonous to Werewolves (aka.Monkshood)*

Language Translations
English (Slang)

Bloody - *Used to express anger, annoyance, or shock, or simply for emphasis*

Bollocks - *Nonsense/rubbish*

Buggered - *Extremely tired*

Chat/Chatting - *Talk/Talking*

Cockney - *London Accent*

Cranny - *A small, narrow space or opening (aka Nook)*

Dump – *Dumping ground (aka garbage dump)*

Fellow - *A man or boy(aka Fella)*

Fiver - *A five pound note*

Geordie - *Newcastle Accent*

Git - *An unpleasant or contemptible person*
Gob - *Spit*

Got Pissed - *Got Drunk*

(Jump) into the sack - *Jump into bed with someone*
Kidding - *Deceive someone in a playful way; tease or joke*

Nab - *Take, grab, or steal something*

Narked -*Annoyed*

Nook - *A corner or recess, especially one offering seclusion or security (aka Cranny)*

Northerner - *Individual from the North of the country*

Mammy - *A child's word for their mother*

Mate - *Pal/Friend*

Mongrels - *A person of mixed descent/Any animal resulting from the crossing of different breeds or types a.k.a Half-Breed*

Pants - *Rubbish/Nonsense*

Pissed - *Drunk or very annoyed (aka Pissed Off)*

Pissed Off - *Drunk or very angry (aka Pissed)*

Prick - *A vulgar word for Penis*
Quid - *One Pound Sterling*
Ringing - *Call by telephone*
Shite - *Shit*
Sod - *An unpleasant or obnoxious person*
Take/Taking the piss - *Mock someone of something*

French

Femme - *Female*
Merci - *Thank you*
Oui - *Yes*

Greek

Ηρεμα, Μαστορα - *Be calm, Master*
Μαστορα; - *Master?*
Αγγελε μου - *My Angel*
Φιλη μου - *My Friend*
Αγαπημενοι μου - *My Loved Ones*
Μητερα μου - *My Mother*
Γιε μου - *My Son*
Καμια λυπη - *No Regrets*
Είναι δυναμικη - *She's Strong*
Γλυκιε μου - *Sweet One*
Τι εγινε; - *What is it?*

Irish

Aye – *Yes*
Daidi – *Father, Da, Dad or Daddy*
Eejit – *Idiot*
Mamai – *Mother, Ma, Mum or Mummy*

Italian

Basta cosi - *Enough/That will do*
Bastardo/i – *Bastard/s*
Bella Mia - *My beautiful one*
Benvenuto – *Welcome*
Brava – *Bravo*
Brutta Sgualdrina – *Ugly bitch*
Cane - *Dog*
Cara Mia – *My dear/honey*
Chiudi la bocca - *Shut your mouth*
Confuso – *Fuzzy*
Contagiata - *Infected/Disease*
Cosa? - *What?*
Disgustosa/o - *Disgusting*
Finalmente - *Finally*
Forza, a lavoro ragazzi - *Go on, get to work guys*
Grazie - *Thank you*
Ho detto vattene - *I said go*
Infetta/o – *Infected*
Lasciaci soli - *Leave us*
Lupo intelligente - *Clever wolf*
Mia - *My*
Muoviti - *Move*
Ora - *Now*
Padrona – *Mistress*
Perdonami - *Forgive me*
Piccola – *Little*
Portatelo via - *Take him away*
Puttana – *Whore/Bitch/Prostitute*
Ragazzi? - *Boys?*

Salve – *Hello*

Sgualdrina – *A female who sleeps around/loose woman/dirty whore*

Si - *Yes*

Sono occupato - *I'm busy*

Sparite - *Move it/Get out/Get lost*

Spostati, cagnetto - *Move, little dog*

Stupido - *Foolish*

Ti prego – *Please*

Ti voglio – *I want you*

Origin Unknown

Boss - *A person in control of a group or situation*

Brick Shithouse - *A person with a well developed body; implies an element of indestructibility*

Chime in - *Interject a remark*

Fella - *Non-standard spelling of fellow, used in representing speech in various dialects (aka Fellow)*

Hovel - *A small squalid or simply constructed dwelling*

Nod/Nodded Off - *To fall asleep or doze momentarily, especially in a sitting position*

No shit - *You Think?*

Piss Off - *Get lost/go away*

Screw you - *Fuck you/Go to hell*

Shitload - *A large amount or number*

Tattled - *Gossip idly/ Report another's wrongdoings; tell tales*

Zoned Out - *To become oblivious to ones surroundings*

Scottish

Aye - *Yes*

Bonny - *Attractive/Beautiful*

Laddie - *Boy or Young Man*
Lass(ie) - *Girl or Young Woman*
Pet - *Term of endearment*
Wee - *Little*

Spanish

Loco - *Crazy*
Mi pequeña asesina - *My little murderer*

Acknowledgement

I'm so happy to finally be able to share the next instalment in the Blood Series. Cross My Heart ended up being a longer work in progress than Blood Secrets was. It was never my intention to take so long to write this boo, but I do hope you find it worth the wait.

Firstly, I want to thank my friend and editor, Zee Monodee who – as always – is full of positivity and support. Once again, she has worked her magic and calmed my inner doubt. Thank you, Zee.

Fiona Jayde, I cannot thank you enough for taking on the challenge of designing the next cover in the Blood Series. I seriously love it.

And lastly and most importantly; my readers, old and new, thank you for taking a chance on my work. Thank you for your patience in regard to this book and well, just in general. I appreciate your support and understanding. I hope you found Cross My Heart worth the wait and are as excited as I am for the final instalment, which I have already started and am aiming to finish sooner than the last two books.

Thank you for your ongoing support, your comments, and your reviews; just thank you. You are truly wonderful, and I hope from the bottom of my heart that you continue to trust in my creative insanity and enjoy my stories.

About the Author

Elizabeth Morgan is a multi-published author of urban fantasy, paranormal, erotic horror, f/f, and contemporary; all with a degree of romance, a dose of action and a hit of sarcasm, sizzle or blood, but you can be sure that no matter what the genre, Elizabeth always manages to give a unique and often humorous spin to her stories.

Like her tagline says; *A pick 'n' mix genre author. "I'm not greedy. I just like variety."*

Away from the computer, Elizabeth can be found in the garden trying hard not to kill her plants, dancing around her little cottage with the radio on while she cleans, watching Netflix or curled up with her three cats reading a book.

For more information on Elizabeth's work, published and upcoming, head on over to her website:
www.e-morgan.com